LAKE TOWN

LAKE TOWN

jane redd

Mirror Press

Edited by Haley Swan and Lisa Shepherd
Interior Design by Rachael Anderson

Cover art by Claudia McKinney: PhatPuppyArt.com
Photographer: Grace Hill
Model: Will Jardell
Cover design by Rachael Anderson

ISBN-10: 1-941145-96-5
ISBN-13: 978-1-941145-96-8

About the Solstice Series

Solstice: Book 1

There are four ways to get Banished from the last surviving city on earth: 1. Cut out your emotion tracker, 2. Join a religious cult, 3. Create a rebellion against the Legislature, 4. Fall in love.

Jezebel James does all four.

Jez is on the fast-track to becoming a brilliant scientist, with one goal—save her city from total extinction. But the more Jez learns about the price of a fresh beginning, the more she realizes that carrying out the plan will lead to few survivors, and among the dead will be those she cares about the most.

Lake Town: Book 2

Jezebel James is on the run after her true abilities are discovered by the Legislature, and the only one who can protect her is Sol. In order to survive, Sol sends her into an underground hideout where she quickly discovers all that she thought was true in her dying world is false. Jez reunites with Rueben and his band of insurgents, and together they escape to Lake Town, only to find that the entire island is preparing to invade the city.

But Sol has been left behind and forced to join the ranks of the Faction, who are working against the Legislature from within. As Jez works with the insurgents and their plan to destroy the city, she learns that attacking the city might save thousands of lives, but it will destroy Sol, the man she knows she can't live without.

Other Books by H.B. Moore

Finding Sheba
Lost King
Slave Queen
First Heist
The Killing Curse
Esther the Queen

Other Books by Heather B. Moore

Heart of the Ocean
Power of the Matchmaker
Love is Come
The Fortune Café
The Boardwalk Antiques Shop
The Mariposa Hotel

It is unnatural for a majority to rule, for a majority can seldom be organized and united for specific action, and a minority can.

—Jean-Jacques Rousseau

CHAPTER 1

Jez

T*he sun will only appear twice a year,* my caretaker told me. *Do not do anything that will prevent you from seeing it.*

I should have asked her, "Like being sent to prison?"

But Naomi was gone. Taken. And now all that was left of the woman who raised me were memories and echoed warnings to keep my emotions hidden.

During the Summer Solstice, I had been locked in a cell beneath the city. Convicted for the crime of reading a book—my grandmother's journal. Except I couldn't refer to her as *grandmother.*

So when I opened the door to reveal Rueben's smiling face, I was stunned to see a giant sun behind him, its light filling the vast underground cavern. I stared at the suspended globe, wondering how Rueben had done the impossible—how he had captured the sun.

It reminded me of Rueben. His hair was golden brown

whereas mine was dark. Even his brown eyes were warm while mine had always been like deep pools of mud. And, somehow, Rueben's skin held a sun-kissed tan in a raining world that left my skin pale.

His breath felt warm against my neck as he stood behind me. Although I couldn't see his smile, I could feel it. That's what I loved about Rueben. His emotions.

"Isn't it beautiful, Jez?" he asked.

The brilliant yellow glow shifted to a warm orange, and I realized it wasn't the sun at all. Of course it wasn't. I blinked at the contrast of the light against the darkness of the cavern ceiling.

"Is it a light bulb?" I asked, unsure.

"No," Rueben said, his laughter soft. The sound of it was welcome, as I'd lived my entire life in a city devoid of emotion, with people controlled by Harmony implants. I was an exception. People like me and Rueben were immune.

"You're seeing millions of glowing atomic particles that are attracted to one another," Rueben continued. "As one divides, another disintegrates, so the mass you see remains the same size. We call it a globe." The orange deepened to a pale scarlet.

"Why does it change color?" I turned to look from Rueben to the other three people who stood in our half circle. I hadn't seen any of these people before, but I could tell they were not from the city.

A female and two males watched me with open expressions and unapologetic eyes. One of them was even smiling. A forbidden expression. Were all of these people like me? Were their Harmony implants inert, too? Had they spent their lives hiding their emotions like I had?

"The atoms are evolving as they multiply," Rueben said

patiently, as if he'd answered my question about changing colors more than once. "But they don't exist long enough to evolve into another form."

Prying my eyes from the globe—or, more accurately, the mass of atoms clinging and multiplying and dying together—I asked, "What is this place?"

His smile was just a hint of what we'd shared in Phase Three prison weeks ago. I never thought I'd see Rueben again. After we were separated, I'd heard that he'd been Demoted, but here he was . . . free.

"We're in an old biology lab that was buried beneath a landslide in the Before." Rueben waved a hand toward the deep recesses of the cavern beyond the bright globe. "They used to run large-scale tests in here. We're still not finished digging it out." He motioned to the people standing by him. "And by the way, this is Becca, Michel, and Gabe." He nodded to me. "Meet Jezebel James."

I lifted my hand in a half wave, a sudden feeling of nostalgia running through me. I missed my own friends. Chalice, my roommate in A Level. Sol, the boy who had my heart. I didn't know if I'd see either again. The people watching me now weren't my friends, but at least their expressions were friendly. Becca wore her blonde hair in a short bob that she'd tucked behind her ears. Her wide, blue eyes watched me closely. Michel was tall and lean. His dark-auburn hair was tied back with a thick string. Gabe seemed to be assessing me, his thin lips quirked into an amused smirk as if he knew something I didn't. Which was entirely true. His black brows arched above his coal-dark eyes, and his equally black hair was short and spiky, with no rhyme or reason.

"Go ahead, look around," Rueben said.

As curious as I was about the new people, I turned from them to look. The room felt immense, as large as the auditorium at the A Level school I'd attended before I was caught with an illegal book. Actually, all books were illegal, but especially the journal written by my grandmother, who had rebelled against the Legislature.

I walked toward the glowing mass of atoms. As I moved closer, I felt the heat from it—not an intense heat, but a mellow, comforting heat. I closed my eyes as I came to a stop directly beneath the globe, and imagined that I was standing outside on the day of Solstice. It had been eight months since I'd seen the sun.

I felt the people watching me, but I didn't care. I'd spent the night in a dark, wet tunnel after being hidden there by Sol. He might have saved my life by telling me to hide, but he had also complicated it by leaving me with a kiss. A kiss that I could have only imagined before. I'd had no idea how much it would bind my soul to his.

As I basked in the warmth and brightness of the globe, I thought of the city above, of the rain that threatened its very existence.

It had only survived for this long because of the Harmony implants that controlled our emotions and suppressed our urges to rebel. They were created by the Legislature for our survival. We needed to work together, with one mind and one purpose. We needed to rise above the civilization that came Before and avoid forbidden activities from the List of Failures, such as thievery, child abuse, prostitution, murder, and government corruption.

Our new world was a better world—at least that was what the Legislature wanted us to believe. But our new world was a dying world, too. One that existed without the sun and flooded more with each passing day. Situated in the former Sawatch mountain range of Colorado, the city was now only five hundred feet above the ocean. And the rain just keeps coming.

And that was why when I first met Rueben and discovered he was from a Lake Town, I decided to learn all I could from him.

My caretaker had entrusted me with a secret—one that had the potential to save our dying civilization. Naomi passed me the Carrier implant, and now it was up to me to accomplish what she couldn't.

The heat on my face from the globe dissipated, and I opened my eyes to see that the colors had changed again. Instead of scarlet red, they were a blue green that reminded me of a rare glimpse of the sky. I turned to see Rueben and the others watching me.

He had called me a Carrier. How had he known? He knew the Harmony implant hadn't controlled my emotions—that I was a "Clinical"—but I didn't know that anyone besides myself and my dead caretaker Naomi knew about Carriers. Naomi had told me that because I had a second implant—the Carrier key—my Harmony implant wouldn't be able to control my emotions. So I'd spent the first sixteen years of my life controlling them on my own and pretending that the Harmony implant worked.

I didn't know if I could trust the others, but I did know that I had to trust Rueben . . . it was the only way. I'd find a way to question him alone later.

Walking about the cavern, I marveled at the size and dryness of the space. Out in the tunnel, everything had dripped with moisture, but in here it was as if there had never been a drop of rain.

The warmth and the light from the globe might be the reason. I stopped at a tarnished and dented metal table covered with rolls of thick paper. *Paper.* It was something that I'd seen in the museum and something I'd held in my hand when I read my grandmother's journal, but it was strange to see it here—out in the open for anyone to touch.

I couldn't resist. I touched one of the rolls. Next to it, another roll had been spread out and anchored by square metal pieces. Leaning down, I examined the lines and circles. "A map," I said to myself. But it was like no other map I'd seen. This one had colors woven through: dark green to denote forests, and yellows to show stretches of sand. This was not the city above the cavern.

Seeming to sense that I had questions, Rueben crossed over and stood by my side.

"Where is this?" I asked.

"Home."

My gaze lifted to meet the warmth of his brown eyes. "A Lake Town?" I examined the map again. "I thought Lake Towns were smaller, more wild." I traced the line of a road that cut through rows of square homes. Judging by the map, this Lake Town called Prairie looked to be a planned community similar to our city, but less congested.

The edges of the map were colored a soft blue. I wondered what it would be like to see the sea that color. Our sea was a cross between an angry gray and a murky green. But between the edges of the sea and the rows of houses and neat roads was open space. Forests, stretches of sand . . . "I thought the population would be larger."

Rueben traced his fingers along the road that ran between the buildings, then his finger continued across a stretch of sand and stopped at the forest line. "Here," he said in a soft voice, "is where the underground facilities start."

I leaned close to the map, looking for what he meant. Another building? A stairwell leading beneath the ground?

"It's not visible from the sky, and it's forbidden to include the facilities on any map," Rueben said, preempting my question. "The underground facilities are built into a rock bed and are where most of the population of Prairie lives."

I looked over at him. "To stay out of the rain? Is it like an underground village or something?"

Rueben gave a casual shrug, but there was a new intensity in his gaze. "That's one way to look at it."

"What is it, Rueben?" I tried not to let my impatience show, but there were so many unanswered questions.

Rueben flashed a smile and grasped my hand. "It's a training facility, Jez. Hundreds of highly skilled people have dedicated their lives to train there."

I arched a single brow. "Training for what?"

"To bring down the Legislature, of course."

CHAPTER 2

Sol

Eleven hours had passed since I opened the manhole cover and sent Jez down the metal ladder into the dark, and now I couldn't stop wondering where she was and what was going to happen. I could only hope that she'd been found by now, that she was safe and warm.

The depths of her dark-brown eyes haunted me still—full of trust, vulnerability . . . and longing. We had kissed. I had touched her skin, felt the cool softness of her neck and her smooth-as-silk dark hair. She had pressed her body against mine, and I had wanted to hold her forever. But the officials were hunting her, and so I let her go.

My face had grown warm at my thoughts of Jez and how she'd felt in my arms, fitting perfectly against me. I needed to cool the heat of my skin. I glanced at the time on my tablet. Seven thirty a.m. Dr. Wells's voice droned on in the committee meeting at the University, his piercing blue eyes scanning the room. As he spoke, his freckled face mutated into varying shades of pink.

Wells was the former director of A Level and had transferred to the University about the same time I did. I had wondered what precipitated the move, and I planned to find out if he was someone I needed to be extra cautious around. I had tested into the highest of his A Level classes; the only one who could have really competed with me was Jez, but that was before she'd been found guilty of reading an illegal book—her grandmother's journal, more accurately. The weeks she'd spent in Phase Three prison had been hard on me.

But this . . . this was worse. Not knowing if she was all right in the tunnels. Knowing she was scared and confused. I had tried so hard not to let my feelings for her grow. I'd befriended her those first days in A Level in order to gather information—to see how far she was in her Carrier process and whether she held securely to the Legislature ideals. Or if I could persuade her to join our resistance.

"Do you have the report, Sol?" Dr. Wells asked, pulling me from my private thoughts. He scrubbed at the neatly trimmed beard on his narrow, freckled face. I'd only spoken to him once, right after I was accepted into A Level, so it was disconcerting to have his focus on me.

I gave a quick nod, pausing to refocus my thoughts, then pulled up the report I'd put together the night before and sent it to the rest of the committee's tablets. The University Informers comprised three students and two professors. I'd been selected as a member after I exposed a religious cult on campus. How was I supposed to know that Chalice would turn herself in, even though she wasn't actually a part of the cult? Chalice had always rebelled alone;

she didn't need a group. But joining the Informers kept me close to any campus disturbances. It was how I knew the Examiner had put out an alert about Jez after they'd discovered she'd found a way to reverse Chalice's altering. There had been little time to hide Jez.

Eleven hours felt like an eternity ago.

"The search has been thorough so far," Wells said, pulling me again from my thoughts.

Of course it had. *I* had hidden Jez, and I knew exactly when to lie and where to steer the authorities. I rotated my tablet, which showed a map of the city. "All apartments in quadrants one through three have been searched. Nothing has been found yet, but a few leads are being investigated further. Quadrant four should be finished by this evening. I'll send out a notice as soon as we find anything important."

"Good work," Dr. Wells said, then turned his attention to the others on the committee. I minimized the screen with the city map and read the correspondence going on between the searchers.

None of the searchers were even close to the small park with the underground entrance. There were other entrances to the cavern, but they were even better concealed—one by the ocean, buried beneath water except during low tide, and the other beneath one of the Legislature buildings. I had never been to that one. Now, as a member of the Informers, I might have easier access.

"Sol?" Wells's voice cut in, and I snapped my head up to look at him. "What are you looking at?"

"The security officers' messages. They just finished with Quadrant four."

"Did they find anything?" he asked.

"No," I said.

Dr. Wells didn't blink, didn't seem surprised. He leaned across the table and lowered his voice. "You knew her the best out of the students in A Level, Sol. Where would she go? What were her resources?"

My pulse quickened at the probing questions, but I didn't let myself seem bothered by it. Wells didn't know who I really was, or how dangerous Jez could be. "My guess was that she'd return to her caretaker's home, but it's been searched. Security has been stationed in the vicinity to keep a watch out in case she travels there."

Wells kept his blue gaze on me. "Where else, Sol? Think hard."

I was ready for him. I'd given him my standard answer first. Now, I paused, pretending to take a moment to consider. The trouble was that I didn't want to implicate anyone else, so I couldn't name a person or a specific place.

"She told me once that she felt sorry for the C Level workers, the ones with the skin conditions," I said in a slow tone, as if I were remembering the conversation as I spoke. "She wanted to help them, to cure their disease."

Another committee member piped in, a boy with thick brown hair and owlish eyes. "Do you think she went to hide there? To live in the C Level and pretend she's a worker?"

Images of the security guards bullying the C Level women with questions raced through my mind. But what other options were there? I could not, absolutely not, let them think Jez would try to escape the city by boat. Of course, there were lookouts posted at each dock, but the focus of the search was inland. Although I didn't want to send security officials to badger the C Level workers, it was a better option than having them find out the truth.

"Yes," I said. "I think that's a very good possibility." My

heart couldn't decide whether to sink or soar when Wells turned to the others.

"We'll send our officials there to search," he said. "They will have permission to use whatever methods of coercion necessary to find Jezebel James. You and I will travel to the C Level factories and aid wherever we can."

CHAPTER 3

Jez

Becca spoke first, and I was surprised at the mellow, rich tone of her voice. Her blonde hair, wide, blue eyes, and delicate features made me think of a fairy story my caretaker had told me once. "We know you're a Carrier, Jezebel. And we've come from a Lake Town to protect you."

"*Protect* me?" I asked Rueben, incredulous.

When he nodded, a flash of heat zipped through me.

"Protect me from going to prison again?"

Rueben grasped my arm. It was just a simple touch, but one that I wasn't used to. "That, among other things. We have a lot to tell you."

I nodded, my mind whirling. When I next met Becca's gaze, she was smiling at me. "We've been tracking you for the past year," she said. "Rueben was sent above when you were put into Detention for reading your grandmother's journal. He broke into a warehouse and let himself get caught so he was sent to Phase Three the day before you arrived."

I was staring at him again, my pulse pounding madly throughout my body. "And Sol? How does he fit into all of this?" My voice was a whisper. Was Sol a Carrier like me? Had I hidden my emotions from him all this time for nothing?

My stomach seemed to rock back and forth as I waited for Rueben's response. "Sol is our leader," he said. The word reverberated through me once, and then again.

How was that possible? I'd known Sol for months. He was a student, studying and taking A Level tests like the rest of us. I had first been drawn to Sol's physical appearance. He was taller than me by several inches, and he carried himself with confidence, as if his knowledge were far greater than those around him. His dark, shaggy hair wisped about his head when it was wet, and I had been tempted to brush it back more than once. But most of all, I had been captured by his murky gray eyes that seemed to mimic the clouds in the sky.

Becca crossed to me and put a hand on my shoulder. In the city above, we didn't touch one another. We didn't comfort anyone or show emotion, so it was strange to feel Becca's hand on my shoulder. But as she gently squeezed, it was like my heart warmed.

"We know it's a lot to take in, Jezebel, but we are glad you're finally with us." One side of her mouth lifted, and I noticed how blue her eyes were. "We've been waiting a long time to meet you."

I opened my mouth to respond but couldn't speak for a moment. And when I finally did, it was to say, "Call me Jez." I looked from Rueben to Becca, then to the other boys, Michel and Gabe. "It's just Jez."

Michel nodded, and, next to him, Gabe gave a small laugh while he scratched his head. "You'll find out that we already know quite a bit about you, Jez. But don't worry, it's nothing personal." The amusement was evident in his voice, and I wasn't sure what to think.

Another nod from Michel, who seemed to be the quiet one of the group.

"What about my roommate, Chalice?" I asked. "Is she a part of your group?"

Quick glances were exchanged, and Rueben said, "No, we don't know Chalice."

"She was Banished," I said in a quiet voice. "For breaking the rules at the University." Just thinking about her made my eyes sting. "She was a good person, and they tried to alter her. But . . ." I looked from one person to the next. They knew my deepest secret, and I decided I could trust them with this information. Had to trust them. "We found a way to reverse the altering."

No one seemed surprised at my confession. Gabe just nodded.

"Sometimes when you know you're different than everyone else, you're willing to try different things," Becca said.

I looked at the map again, wondering how far this Lake Town was from our city. Suddenly, hope burst through me. "Do you think my friend Chalice could have been sent here?"

"It's hard to know," Becca said. "Once someone is Banished, their records are no longer available."

Becca glanced over at Rueben, as if asking for his permission to speak.

"We wanted to wait a little longer to bring you down," Becca said. "But Sol said that it had become too dangerous for you."

"Yes." My voice was little more than a whisper.

There was a lot of information to process. The boy that I'd been in love with for almost a year was the leader of this underground group. And Rueben had been sent to Phase Three to *protect* me? And now I was in this cavern, sent by Sol, but I was early. What was the plan? And how did I fit in?

A deep ache had started in my heart. "Where is Sol?"

Becca again glanced at Rueben. This time, he spoke. "We'll let Sol tell you more when he joins us."

"So he's coming here?" I had to hope. "To the cavern?"

Rueben glanced at Becca. Why did they keep looking at each other? What were they not telling me?

"He's coming, but we won't know when," Rueben finally said, apparently able to tell me that much.

I felt some relief, but still worried. Sol was coming here. Surely he was in danger. Something could happen to him—anything could happen to him.

I pushed away the anxiety that was growing by the minute. Over Sol. Over Chalice. Over the fact that I was a hundred feet below the city and had no idea what my future would bring. "Tell me more about this training facility."

Becca's gaze flickered to Rueben, then back to me. I wondered if she was worried about saying the wrong thing, about giving me too much information. "It's a complicated process."

I motioned for her to continue, making it clear that I was happy to hear her out. "Tell me how these people plan to take down the Legislature, and what they are going to replace it with? A new leadership?"

Rueben moved to Becca's side, as if standing next to her in support. "That's exactly what we're doing," he said. "The new leadership will remove all Harmony implants, and society will return to the humanity that it deserves."

I'd grown up in the city and its controlled environment. I'd learned why we had to do certain things in order to survive. But I'd also seen the misery of a life without emotion, without joy. I'd watched people disciplined and Demoted to lower levels of society. Men and women at C Level could marry, but they could only have one child. And then when the end of their life cycle came, they were Taken.

My world was a world without choices. A harsh reality of survival through uniformity. The rain had been relentless for dozens of years, destroying city after city, country after country, until only a few landmasses were inhabitable. We had to protect what we could still hang on to. But what good was a life without happiness, love, or fulfillment?

Gabe suddenly cursed from several paces away where he and Michel were huddled over a tablet.

Rueben crossed to them, leaving me standing with Becca.

"What's going on?" I started to walk toward Gabe, but Becca grasped my arm.

"Wait," she said.

I looked at her. "Why?" I wasn't going to let these people keep secrets from me.

"You don't want to—"

Gabe cursed again and I pulled from Becca's grasp and jogged over to the boys. I sidled up to Rueben to see what they were all looking at. A message flickered across the screen, and I knew instinctively that it was from Sol. The words had to be his.

I was elated to see anything from him, but his message both chilled and confused me.

Take her to the Lake Town ASAP. The authorities are getting too close. I can't keep them from the water much longer. Don't wait for me.

Gabe's eyes lifted and locked with mine.

"He wants *me* to go to the Lake Town?" I asked, leaning forward. "Is that why you're all here? To take me there?"

Becca came up on my other side, her eyes wide. "It's too soon," she said. "We don't have a boat secured, and—"

"We're going," Rueben said, cutting in, and everyone looked at him. "Sol wouldn't have sent this if he didn't think Jez was in real danger."

Becca blew out a breath of frustration. "What's the timestamp?"

"Ten minutes ago," Gabe said, looking down at the tablet. He switched the screen over to a map of the city.

Intrigued, I moved past Rueben to get a better view. The map was divided into quadrants, and one of them was flashing. "What's going on?"

"This is the security grid," Gabe explained. "They're searching Level C right now. The other quadrants of the city have already been cleared, but if they don't find something in Level C, they'll likely start all over again."

I stared at the blinking lights, and my stomach went sour. "All of this just for me?"

Becca joined me. "They know enough about you to know you're dangerous. They can't risk you running around free in the city, *or* leaving the city."

I watched the blinking lights move as the security officials searched the buildings and homes. What were they saying to the people? What damage were they doing in their search? "What happens if they catch me?" *Or I turn myself in so that others won't have to suffer on my behalf?*

"They'll alter you, at the very least," Rueben said. "As much as you're willing to be a martyr, future generations will thank you for not turning yourself in right now."

Rueben always could read me.

"They're looking for you, Jez." Rueben looked at the others. "They don't know about us . . . or at least they think I'm already gone. If they knew that we were all hiding down here, they'd be after all of us. So this warning from Sol isn't just to get you to safety. We all need to leave. We need to keep the location of this cavern a secret so that we have a place to come to when we return to the city."

Michel scrubbed a hand through his long hair. "I'll wire the door to the tunnel opening."

"Wire it?" I asked, unable to stop my outburst. "So that it will explode?"

"Only if someone tries to force it open," Rueben said without looking at me. He was typing into the tablet. "Hopefully Sol will get this message."

I looked at the screen. He told Sol that we were leaving and, if he could meet us in an hour, we could all travel together.

Becca also saw the message before Rueben sent it. "What about the boat?"

Rueben shrugged. "We'll have to improvise."

"What does that mean?" I asked. I'd never been in a boat or on the water, except for the swimming test in Phase Three that almost killed me.

"Our Lake Town boat is anchored too far out to make it in time," Rueben told me. "We'll have to find a different one. Come on."

It wasn't like I was going to stay behind, but I did wonder what I was getting myself into. Gabe, Michel, and Becca were stuffing some sort of equipment into thick canvas bags and hoisting them over their shoulders.

"Can I help?" I asked, just as Becca handed me a bag.

The weight of it surprised me—had they filled it with rocks?

But I didn't have time for more questions because Rueben was telling me to follow him across the cavern. He handed me a rain jacket, and I pulled it on, knowing that once we got out of this place, I'd be facing a world of rain again.

CHAPTER 4

Sol

Sliding my arms into the sleeves of my raincoat reminded me that Jez was probably doing the same thing as she fled with Rueben and the others to the ocean. But instead of fleeing to the shore to meet her, I was accompanying Dr. Wells to the C level manufacturing plants. There was a reason I had avoided the C Level area, and if Dr. Wells found out, I would no longer be a free man. But I had no choice but to follow Dr. Wells out of the classroom, our shoes clapping on the tiled floor until we reached the exit.

Outside, the wind had picked up, and rain drove straight into my face. Dr. Wells snapped his umbrella open and angled it to share with me, but it didn't offer much protection for two men.

As we hurried along the wet pavement toward the tram station at the west end of the University campus, I knew that with every passing moment, the chances of catching up with Jez were getting slimmer. If I made a break from Wells, he would notify the authorities, and I would jeopardize the identity of the other Lake Town people.

I'd be tracked down like a varmint, and I wouldn't be released until it was far too late. Dr. Wells had already asked too many probing questions. And the fact that he was making me accompany him didn't bode well. I followed Dr. Wells onto the tram, and it soon lurched into motion. I held onto the overhead strap and remained standing, watching the darkness race by.

With each passing building, the stress built up inside of me. I could only hope that Jez was safe with Rueben and that they were getting on a boat. One that would get her far away from the danger of the city authorities. The tram rattled as it bent around a corner and the wind whipped against the windows. It was a terrible night for a storm—I worried that it wouldn't be safe to launch a boat.

Finally, the tram started to slow, and I reluctantly got off with Dr. Wells. I hoped Wells would get caught up in helping security so I could slip away unnoticed and catch the tram back to the University, where I could sneak into the Legislature building. There was a hidden access to the beach in the basement, and if I hurried, I might be able to catch up to the boat.

The C Level warehouse was fully lit—odd for this time of night. The night-shift crew usually worked under half light in order to reduce electrical use. The full lights must mean that they were actually inspecting the warehouse.

Sure enough, we stepped inside to see a row of workers lined up against a wall as security officers took notes on their tablets and asked questions. The first thing I noticed was that they were all women. Had they already questioned the men?

Most people didn't realize that these plants were the

hub of the city. It was where their electrical power came from, and if the equipment wasn't maintained, the whole city could be at risk. The C Level people might be the least educated in the city, but the functions they performed were essential to survival. I had spent my early weeks in the city learning to maintain the equipment.

It wouldn't matter how many Carriers we had—if the power went down, the secret generators couldn't be unlocked. But Jez was the only known Carrier. And if the Legislature discovered that Lake Town people had created a rebellion and were attempting to take over the city, the first thing they'd do is cut off the power.

I scanned the large room. It wasn't the same place I'd worked, but the layout was similar. The ceilings were high and the walls bare, and long tables stretched across the room, covered in piles of scrap metal that had been salvaged from the ocean. The workers would oil the scrap metal and sort it. Pieces that couldn't be used to build something else were melted down and refashioned into new ones.

I shouldn't have been shocked to see the physical condition of the women. They were C Level, after all. And it was their job to work in the rivers and the edges of the ocean and collect the metal. But their thinness still surprised me. The women wore their hair pulled back, which only emphasized their gaunt faces. The skin on their arms looked red and scaly from constant exposure to water, and some of their hands were swollen and discolored, which could lead to a more serious illness called River Fever. Jez had been trying to help these workers by creating an ointment from Lemon Balm to protect their skin.

I swallowed against my thickening throat, worrying even more about Jez. Was she already on a boat? Was Rueben taking care of her like he said he would?

Dr. Wells crossed to one of the security officers and introduced himself. Then he motioned for me to join them.

"Sol is with the University Informers," Dr. Wells told the officer. "He's also acquainted with the missing person. I'd like him to review the notes you've taken so far during the questionings, and he can see if anything stands out."

There was nothing I could counter, so I walked with the security officer to a table and chairs in one corner of the room. The officer pulled up his notes, and I scanned the testimonies that had been given by the women so far. I was surprised that a few of the women claimed to remember Jez from her visits to the C Level.

One woman had said, "Jezebel looked me straight in the eye, which I found very unusual."

I continued to read, knowing I wouldn't find anything that would give away Jez's hiding place. No one in C Level could know where to find her. I glanced over at the security officer, then scanned the room until I found Dr. Wells. He was hunched over a tablet, scrolling through information.

I tracked the distance to the exit. I'd have to walk past Wells. That wouldn't work. "Is there a bathroom in this building?" I asked the officer next to me.

The man nodded and pointed to a recessed door in the far wall. I didn't think there was another way out of the bathroom, but it would at least give me a chance to see more of the area.

"Sol," Dr. Wells called out, and I stopped, turning slowly.

"This officer says he recognizes you. Said he knows your caretaker."

I didn't recognize the dark blond man with a thick mustache. "I don't think I know you."

The officer narrowed his eyes. "You were here about a year ago, working in the warehouse, when you disappeared one day." He held up his tablet to reveal a report that had my picture on it.

I didn't have to read it to know what it said. There had been a search put out for me, but it was short lived since I was C Level. I had hidden out until I'd grown my hair longer and could infiltrate into the B Level society with a confiscated Harmony implant.

"I was promoted," I said. "You must have old information." I refused to look at the professor and kept my eyes on the security officer. "If you look up my name on the WorldNet, you'll see that I was top of my A Level classes and I'm a student at the University."

The officer finally dropped his gaze. But my heart was still thumping. "The bathroom is that door?" I asked, pointing, and not really speaking to either man.

"Yes," the officer said, and I took that as a dismissal.

I strode toward the bathroom door, past the line of women being questioned. Just before I reached the door, one of the women moved toward me. I stopped in surprise when she spoke to me.

"Sir," she said, her voice raspy. "Don't let them take her."

"Are you talking about Jezebel?" I asked in a low voice, glancing around to see if Dr. Wells was watching. But Wells was speaking with another woman, and a nearby officer typed busily into his tablet.

"Yes," the woman said. "She only tried to help us, and if she's in trouble, I don't want them to do anything to her."

I stared into the woman's pale blue eyes. "Do you have any idea where she is?" I asked.

"I don't," the woman said. "But I can see that you aren't like the others."

"What do you mean?"

"Your eyes are alive," the woman said, her voice falling to a whisper.

I looked past her to see Dr. Wells approaching.

"Go help her," the woman pressed. "I can create a distraction so that you can get out of here."

"It's not that easy." If I were caught trying to reach Jez before she left the island, it would only make everything worse, and I'd be sent to prison.

Dr. Wells was getting closer. "Sol!" he barked. "We need to talk, now."

I gave the woman an apologetic look and walked with Dr. Wells back to the table and chairs.

"Tell me about when you were at C Level," Wells said, his words drilling into me. "And don't leave anything out."

I fought against the rising heat in my neck and tried to keep my voice steady. "My caretaker worked in C Level, but I had tested into B Level classes. But my caretaker was Taken before I could be promoted, and that's when I took over his job for a short time."

Wells's eyes narrowed, but he didn't say anything—just waited for me to continue.

"I excelled in my tasks, and because of my age, I was allowed to attend B Level classes," I continued, trying to stay as close to the truth as possible. In reality, I hadn't come to the city until I'd been sent by the Prairie citizens. Then I'd waited until a man with no offspring was Taken, and I pretended to be that offspring. It hadn't taken long to create a personal record on the WorldNet. Otherwise, the promotions to B Level and then A Level were true.

"It seems that you have more in common with Jezebel than I thought," Dr. Wells said.

I didn't like the intensity of his gaze. I thought I'd already convinced him that Jez and I were just classmates, but he had clenched his jaw and curled his hands around the edge of the table. I was trying to come up with an answer that would appease him, when a woman started yelling.

Both of us turned, and the woman who'd told me to go find Jez was crouched on the floor. "I'm burning up!" she cried out.

I rose to my feet, wanting to help her. Both Dr. Wells and I hurried over. One of the officers had already bent down to grasp her arm.

But I could see that Wells was more hesitant about touching her. What if she were ill and contagious?

I flinched as she cried out again. The next thing I knew I was bending toward her and reaching for her hand, but she just twisted away from me.

"It's burning all over," she cried again, real tears running down her cheeks.

Everyone in the room was staring.

I was about to tell one of the officers to contact a medic, but then the woman's gaze met mine. In that brief moment, I understood. She wasn't really afflicted—she was creating a distraction so that I could leave.

I stepped away from the writhing woman and the officers who'd gathered around her, Dr. Wells in their midst. With Wells distracted, I walked toward the exit. I didn't run or hurry. I walked as if I had permission to leave the scene.

Pushing the door open, I stepped out into the wind and rain. That was it? Could escaping Dr. Wells really have been so easy?

I hurried to the next tram stop and jumped on a tram that was ready to pull away. As the doors whooshed behind me, I finally caught my breath. This tram was headed to the bottom of the C Level, then would turn around and head to the B Level residences. But as the tram came to its final C Level stop, I jumped off and headed toward the row of tall apartment buildings. I knew the maps of the city well enough to know that behind the apartments ran a high wall that edged the rocky beach.

I strode toward the apartments, then slipped between two of the buildings. As I walked deep into the narrow alley, the light from the street lamp started to fade. Moments later, the wall rose above my head.

I ran my hands along the cement blocks. They had become smooth with years of rain, making them as slick as metal. Tilting my head back, I peered at the top of the wall, its dark form a faint outline against the sky. I moved sideways, using both hands now, the cement cold and wet against my palms. There was nothing to hold onto, no foothold, no opening.

I ran through the city map in my head, looking for details that I might have missed, but I knew that any open access to the ocean was manned by security officers. I either had to get past them or find a way to scale the walls.

I hurried out of the alley and ran along the sidewalk, turning the corner of the next building. The second alleyway was much like the first, but as I reached the wall, I knew I had a better chance here. There was some inconsistency in the cement, and I was able to hoist myself up the wall, grasping at a protruding block about halfway up. For a smaller person, the climb would have been easier, but my size made the task arduous.

Just as I slung my arm over the top of the wall and started to pull myself up, a light flashed in the edge of my vision.

Someone stepped into the other end of the alley.

I couldn't move. Three forms wearing glowing wrist lights were moving toward me, zeroing in.

I knew it could be literal seconds before one of them trained an agitator rod on me. Without any time to think, I maneuvered my body over the top of the wall and dropped down to the other side.

But I didn't land on a rocky beach as I expected. I hit the ground hard, my feet sliding out from under me as I skidded along smooth pavement. I'd fallen into a courtyard of sorts, which meant that there was probably access to it from inside a building. It also meant that I was now surrounded by walls.

I scrambled to my feet and ran my hand over my face, blinking against the rain pelting me. The darkness made it hard to decipher where I could go.

I heard shouts on the other side of the wall. Would the men try to climb the wall, too, or . . . I spotted the door that led to the building. I rushed across the courtyard and tugged at the handle. Locked.

I scanned the courtyard. I saw no other outlet—only looming walls. Knowing I really only had one choice, I began to move my hands along the cement blocks. Time and time again my hands slipped, until finally I found purchase. I was about halfway up the wall when I stopped. There was nowhere else to catch hold.

But it was too late anyway. The building door opened, and a man's voice said, "You should come down from there."

A jolt of pain burst through my limbs, and I lost my hold on the wall, falling to the ground.

CHAPTER 5

Jez

"We need to go now," Rueben told us.

I hoisted the pack higher on my shoulder and followed him across the cavern. The farther away we moved from the globe, the cooler the air grew. Rueben opened a low door on the far side of the cavern that I hadn't noticed before, and I had to stoop to pass through it. The tunnel beyond was dark and pungent with the damp.

Rueben switched on his wrist light, and I fell into line with the others, Michel bringing up the rear, already having wired the other entrance with explosives.

I hadn't ever been particularly claustrophobic—not even when I'd been locked into a dark cell in Phase Three—but this low-ceilinged, narrow tunnel seemed to have no beginning and no end. At one point, Rueben whispered to me, "It's all right. We won't be much longer."

But for the most part, everyone was silent, and I could only hear footsteps and jagged breathing as we moved quickly through the tunnel.

The ground rose and fell, and several times we had to climb over large rocks. When the tunnel narrowed even more, we had to remove our packs and turn sideways to fit through. I found myself trying to push away the panicked thought that I was far beneath the city roads with hundreds of tons of rock and dirt above me. A cave-in would mean certain death.

The change in the scent of the air was the first indication that we were almost out of the tunnels. When the dark softened to a light gray, a weight seemed to lift off me. Without Rueben saying anything, I knew we were close. My stomach ping-ponged with a mixture of worry and anticipation.

Rueben stepped out of the tunnel before me, then said, "Stay against the rocks. The searchlights are already on."

I exited the tunnel and stepped into the night, and the first thing I noticed was the heaving ocean pushing against the shoreline like a black mist. The second thing I noticed was the yellow sweep of light traveling along the shoreline toward us. I flattened myself against the rocks behind me, huddling with the others as the light moved closer. Its arc skimmed our feet, then moved on.

My eyesight wavered as I tried to see beyond the searchlight through the driving rain. The rain was fierce, making visibility poor, and the wind pierced right through my rain jacket. The searchlight, mounted to a floating barge close to shore, circled back, this time higher.

"Get down!" Rueben hissed, grasping my arm and pulling me down with him.

The light moved faster this time, and we barely got out of the way before it passed right where our heads had been.

After the light moved on, I sagged against Rueben. I didn't know how much more of this my heart could take.

"We have to get to that dock before the patrol changes over," Rueben told the group in a strained voice. "If any of us are spotted, you need to run the opposite way to draw the attention away from Jez."

My questions stuck in my throat.

"There's too many of us to stow away on a barge," Becca said.

Rueben gave a brisk nod. "We'll have to see how many of us make it to the dock."

"What will happen if we get caught?" I asked, though I was afraid of the answer.

"We won't let *you* get caught," Rueben said. "It would destroy all of our plans."

"But I can't let you all take so many risks just for me," I said. "I can hide here until it's safer for all of us to leave."

"It will never be safer," Rueben said. "The only way we can protect the only Carrier is to get you off this island. If you're captured, then all the operations will come to a stop."

I exhaled, thinking of the Carrier implant that my caretaker Naomi had given me. Why had *I* been chosen? Shivering in the middle of the night while I crouched on a cold, dark shore, running from the Legislature, it didn't seem like such an honor.

"So, we're going to sneak onto a boat and hide until we reach your Lake Town?" I whispered against the trembling that had started in my voice. I imagined us hiding behind a crate or beneath a bunk bed as the boat moved across the churning waters. My stomach tumbled just thinking about it.

"We won't be hiding, necessarily," Rueben said. "We'll be taking over from the captain."

Becca straightened, pointing out to sea. "There's a second spotlight coming this way."

I looked to where she was pointing, and I could see two barges now out on the dark waves.

"Damn them," Rueben said. "We have to go now. Two spotlights leave us no way to dodge them." He grabbed my cold, trembling hand, pulling me to my feet.

I stood shivering next to him as he directed the others how we would spread out. Next, he turned to me, "You'll stay with me. Don't let go of my hand for any reason."

I could only nod—my teeth were chattering with cold.

The spotlights had begun another sweep of the shoreline, one light at one end, and the other light coming from the opposite direction. When they met in the middle, it would be too late to escape our rocky enclave. Rueben tugged at my hand, and suddenly there was no turning back.

Together, we ran across the shore, Becca in front of us, leading the way toward the dock, and Gabe and Michel behind.

My heart pounded so hard that I thought it might leap right out of my skin, and the sound of our running footsteps on the wet ground seemed to reverberate across the shore. Despite the growing ache in my legs as we ran, I pushed forward, not wanting to slow Rueben down.

"Get on the ground!" Rueben called out.

The two searchlights had already crossed each other, and one of them seemed to be following us step for step. Rueben tugged me just enough that I landed next to him. We both buried our faces in our arms as the light passed right over us, skimming our clothing. I couldn't move. They had to have seen us.

But the searchlight continued moving.

"Come on." Rueben tugged my hand again, and I scrambled to my feet.

This time as I ran, the ache was so deep that my thighs burned. But I wouldn't have slowed down for anything. I ran, keeping up with Rueben and the others, my pulse thundering in my ears, blocking out the sounds of the waves.

It wasn't until I heard a scream that I realized how close we were to the dock.

"Becca!" Rueben called, as Becca collapsed in front of us.

We raced to her side. Becca lay on the sand, gripping her leg, her face contorted in pain. "Go!" she rasped. "You have to keep running!"

Something whizzed past me, and I dropped to the ground. We were being shot at. Becca had been shot. By a range bullet? I didn't think they were used anymore. Bullets were nightmares of the Before.

Rueben released my hand and started gathering Becca in his arms.

"No," Becca screamed at him. "Remember the plan! Get Jezebel to the boat!"

But Rueben didn't stop, and as I watched him scoop her off the ground and stagger until he adjusted to her weight, I realized there was something going on between them. Something I hadn't noticed until now. Rueben cared for Becca. I didn't know how deep his feelings ran, but it was clear that he wasn't doing all this work to change the world just to get back at the Legislature. He was doing it for those he loved as well.

I ran alongside Rueben, refusing to go ahead of his slower pace. I didn't want to leave either of them behind, and

I didn't want to get on a boat without them. Gabe and Michel had kept moving when Becca went down and were now somewhere ahead of us. Just as we reached the dock, both spotlights landed on us.

Everything in the space around us glowed white. We'd been found.

CHAPTER 6

Sol

The electricity of the agitator rod rippled through my skin, through my muscles, into my bones. I'd been shocked before, but it seemed the technology had intensified since then. I literally couldn't move, and as I was lifted from the ground, I blinked up at the men who were holding me. They were definitely security officers, but I didn't recognize them. I was helpless against their strength, and as they carried me through the building and out onto the street beyond, I could only hope that Jez had gotten away, that she was safe. I knew that Rueben would be able to take over if something happened to me.

The men carried me into the tram and set me on one of the long benches. Dr. Wells peered down at me.

Although my body was still inert from the shock and pain of the agitator, my mind was surprisingly on high function.

"Where were you going, Sol?" Wells asked, in a way that

let me know he wasn't going to wait for an answer. "It seems that you haven't quite told me everything." His blue eyes seemed to brighten. "We have plenty of technology that can tell us what we need to know. I wish we didn't have to use it on you, but you've given us no choice."

He drew a narrow object from within his raincoat and then pressed it against my arm.

The pain of the prick against my shoulder was brief, but within seconds, a haziness filled my mind, and I wasn't sure where the line was between reality and dreams.

Whatever Dr. Wells had inserted in my bloodstream made me feel like I had woken up after a too-short sleep—suspended between the wakeful world and the sleeping one.

They carried me off the tram and into a building that I realized was the same place I'd been taken to meet Jez after she'd escaped Phase Three prison. I was transferred to an empty patient room, and when a medic came in and started me on an IV, I had no strength or willpower to protest.

Whatever liquid was in the IV burned hot, then cold, but it cleared my mind so that I felt wide awake—almost euphoric. Every sound became amplified, and as the medic moved about the room, adjusting a large monitor, I winced at every sound.

Dr. Wells came into the room and hovered near the doorway, and although he was whispering to the medic, I could hear every word.

"How long will it take for the serum to work?" Wells asked the doctor.

"Minutes," he replied. "You can start your questioning right away."

I tried to lift my head, but I realized I was very comfortable. And I realized that I wanted to confess everything to

Dr. Wells. He didn't even need to ask me any questions. I had been foolish to spend the past year trying to learn the inner workings of the city. Why had I been trying to take down the Legislature? We were all part of the human race and needed to work for the common good—together. Yes, some choices were hard, but that was the only way to continue surviving in our flooded world.

Dr. Wells deserved the truth, as did the rest of the government officials. And I was willing to be the person to tell it to them; for who knew better than I about the movement operating in the Lake Town?

As Dr. Wells approached the bed and sat in a nearby chair with his tablet in hand, I smiled. The first time I'd smiled openly since arriving in the city. But I didn't mind that he knew that I wasn't controlled by a Harmony implant. I was ready to share my story.

CHAPTER 7

Jez

"Keep going," Rueben called above the deep voice shouting through a loudspeaker. *Security breach! Security breach!*

I climbed onto the dock. There were two boats docked—both fishing boats. One was dark, the other had a light on at the captain's wheel. I could see three men. I ran toward the boat, and as I neared, I realized that two of the men were Gabe and Michel. The third was an older man—the captain—and he did not look happy about being tied up.

I leapt onto the rocking boat, and Rueben followed. I helped him set Becca down, and Rueben handed me a life jacket. "Put this on her."

I crouched to lift Becca's limp arms and slid each one through the jacket, then buckled it in front. Her head lolled to one side, her eyes open and staring, but not seeing. She was so pale.

"Here," Rueben said, handing me a piece of cloth he'd ripped from his shirt. "Tie it around the wound."

I had been so focused on her face that I hadn't seen how much she was bleeding. The blood had seeped through her pants. I couldn't take the time to see if the bullet was still in her leg. I tied the cloth around her thigh and knotted it securely. Just as I finished, the boat's engine roared, and the boat jerked away from the dock.

I nearly toppled onto Becca. I grabbed at a nearby bench and hung on as the boat pitched from one side to the other, moving in and out of the spotlight that was tracking our progress.

The captain was shouting curses at everyone until Gabe marched him to the edge and untied the ropes from his hands. Then Gabe shoved the captain over the side. He flailed, then splashed into the water. I stared in horror as the boat jetted away from his screams, and his bobbing head was the last thing I saw as the spotlight passed over him.

"He'll drown!" I shouted at Gabe.

He didn't even look at me as he took over the steering wheel. "He's close enough to shore to swim."

Rueben and Michel were bending over Becca, feeling her pulse, counting her heartbeats. I looked behind us at the two security boats speeding after us. I had a feeling that their engines were much more powerful than ours.

I scrounged around for another life jacket and pulled it on, buckling the clasps with trembling fingers. With every passing second, the boats gained on us, but the others didn't seem too concerned about our pursuers.

I tried to walk across the deck toward Gabe but fell after the second step. Never having been on a boat before, I had no idea they were so hard to walk on. I grasped at whatever I could until I'd made it to the captain's wheel.

"What happened back there?" Gabe asked me, his spiky dark hair blowing nearly flat in the wind.

"We were shot at," I said. "They got Becca in the leg."

"And you stopped for her?" Gabe looked away from me, moving his focus back to the ocean. "We could have all been killed."

He was reprimanding Rueben, I knew, but I somehow felt responsible. Sol's message about getting me out of the city was the reason we were all on this boat, racing across the water in the middle of the night.

Before I could come up with some sort of reply, Gabe said, "You'd better find something to hold onto. It's about to get rough."

I was already holding onto a nearby rail, so I clamped both of my hands around it.

Suddenly, everything on the boat went pitch dark. Gabe had switched off all the lights. The engine accelerated, rumbling the boards beneath my feet. The boat lunged forward, speeding even faster, although I knew the security boats would still be gaining on us. Then Gabe turned the boat sharply, and I nearly lost my grasp on the rail. My feet slipped out from under me, and I was pitched sideways, hanging on with only my hands as the boat cut through the water at an angle.

I might have screamed if the wind hadn't made it so difficult to breathe. And then just when I didn't think I could hang on to the rail any longer, the engine cut out. Completely stopped.

Pulling myself to a sitting position, I looked around. Gabe was hunkered beneath the captain's wheel. Rueben was by Becca, clutching her close and holding onto the far rail. And Michel was nowhere to be seen. I didn't dare ask any questions, though.

In the distance, the security boats moved in slow circles. Somehow—miraculously—they'd lost our trail.

I heard a faint moan, and a movement caught my eye. Toward the back of the boat, Michel rose to his feet. He must have slid all the way over there.

"Get down," Rueben hissed at him.

Michel said something that sounded like a curse word and dropped onto a bench. He stretched out on top of it.

I didn't dare move from my crouched position as the boat drifted in the water. Looking back at the circling boats, I caught glimpses of the shoreline of the city. I was really leaving. It was hard to believe that I was away from the place I'd lived my whole life, surrounded by a vast gray ocean, relying on a group of people I barely knew to take me somewhere I'd only heard about.

I was about to find out if the myths about Lake Towns were true.

Time passed. It must have been about an hour before Michel and Gabe finally rose and started moving about the boat. Rueben crossed over to me and grasped my hand, helping me to my feet. "Are you all right?" he asked.

I was exhausted, cold, wet, and hungry, but I said, "Yes."

"Becca's awake. Take her below and you two can dry off," he said. "See if you can find a first aid kit and clean her wound. I felt around the wound, and I don't think the bullet is still in. There also might be something down there to change into."

"Do you need help up here?" I asked, glancing at the others. Gabe was at the captain's wheel, and Michel was coiling up rope.

"I'll let you know if we do," Rueben said. "But for now, take Becca below."

I understood the concern in his voice for Becca, but I knew very little about first aid. I crossed over to her and was glad to see that she was awake. The fabric scrap I'd tied around her leg was stained with blood, but the stain hadn't spread much farther. "Let's get you below," I said, wrapping an arm around her.

I could hardly support her weight, and Rueben ended up rushing over to help me get Becca down the few stairs to the small cabin below deck. He turned on an oil lamp, then rummaged through the cupboards while I sat Becca on one of the two cots.

"How are you feeling?" I asked Becca.

She blinked at me, and even in the dim light of the oil lamp, I could see that her cheeks were too pink, her eyes too bright.

When Rueben came over to us with a first aid kit, I looked at him. "Do you think she's in shock? Or maybe an infection has already started?"

"I don't know," he said, his normally warm eyes dark with worry.

I'd never seen Rueben be anything but confident. So now that he was worried, I felt it acutely as well.

"Let's lay her down and look at the wound," I said.

Becca didn't resist as I moved her into a prone position, but she winced when I lifted her pant leg to reveal the gash in her leg.

Rueben sat on the edge of the bed, his face going deathly pale.

"Are you all right?" I asked.

He swallowed, then nodded. "I'm just light-headed."

"I think you're right. The bullet's not in there."

"Good," Rueben said. His color started to return.

He must have expended a lot of energy carrying Becca. When we'd been in Phase Three together, Rueben hadn't had any issues with the sight of blood. "I'll clean it, and then we can be sure," I told him.

"Right," Rueben said, helping me prepare the supplies.

While I cleaned the wound with gauze and disinfectant, Rueben held Becca's leg still. She kept flinching at the application but kept her eyes closed. I didn't think that was a very good sign, but once the wound was clean, Rueben agreed that there wasn't a bullet in her leg after all.

I sensed his relief, as palpable as mine.

"But why is she so out of it?" I asked him.

Rueben stood and walked to the top of the bed so he could peer down at Becca. "She's probably exhausted." He glanced at me. "Like we all are."

I bit my lower lip. Becca's face was still flushed pink. Something wasn't right. "Do you know what kind of bullets they were shooting?"

Rueben's brows arched. "Probably the range ones—those are the only ones in the city, although I thought they were illegal to use, even for the security officers."

"Have you ever heard of poisoned bullets?" I asked. "It might explain how she's acting."

Again, Rueben's face paled, and I wished I could reassure him that Becca hadn't been poisoned, but she was acting very ill for having only received a surface wound.

"What can we do?" Rueben asked in a hushed voice, but I saw the panic in his eyes.

"Try to flush it out," I said. "Is there any drinking water on board?"

"I'll find some," Rueben said, jumping to his feet and rushing back up on deck.

While he was gone, I gathered up the first aid supplies, keeping an eye on Becca's breathing. It was steady, so at least there was that. I wished I could access the WorldNet and look up her symptoms.

It wasn't long before Rueben came tripping back down the stairs with a canteen that looked like it had been around in the Before. As I took the canteen from him, I asked, "Is this water clean?"

"I tasted it first," Rueben said, casting me a rueful look. "I filled it from a water barrel up top, so there's plenty."

"All right," I said. "Can you hold up her head?"

Rueben did, and I pressed the canteen opening against Becca's mouth. She coughed at the first bit, but her eyes opened. She didn't exactly focus on me, but I told her, "You need to drink, Becca." She dutifully took a couple of sips, swallowing the water down, but then tried to pull away. "No, drink some more. It's important."

I gave Rueben a nod.

"Becca, we think you were hit with a poisonous bullet," he said. "We need you to drink as much as possible in order to dilute the poison."

Becca's eyes fluttered open, and for a moment, I thought she'd understood us. But then her eyes shut again. I poured more water into her mouth and watched it dribble off her chin. "Let's try again in a few minutes," I said.

Rueben let her head relax back onto the cot. "Is there anything else we can try?"

"I can ask Michel and Gabe if they have any ideas," I said, then handed the canteen to Rueben. "Try again in a few minutes. Even one swallow of water would be progress."

He nodded and said nothing as I left the cabin. Up on deck the rain was coming down hard. Even though it was dark, I could see the rolling storm clouds up ahead. It appeared that we were moving straight for a storm.

Gabe was still at the captain's wheel, and Michel was right beside him. When they saw me emerge from below, Michel crossed to me. "How's Becca?"

I filled him in, but he had no more advice than giving her water. Gabe said that if she could hold on until the Lake Town, we could get her medical care. I walked around the deck, holding onto the rails to avoid slipping. I stood at the back of the boat to see if I could make out any part of the city, but it was either totally obscured by rain or we were too far away now. We were surrounded by the dark void of the churning ocean.

The boat pitched, and I grabbed the rail. We hit another wave, and I groaned at the echoing lurch in my stomach.

"Get below!" Gabe shouted at me over the increasing wind.

I didn't need to be told twice. I moved as quickly as I could, but the boat's movement caused me to stagger more than once. When I made it down to the cabin, Rueben was busily securing items by locking them in the cupboard.

Becca's face was still flushed and her eyes closed.

"Are we headed into the storm?" Rueben asked, raising his voice to overpower the increased noise from above.

"Yeah," I said, clutching my stomach and sitting next to Becca on the bed. The boat tilted at a deeper angle, and I let out a groan.

She opened her eyes, and they were clearer than they had been before. "What's happening?" she asked, looking about the cabin wildly. "Are we going to sink?"

Rueben was by her side immediately, grasping her hand. "We're heading into a storm. How are you feeling?"

Becca looked at me. "Was I poisoned?" she asked.

"We're not sure," I said, grateful that she was looking a lot better, although the rocking of the boat wasn't helping my rising nausea.

The boat lurched violently, and Rueben grabbed onto both of us, and we huddled all together on the bed.

"Please, God, spare our lives," Becca said.

I was feeling too sick and scared to be shocked that she was offering a forbidden prayer. If I thought there was a god, I'd be praying, too.

CHAPTER 8

Sol

Dr. Wells's blue eyes were kind, even friendly, and I'm not sure why it surprised me so much. He'd never been cruel to me; he'd only wanted to do what was best for the city. And he, along with the Legislature, deserved to know the truth. As Dr. Wells began to ask the first questions, I wondered why I had spent so many months trying to keep secrets. It had been exhausting.

"Where are you from, Sol?" Dr. Wells asked.

It was a simple question, really. One that I hadn't ever been asked that I could remember. Everyone in the city had always assumed that I'd been born there like they had. But now I realized that not even Jez knew the truth about my childhood.

"I'm from a Lake Town," I said. Rueben and I had been friends as young boys, and we'd been part of the original plan. I'd come to find the Carrier, and once I found her, Rueben made his preparations.

"Who was the man who raised you after your caretaker was Taken?" Dr. Wells asked, not looking very surprised at my answer.

"His name was Zed," I said. "I don't remember my natural mother or father. They died before I was three."

The edges of Dr. Wells's mouth lifted as he tapped something into his tablet. "Do you know why your parents died, Sol?"

I had asked Zed this same question many times, but he had never answered it.

"They came to the city," Dr. Wells said, as if he already knew that I didn't know the answer. "We discovered that they were trying to infiltrate the government."

Something deep inside of me went on alert, but Dr. Wells was speaking in a calm, soothing voice, and I knew I had nothing to worry about.

His mouth almost curved into a smile, although I knew it wasn't a true smile. "We locked them up and gave them a chance to tell us what they were really doing in the city. Why they'd come and why they were breaking the rules and risking the safety of our civilization. Your female caretaker hacked into the WorldNet and added illegal warnings. We caught them before they could be downloaded by our citizens. And your male caretaker." Dr. Wells paused, his mouth turning down. "He was an expert mechanic, and he altered some of our machines in the electrical department. He was trying to manipulate our power output."

That's why I'm *here,* I was about to say, when Wells continued, "They were Executed for breaking the rules and putting our citizens in jeopardy."

I was shocked. My parents. Executed.

Dr. Wells leaned closer. "If you share what you know,

and why you're really here, Sol, you can escape the same fate."

Of course I would. I had no intention of dying. I was more than willing to tell Dr. Wells anything he wanted to know. Then my skin started to tingle, and I looked at the IV attached to my arm. Another dose of whatever they were giving me was flowing into my body, and my veins began to burn. I squeezed my eyes shut as the pain intensified, and then suddenly it eased.

"I came to finish what my father started," I said. "I've been learning how to run the electric power machines and generators, and I've been memorizing the codes to get me through security."

Dr. Wells tapped into his tablet again, then looked directly at me. "Tell me why."

"We are planning on taking over the Legislature and restoring humanity to its former self," I said.

Wells's brows arched. "How?"

I linked my fingers together. "We have invented an atomic bulb that evaporates water and doesn't send the moisture back into the atmosphere. But in order to create enough power to run it, we need the generators."

This time Dr. Wells's face showed surprise. "How do you know about the generators?" Then he lifted his hand and said, "Let me guess: Zed."

I nodded, and Wells continued, "It's impossible, you know. They haven't worked for decades. The keys have been missing since the Before."

Excitement blended with the euphoria of the liquid coursing through me. I lowered my voice as if I were about to tell Wells the greatest secret—which, in fact, I was. "The keys weren't lost. They were hidden, inside of people. People we call Carriers."

It was thrilling to tell Dr. Wells something he didn't know.

His eyes widened. "Where are these 'Carriers'?"

I smiled, happy that I could answer his question. "We've only been able to locate one Carrier so far. And she's being taken to a Lake Town for training."

"Who?" Wells asked.

I could see the realization dawning in his expression even as he asked.

"Jezebel James," I answered.

CHAPTER 9

Jez

I had never thought I'd be so glad to see a stretch of land in the middle of the ocean. The boat trip had taken two full days, and even after the storm faded into a calm sea, my stomach felt like it had been through a battle. At least Becca was awake and feeling better. As I stood out on the deck helping the boys prepare for landing, my heart both soared and plummeted. Soared because I'd safely escaped the city and the officials chasing us; plummeted because Sol hadn't joined us, and I worried about him.

Rueben assured me that Sol was probably being very careful, and if he didn't have a safe way to leave, he would have stayed behind so he wouldn't compromise my escape. At any rate, Sol had been aware enough to warn me and Rueben to get out, so he must have been able to stay safe himself. At least that's what I had to tell myself.

I almost lost my balance when the boat bumped into the extended dock reaching from the shoreline. Where I'd expected to see tall, gray buildings outlined in the rain like in the city, this island looked desolate. As far as I could see, trees and jungle-like foliage stretched across the land. Not a soul was there to greet us, either.

"Are you ready?" Becca asked, coming up behind me. She clutched a raincoat about her thin form. Her face had returned to its normal color, and her eyes were bright. It was good to see her walking around.

"Where is everyone?" I asked.

"Beyond the trees, out of sight from the shoreline," she said. "You won't see a welcoming party at our Lake Town, but, believe me, we're being watched."

I scanned the trees and bushes as if I would be able to see faces peering back at me. But there was nothing.

"Come on," Becca said, shouldering a bag of the equipment we'd brought and limping as she walked ahead of me.

I picked up one of the bags and hoisted it onto my shoulder, wincing as the strap cut into the bruises I'd sustained sliding around the deck, banging into things aplenty. We crossed to the side of the boat where Gabe had secured it to the dock. Rueben had already stepped off, and extended his hand to Becca. She took it, and I followed.

My legs still felt wobbly as I walked along the wet dock with the others. But for the first time in two days, my stomach started to feel better. The rain was a soft drizzle, and the sky a light gray. The air felt and smelled different out here. Maybe it was because we weren't surrounded by the infrastructure of the city. In this Lake Town, the scent of ocean water mixed with the smell of the trees up ahead.

"Why aren't there other boats tied up to the dock?" I asked Gabe as we walked.

"They're on the other side of the island," he said. "Once

we get you to the compound, I'll come back and move the boat around. But here, we are much closer to the compound, and it's less of a walk for Becca."

I had more questions, but I was too curious to see what lay beyond the first line of trees. Rueben led us along a well-worn trail that weaved around a group of trees, and suddenly, we faced a tall wall that I hadn't seen at all from the dock.

It reminded me of the wall in the city, although this one was built from planks of wood instead of cement blocks.

We walked along the edge for a few paces, then Rueben stopped and said, "Here we are." He unlatched a lock and pushed open a gate-like door.

We stepped through and came face-to-face with a circle of men and women who stood close together, knives in their hands. They wore long raincoats that looked to be made of tanned animal skins.

One of the women stepped forward. "Rueben, welcome back."

He smiled, then moved to embrace her. The woman then greeted Becca, Gabe, and Michel.

When the woman looked at me, I was grateful to see only curiosity, and not suspicion, in her gaze. "You are Jezebel James?"

She knew my name? "Yes," I said, full of curiosity myself.

"Welcome to our Lake Town," she said.

I scanned the other faces of those gathered, and was surprised by the coloring of their skin. It wasn't exactly dark, but bronzed, as if they'd lived beneath a sunny sky. But the Lake Town had plenty of gray clouds and rain, just like the city. I wondered if they'd had sunshine during more than just the Solstice days twice a year.

"Come with me," the woman said, motioning for me to follow her.

I glanced over at Rueben, and he nodded and then turned back to the man he was speaking with.

"My name is Martha," the woman said. "We're glad you finally made it. With you secured, we can begin our final plans."

I was full of questions, but just then, she stopped in front of a glass atrium of sorts. It reminded me of the Agricultural Center in the city. She swung the door open and ushered me inside. A bright light nearly blinded me, and I squinted, trying to take in my surroundings. The atrium's warmth felt wonderful, and I wanted to somehow wrap my arms around the whole of it, let it all consume me in delicious heat.

I looked over at the walls. Outside, the rain pelted against the glass, but inside, it wasn't humid at all, but dry like old paper, and I couldn't see any plant beds. My gaze traveled upward where the ceiling of the atrium shone a brilliant yellow, and I realized I was looking at the same type of globe that had been at the top of the underground cavern in the city.

Martha slipped off her long raincoat and draped it over a nearby bench. Her dark blonde hair fell down her back, longer than I expected. In the city, most women kept their hair length to about their shoulders and pulled back from their faces. I looked about the atrium and realized that it was dotted with benches, and other people sat quietly, their eyes closed, as if they were just basking in the warmth of the globe.

I took off my jacket as well and immediately felt the drying effect of the yellow globe. The heat was remarkable, really. “I didn’t realize there was more than one globe,” I told Martha. “I thought the one in the cavern in the city was the only one.”

Martha came to stand beside me, crossing her arms. She wore short sleeves, something I’d never seen on anyone. But I was starting to feel warmer and warmer and felt overdressed now.

“Can you imagine what will happen when we have dozens of these set up throughout the city?” Martha asked with a smile in her tone.

I stared at her. “Is that your plan?”

She arched her eyebrow, as if she were surprised I didn’t know. “Of course. It will take years, you know, to start the flood receding. But if we have enough of these globes powered up and running, we can start to dry out the city and reclaim landmass. It won’t stop the rain, of course, but it will reduce the moisture evaporating and returning to the atmosphere.”

I was stunned into silence. Everything was fitting into place. “How much power does it take to run a globe?”

“Running several will take all of the city’s power,” Martha said. “We’d need more. A lot more.”

“Like the power the generators can provide?”

Martha smiled, and her whole face lit up. “Yes.”

“And that’s why you need a Carrier, to power on the generators,” I said in a quiet voice. “How many generators are there?”

“We’ve estimated that there are about fifteen in the city alone,” Martha said. “There may have been more in other locations, but those are flooded out.”

“And we can’t talk the Legislature into cooperating?”

Martha released a laugh. The sound buzzed through me.

"Many people tried that approach already, including Sol's parents. They never returned to our Lake Town."

The information sobered me.

"Power and greed have a strange control over people," Martha continued. "Even if a solution to our problem is presented, the Legislature is more concerned over losing its power."

"We've been sending over recruits for years," Martha said, "to learn how to run the power plants, because once we take over the Legislature, we don't know what they'll do to the citizens. They have control over them through their Harmony implants."

The magnitude of it all started to overwhelm me.

"Jezebel," Martha said, placing a hand on my arm. "We need you. Not only are you a Carrier with the key to the generators, you have knowledge of the city and the Legislature." Her eyes held mine. "We will do everything to protect you, but other lives may be lost. We'll have to use force to take down the Legislature."

I swallowed against the thickening in my throat.

"But," Martha said in a soft voice, "once it's all over with and the globes are expanding, civilization will start to heal. In a decade or two, our children will have a better life."

I nodded. She was right, I knew that. But at what cost?

CHAPTER 10

Sol

The handcuffs they strapped my wrists into weren't metal but a thick plastic that was just as unbreakable. I'd been in a holding room for hours, perhaps days. The truth serum had worked all too well. I told them everything. I told them the plan to take over the Legislature. I told them that Jez had escaped to a Lake Town with Rueben and the others. I told them that Jez is a Carrier and possesses the only key in existence to the generators.

And now they were preparing for war. Against my friends, and against the girl I love. The minutes and hours dragged on, and my mind was a tortured abyss of regret. Because of me, everything would fail. The Legislature was planning to wipe out the boats arriving from the Lake Town as soon as they come into sight.

Dr. Wells had me pumped with the truth serum for two straight days, and I babbled about everything—about how the Lake Town was structured, about our master plan to restore humanity, and how my own parents were the first ones sent over as the initiates of the rebellion. I told Dr. Wells how I had replaced them, and how we were training the Lake Town citizens to infiltrate the city.

The door of my solitary cell opened, and Dr. Wells entered with two security officers. I didn't know whether I was relieved or terrified. Would they pump me full of more truth serum? I honestly couldn't think of anything I hadn't already confessed. The two security officers dragged me to my feet, which wasn't hard in my weakened state.

Their hands clamped around my upper arms, and, with my handcuffs on, it was easy for them to control my every movement. Not that I had a plan to escape, yet. I knew that I needed to reverse the damage I'd caused, but I didn't know how. If I found a way to escape and live as a fugitive, I would be useless. I had to act like I was under their control, on their side.

My greatest fear was that they'd alter me. But it seemed that their chemical experimentation was over, and I was led into a court room.

Fourteen judges sat upon the upper bench, eight men and six women, all with their eyes on me. I remembered Jez telling me about when she faced the Council and they handed down her conviction. There were others in the room, sitting in a row of chairs, waiting for their turn.

I took my seat at the end of the row, flanked by the security officers, and Dr. Wells sat behind me. I felt his gaze on the back of my neck, determined to analyze every movement I made.

The judges refocused their attention back on the young woman who stood before them in handcuffs. The woman reminded me of Jez—not in appearance, but in vulnerability.

She was convicted of doing illegal research on the WorldNet. I found myself straining to hear every soft-spoken word she said.

"My caretaker has been ill, and the medicines from the medical center haven't helped," she said. "I wanted to see if there was another remedy that could cure her."

None of the judges looked very convinced. A middle-aged man with a nearly bald head leaned forward and said, "Your searches came up as classified. You are not a medical professional, and any medication or treatments need to be directed by the medical staff, not by a regular citizen."

The woman hung her head, and I noticed how thin her shoulders looked.

"What's the age of your caretaker?" the male judge asked the woman.

Her head snapped up, and her whole body tensed; I could tell she didn't want to answer the question.

"Sixty-two," she finally said.

The judges exchanged glances with one another, then one of them said, "We will speak to the medical center about your caretaker's treatment plan. Now we will move on to sentencing."

A female judge stood and cleared her throat, then read from her tablet. "You will be sentenced to six months in Phase Three prison."

Abigail cried out, and I felt as if I'd been punched in the stomach. The punishment for illegal research used to be a month spent in C Level labor, or perhaps several days in Detention. Six months was extreme.

She was led away in cuffs, and the next person was called to face the judges. I watched as each person listened to their charges and then were quickly sentenced.

No one had come in after me, so I was the last person to the bench. I was quite sure this was deliberate. The judges likely didn't want the others to know how far I'd infiltrated their treachery. And now, I'd have to do the most difficult thing of all.

"Solomon," one of the judges said. "You've been brought before us to be handed your sentence." He looked down at his tablet, seeming to read my charges, but his eyes didn't track any words. When he lifted his gaze, his face was a façade of calm. But the man's pale eyes seemed to pierce right into me. "Your crimes have exceeded any in the past decade, and your punishment calls for Banishment or Execution."

The words rocked through me, although they didn't come as any surprise. I kept my back straight, but inside I was burning with humiliation. Not for the punishment that was sure to come, but for the wrongs I'd brought upon the people of the Lake Town.

"You have cooperated and confessed much that has been very useful to the Legislature," the judge continued. "And for your continued cooperation, they have requested that you not be altered yet."

The words echoed in my mind. So I would not be altered, but I might be Banished or even Executed. There was little comfort in that. At least altering was reversible. It seemed that the Legislature didn't know that Jez had shocked Chalice with an agitator rod and reversed her altered state.

I thought of my role as an Informer, of my need to stay as close as possible to any secure information, and knew I had to convince the judges to trust me.

"What do you have to say for yourself?" the judge asked me.

I lifted my chin and lied. "I have told Dr. Wells everything I know, and in doing so, I've realized the serious error of what I was taught to believe. The Legislature is not anyone's enemy, and I will help wherever I can to right my wrongs. I know it might take a while for anyone to trust me, but I will undergo whatever tasks or punishments you deem necessary."

I saw in their eyes that it would take a lot more than that for them to trust me again—that it may never happen at all. But I was running out of time. If the government was investigating any of the information I'd so readily given them under the spell of the truth serum, I had to find a way to warn Rueben and Jez and the others at the Lake Town.

"Your punishment has not been decided yet," the judge said. Then he looked at the security officers next to me. "Return him to his cell."

The security officer to my left clamped a hand down on my arm. Returning to the cell was punishment enough. I'd be completely isolated, and the constant turning of my thoughts was the worst torture of all.

The officers moved me swiftly out of the courtroom, as if they couldn't stand being there, either. Dr. Wells stayed behind, and I wondered what he was speaking to the judges about. I didn't have to wonder long, because about an hour after I'd returned to my cell, the door opened, and Wells walked in.

He came in alone and closed the door behind him. I was no danger to him in my handcuffs, unless I had a sudden burst of energy to head butt him—but that would hurt me just as much as him.

"The judges want you altered now," Dr. Wells began with no preamble. "But the Legislature thinks you are still useful; that you haven't told us everything."

I'd told them everything, unfortunately. Or I'd at least given the answers to all of Dr. Wells's probing questions, which was enough information to doom the Lake Town. I had to find a way to warn them, to stop them from coming. Then at least they could continue living in the Lake Town, and not risk the battle that would meet them in the city.

"What is it?" Wells asked, peppering my thoughts. "Have you told me everything?"

"I have," I said, hoping that my voice sounded confident. He knew enough. What I didn't tell him was that, if given a tablet, I could hack into the WorldNet and make things interesting for the Legislature—send them on a wild goose chase after false leads. Thankfully, he hadn't asked me those questions. Or about where I had hidden out between my transfers to the different levels.

And if I'd told Dr. Wells about the cavern, I wouldn't be alive right now. The Legislature would know I'd given up all my secrets.

"Have you ever heard of the Faction?" Dr. Wells said, lowering his voice.

I stayed still and was about to deny that I had, but Dr. Wells had already seen the answer in my eyes.

"You have," Wells said. "Very good. I knew that you have more to offer." He clasped his hands together. "I have an agenda, you see, and if you know what the Faction's mission is, you'll understand."

"You're a Faction member?" I asked.

His single nod said it all.

Dr. Wells's revelation could either be very good or very bad. But, either way, it completely changed everything. He was a rebel in his own right, although I didn't know if the Faction was much better than the Legislature—whether it was for or against someone like me.

Every few years, news broke about a member of the Faction being exposed. The penalty for membership was immediate Banishment. In fact, a few of them had made their way to the Lake Town, but were always sent away. Anyone who'd been part of the Legislature and then betrayed it from within couldn't be trusted. And Faction members were members for life—their blood oaths were stronger than any religion or family connection.

"I can see you're interested," Dr. Wells said. "Helping me would be better than sitting in this cell waiting to be altered whenever the Legislature gets tired of asking you questions." He shook his head. "You haven't given them much new information, anyway."

Now, that surprised me. "What do you mean? They already knew about the Carriers?"

"Of course," Wells said. "That's why Phase Three prison was developed. We send anyone who is immune, Clinical, or a potential Carrier there for testing."

I sobered at this thought. Jez had been there for several weeks. The Legislature had been watching her closely for much longer than I thought. Then another idea occurred to me. I snapped my eyes up to meet Wells's. "How long has the Legislature been tracking me?"

A corner of Wells's mouth lifted, although I knew it wasn't a smile. "You've been elusive until a few months ago, when you went into Detention to try to distract the authorities from Jezebel's illegal journal."

It made a strange sort of sense.

"As far as the Legislature knows, you are wiling away your days in this cell. But after midnight each night, I'll come and collect you." Dr. Wells arched a brow in my direction.

What could I do but agree? And leaving the cell would

open up a new opportunity. If Dr. Wells thought I'd keep his secret about being a member of the Faction, then he'd developed a misplaced trust in me. Did he know that my speech before the judges was completely false? Or was he leading me into another dead end?

Wells shut the door and promised to be back at midnight, and I closed my eyes against the dim light of the cell, having no doubt that he would.

CHAPTER 11

Jez

Martha led me through the atrium to the opposite side. We stepped through a door that opened to the outside and into the familiar rain. It felt colder and wetter than I remembered, even after such a short time in the dry atrium.

I walked with Martha along a rocky path through a copse of trees until it opened up into a wide square surrounded by low, black buildings that connected to one another. We only passed a couple of people, and I wondered where everyone else was.

Martha kept moving quickly until we reached a thick door that she pushed open. Inside, it was nearly black, and I stayed close to her as I followed. "What is this place?" I asked in the deep silence, almost overwhelmed by a strong odor. It smelled like a combination of rotted wood and a conglomeration of chemicals.

"It's a decoy," she said. "If our island was invaded, the

soldiers would come to these buildings looking for people. Or if the invasion were aerial, they'd drop their bombs on these structures." She turned on her wrist light and shined it about the place.

The building was low ceilinged, and I imagined that Rueben and Sol would have to stoop in here. The ground was barren and slightly muddy. "What's on the walls?"

"Tar and petroleum," Martha said. "If a bullet or bomb hits a wall, it will create a terrific fire."

I stared at the thick, black substance smeared on the walls. "Isn't that dangerous for the people here?"

"Another decoy," Martha said. "These buildings explode, and we escape through the other side of the island." She crossed to the center of the room and crouched, shining her wrist light on the ground.

"See this handle?" she asked as I reached her side.

A metal, curved handle showed through the dirt, although it was level with the ground. Martha placed her palm flat on the handle. I stared as a door slid open in the middle of the wall.

"Come on," Martha said with a chuckle. "The first time into the cavern is always the most nerve-racking."

When I stepped past the door with Martha, my eyes could hardly adjust to the even deeper black. It was like staring into a bottomless pit.

"Don't worry," Martha said. "You'll get used to it soon enough. Just hang on to the ropes."

Martha stepped down and turned on her wrist light, casting light against a series of stairs—but the stairs weren't made of cement or wood. They were of woven ropes that swayed as she stepped onto them.

"They're strong and secure," Martha said. "Once you get the hang of it, it's easy to keep your balance."

So I followed her, and after about my third step, the door slid noiselessly behind us, leaving us in a deep black punctuated only by the narrow beam of Martha's wrist light. Except this darkness wasn't as silent. Voices echoed somewhere below us. Women and men, and even younger voices—children.

The air was surprisingly dry as I carefully followed Martha down the rope steps. We were in a narrow shaft, and if I wanted to reach out, I could have touched the walls, which appeared remarkably dry as well. The shaft began to turn, and Martha turned off her wrist light, no longer needing it. Light flooded upward from somewhere below, and I guessed it was another globe. Maybe even more than one, gauging by the amount of light.

A couple more turns along the rope stairs, and the underground cavern opened up. The room was smaller than I anticipated, and indeed, a globe was suspended near the top of the room. But then I realized that the room was the first of many. As we walked past several dug-out rooms along the winding, dry corridor, I glanced into each space. Each room contained a smaller version of the globe inside. One room was set up with wooden tables and chairs, with children sitting at the tables, all intent on drawing.

"Wait," I said to Martha. "Are they drawing on paper with pencils?"

"Yes," she said with a small laugh. "I'm sure it's fascinating to you."

And it was. I paused in the doorway and watched the children's pencils moving fluidly along their pieces of paper. At first, a panicky feeling swept through me. They were wasting precious paper and pencils, which we only had in museums in the city.

"We make the paper and pencils ourselves," Martha said, the sound of amusement still in her voice. "But don't think the children are being wasteful. They're replicating machine designs. We've found that the best way to start learning mechanics is to draw the machines from the inside out and include each detail."

I continued to stare, amazed.

"Come on," Martha said. "I think you'll like the next classroom as well."

The corridor sloped as we continued, and the air started to feel different. Moist. When we reached the next "classroom," I understood what Martha meant. A pool of water carved out the middle of the room, and although the width wasn't more than two dozen feet, Martha said, "The pool is fifty feet deep."

I started as a masked head surfaced above the water.

"That's Jude," Martha said. "He's doing his diving training."

The man climbing out of the water wore black, form-fitting pants, but his torso was bare. His face was obscured by a mask that had a tube running to a metal container on his back.

"Scuba diving," I said. "He's scuba diving?" I'd read an article once years ago about scuba diving. When I tried to find it again on the WorldNet, it had been deleted.

"It's one of our training requirements," Martha said, giving me a meaningful look.

As much as I wanted to see how Jude managed to detach himself from the equipment, I took a step back. I wasn't going to get into water anytime soon. My near drowning experience in Phase Three overpowered any curiosity that I might have.

"Are you the new girl?" Jude asked, popping off his mask.

I stared at him. He reminded me of Sol: similar height, dark hair, and those eyes—a deep gray that I imagined would lighten on a sunlit day. Then I realized that I was still staring, and I blinked.

Jude smiled, and something inside me fluttered. He did look like Sol, but I had never seen Sol smile. This was a different man, and a much different vision before me.

"You must be Jezebel," Jude said. "Because I could only imagine one girl that would stare at me like that."

I glanced over at Martha, not understanding how Jude knew anything about me. Or why he would say that to me. But Martha simply said, "How's the training going, Jude?"

He reached behind his back, and I couldn't help but notice the way his arm and chest muscles flexed at his movement. He might look like Sol, but his body was conditioned like that of a soldier's. "I can stay down for nearly thirty minutes now," he said as he unstrapped the metal container from his back. "We need bigger tanks."

Martha nodded thoughtfully. "They're already in production, but the weight of them might be too much for the women."

Jude watched me openly, and I felt my face heat up under his scrutiny. Why was I reacting this way to him? I didn't know him; I'd never met the man, yet I couldn't seem to take my eyes off him.

"Should we tell her?" Jude asked Martha, although he was looking at me.

"Of course," Martha said, and I could hear a smile in her voice. "She'll likely figure it out soon enough anyway."

Jude stepped off the deck that rimmed the pool and

walked toward me, water dripping from his hair and torso. His skin was the same color as Rueben's—bronzed as if he'd lived under the sun. An impossible feat, I knew. He extended his hand. "Nice to meet you at last, Jezebel."

I grasped his hand. "Hi," I said in a slight croak. Even my voice was failing me.

"Welcome to our Lake Town," Jude continued. "I've been looking forward to meeting you ever since my younger brother told us about you."

"Younger brother?" I asked.

"Yes," Jude said, releasing my hand. "Sol's my younger brother. Hasn't he ever mentioned me?"

The breath left me. Sol had a brother? Now the resemblance made sense, and I understood my reaction to him. "He . . . only told me about his caretaker and his caretaker's grandfather."

Jude just nodded, apparently unsurprised. "Of course. You probably don't know Sol as well as you thought you did. I forget that all of this is new to you." He waved a hand as if to include the entire compound.

"I don't . . . I didn't know much about your Lake Town until Rueben told me," I said. "In the city, we're given a different perception of the outlying islands."

"Ah, Rueben," Jude said, his eyes shifting a little darker. "I guess we can give Rueben some credit for bringing you to our Lake Town safely."

"Yes," I agreed. I wanted to know what Sol had told Jude about me, though. I wanted to ask him questions about Sol, too.

At our A Level school, Sol and I had talked every day, yet it seemed there was so much I didn't know about him—so much he didn't tell me. And I could see that Jude realized that, and that he was interested to know why Sol and I hadn't revealed more of ourselves to each other.

Maybe people in the Lake Town didn't understand that I'd been living in fear most of my life. Fear that the government would find out that I was a Carrier. Fear that my teachers and classmates would discover that I was immune to the Harmony implant that was supposed to be suppressing my emotions. For a long time, I'd thought I was the only one struggling to put on a different face every day. To act differently than I felt and to pretend not to feel anything. That was until I met Rueben in Phase Three. He showed me that what I was feeling was a part of who I was, and he showed me that it was all right to smile, and laugh, and care, and love.

The last time I'd seen Sol, he'd pulled me into his arms, and my body burned at the feel of his body against mine. I still remembered every nuance of that embrace, and I could certainly never forget what happened when I pressed my lips against his. I had never thought that kissing someone could ignite such an intense longing and at the same time expand my heart until I thought I might float to the heavens. My memories of Sol and the reality of the man standing before me who looked so much like him collided together into a swift thump to my emotions.

Stop staring at Jude, I told myself.

He seemed to quite enjoy the attention, and the corners of his mouth lifted as he continued to study me. "I'm looking forward to getting to know you," he said in a low voice that I was pretty sure he meant for only me to hear.

CHAPTER 12

Sol

Dr. Wells plied me with more reading material than I expected, but I didn't mind in the least. I had a tablet back in my hand, and although we were cloistered together in Wells's University office in the dead of the night, I'd miss a thousand hours of sleep if it meant finding a way to reverse the damage I'd caused.

Dr. Wells sat in his chair, his eyes half closed, while I scrolled through the reading material he'd assigned. My hands were still cuffed together, although in front now, and Wells held an agitator rod in his hands. The door was locked with a combination that only Wells knew. So even if I was somehow quick enough to get the agitator rod away from Wells, and then shock and incapacitate him, I'd still be stuck inside the office, or at the very least on this second floor of the University building. The outside entrances were also locked.

"What do you think so far?" Wells asked.

I wasn't expecting such a friendly question—it was as if Wells considered me a comrade instead of an enemy or a prisoner.

"I told you that I'd heard of the Faction, but I didn't know how sophisticated it was," I said, looking up and meeting his eyes. The comment seemed to please him. "How long have you been a member?"

"Since birth, really," Wells said. "My caretaker and his caretaker were members. You could say I was grandfathered in. Just like you in the Lake Town."

We had something in common, it seemed. If I'd been born into another family—perhaps Wells's family—would I be battling for a different cause?

Wells leaned forward, his thick arms resting on his desk. "We're really on the same side, you and me."

"There are some significant differences," I pointed out. The people of the Lake Town wanted to make the world more habitable and stop the government manipulation so that citizens would be free to choose their own destinies. With the atomic globes in place, we might even be able to reverse the deadly flooding. The Faction just wanted to take over the government and have their members in power—nothing would change for the citizens. The world would continue to flood, civilization would continue to erode, and desperation would only increase year by year.

"Our differences aren't as significant as you might think," Dr. Wells said, steepling his hands together. "Once you finish reading those documents, we'll start your initiation."

I nodded, my heart thumping at the word *initiation.* I didn't know what he meant by it exactly, but as long as it wasn't altering or another chemical injection, I would find a way to send a message to Rueben. He had to know what I'd done, as painful as my guilt was.

I continued to read through documents, which amounted to a warped mission statement that was actually very close to the Legislature's. The Faction claimed that they wanted to restore "humanity" by giving the people voting power, like in the Before, yet the Faction would still have final decision-making power.

While reading about members of the Faction and their accomplishments, I also half watched Dr. Wells, hoping that his eyes would slide shut long enough for me to send a message through the tablet. The only trouble was that an encrypted message would only be active for a short while, and if Rueben didn't see it in time, the message would be lost. But as long as I had access to a tablet, I was going to keep trying.

Dr. Wells's eyes didn't shut, but he seemed to be gazing at nothing, so I opened a new page and tilted the tablet upward as I leaned back in my chair. I hoped he'd see it as the casual action of settling in for more reading. I pretended to scroll through the document, when in reality, I typed in the encrypted code, then a very short message.

Abort plan. City knows all.

I sent the message, then closed down the page and went back to the article. I'd have no way of knowing whether or not Rueben would get the message. I might never know. Continuing to read, I thought through the path we'd taken to Wells's office. We'd have to return the same way, and as I reviewed the steps in my mind, I looked for an opportunity to escape. The problem would be putting enough distance between me and Wells to reach the underground cavern before I was caught.

Wells seemed to know that I wasn't fully concentrating on my reading because he straightened and snatched the tablet from my hands. "That's enough for tonight," he said, picking up the agitator rod and motioning for me to stand.

I rose to my feet, my muscles cramped from sitting so long—although it was much better than sitting on the floor of my cell. I turned toward the door, and Wells activated the latch so that the door slid open. With the agitator rod pressed against my back, Wells prodded me out of the door and into the dim corridor.

It took a moment for my eyes to adjust, but I was already being nudged down the corridor to the building exit. Outside, the wind was cold, but it felt good on my face. The rain was soft, almost lazy, as if it were resting for the night.

We moved across the silent campus until we reached the Detention Hall, and before I knew it, I was back in my cell, with Wells's parting words echoing in my mind: "Get as much sleep as you can. Tomorrow night, I'll be collecting you again."

The next few days repeated themselves as Wells took me out of the cell in the middle of the night, gave me material to read about the Faction, then sent me back to my cell. During the day, Wells questioned me on behalf of the Legislature. None of the questions were new, but just asked in different forms. But this time when I was forced to answer them again, I was no longer under the numbing influence of the truth serum, and I knew full well who and what I was betraying.

Wells said that reporting my answers while waiting for the Legislature's decision would benefit me—make it look like I was still fully cooperating. And it would give Wells more time to use me for his purposes, which still weren't entirely clear.

It was on the fourth day that the pieces came together. Instead of leading me to his University office, Wells took me the opposite direction, and we ended up in an apartment building a short distance from campus. We passed through three sets of doors until we arrived in a narrow room with a long table. The two men in the room looked up from where they were sitting as we entered.

"This is Solomon," Wells said. "Our new recruit."

The two men gave me long looks, then turned back to the tablets on the table. On the wall was a large screen that showed a map of the entire city. The size of the map fascinated me. I'd never seen the entire city at once since I'd only been able to work off tablets.

"You've read Sol's confessions that I sent over," Wells continued. "And now that he's been educated on our history, we'll put him to work."

"How long do we have?" one of the men asked.

"A few hours each night," Wells responded.

The same man pointed at a chair next to him. "Then let's get started."

I joined the man at the table, and he gave me a brief nod. "I'm Thad. We're systematically creating power surges that have to be fixed by the citizens. But we don't want to create too many, or we'll arouse suspicion. We're tracking the maintenance response and recording which citizens are trained to fix the power machines. Those are the citizens that we'll have to imprison when we breech the entire system."

Thad pointed to the large screen on the wall. "The red lights indicate the power systems that we've glitched. When the lights turn green again, that means they've been fixed. We try not to do too many at once, or else the Legislature will issue a state of emergency."

I counted seven red lights spread across the map. As I watched, one of the red lights switched to green.

Thad tapped a few commands on his tablet, and another red light popped up on the east side of the city. Then he opened another page on his tablet, and I saw the repair report and a citizen's name at the bottom.

"You'll record the names and do research on who the citizen is," Thad said. "We've created a master list of the maintenance crew members so that we'll be able to sequester them when we aim for blackout."

"How long have you had this plan in place?" I asked. It sounded eerily similar to what the Lake Town group had planned.

"Only a couple of weeks," Thad said. "We have *you* to thank for the idea." His eyebrows lifted. "Once Wells told us what you'd revealed, we realized it was brilliant. If the power from the city can be completely shut down and we've sequestered all of the mechanics, the Legislature will have no defenses against the Faction. We can stage a complete takeover."

I thought about the population of the city and the number of men and women who had mechanical experience. If you counted all of the generations, the number was probably in the hundreds. "What about the members of the Legislature?"

Thad wrinkled his brow. "What are you asking?"

"It's possible that members of the Legislature had mechanical experience in their earlier years; and there may be others who have moved up and no longer work in the C Level."

Thad went quiet.

"Are you glad I recruited Sol?" Wells asked, an edge in his voice.

"We'll start now," Thad said. "How good are you at research?"

"Excellent," I replied.

And I spent the next hours meticulously researching records and adding names to the master mechanics list. By the time Wells said we needed to leave, I'd added two dozen names.

Back in my cell, I dropped to the ground, exhausted yet exhilarated. I'd been able to send another encrypted message to Rueben. I could only hope he'd get it. If not, he'd be arriving to a city in chaos.

CHAPTER 13

Jez

I had never been so glad to see Rueben as I was when he came around the bend ahead of us in the corridor. Jude turned at the sound, and the tension between the two men was palpable.

"Coming to find Sol's girl?" Jude said to Rueben.

Rueben exhaled slowly. "It's been a long time, Jude."

Jude folded his arms across his broad chest, which was still wet from the pool. "We'd nearly given up on your little expedition," he said. "I told Martha and the others that we should have sent someone with more experience."

"Like who?" Rueben said, stopping in front of Jude.

When the two men stood right next to each other, Jude didn't look as imposing. Rueben was just as tall—maybe not as thickly muscled, but definitely no weakling.

Jude barked out a laugh. "Like *me*. I could have returned in half the time, with *everyone*."

"We barely got out of there alive," Rueben said. "I'd say we did a pretty good job."

"You got out alive," Jude said, his dark eyes narrowing. Eyes that were so much like Sol's. Jude lowered his voice. "But where's my brother?"

"He didn't make it out at the same time," Rueben said. "But he knows the city, and he knows the boats and docks. He'll be here."

"I hope you're right," Jude said, stepping closer to Rueben.

I didn't know if I was relieved or worried that Rueben didn't back away. He and Jude were toe-to-toe now.

I glanced at Martha, wondering if I should say something.

She gave a slight shake of her head, as if to say, *Stay out of it.*

In the city, men didn't argue or confront one another like this. Fights were quickly quelled and reported to authorities, and the men would be taken before the judges for sentencing. Because a contentious man meant his Harmony implant had malfunctioned—or worse, that he was immune.

"Look, Jude," Rueben continued, unwavering. "I wanted Sol to leave with us, too. But I couldn't wait any longer. If I had, then all of us would have been lost. We just have to trust that Sol can take care of himself."

Jude puffed out a breath. "I know my little brother can take care of himself. He has no other choice. But my point is that you failed in your mission. You shouldn't have been sent in the first place."

Rueben's face colored, and I wanted to push the two men apart. I could understand Jude's concern for his brother, but I had been in the city, and I knew that Rueben hadn't deliberately left anyone behind.

"What did you bring back?" Jude asked, his arms still folded across his chest.

Finally, Rueben took a step back, and I was glad that Jude didn't try to close the distance again.

"Come with me," Rueben said, looking over to include me in the invitation.

Jude grabbed a towel near the pool and wrapped it around his shoulders to stop some of the dripping. Together with Martha, I followed after Rueben along the corridor. We passed several other rooms, but we didn't slow down enough for me to really get a good look at what was going on inside any of them.

When we came to a room with a couple of tables in it, I recognized Michel and Gabe. They'd cleaned up from the boat and had their paper maps of the city spread out on the tables. The packs they'd brought were propped in the corner of the room.

"Where's Becca?" I asked Rueben.

"She's with a medic," he said, glancing over at Jude.

"What happened to her?" Jude asked.

While Rueben explained our harrowed escape and how Becca was shot with a poisoned bullet, I could see the news was only making Jude more agitated. "You're a sloppy recruit, you know that?"

Rueben shook his head and crossed over to the table. "We brought back the maps of the city and several tablets."

Martha picked up one of the tablets and powered it on. I hadn't known about the tablets. Was there a way to stay in contact with those in the city? To track my friend Chalice, or to send a message to Sol?

I reached for one and powered it on. The signal for the WorldNet popped up, surprising me. "The tablets can link in down here?" I asked.

Rueben looked over at me. "Our technology in Prairie is just as sophisticated as the city's. And we can spend more time on new technology since we don't have such a large population."

"Like creating globes," I said.

"Exactly," Rueben answered. "Although we can't create new ones without a larger power grid. Once they're running, they're self-sustaining through the atomic molecules. But to create them, we need a lot of power."

I nodded and glanced at Jude, who was drilling Gabe about what they'd left behind in the cavern under the city.

"Can we send a message to Sol?" I asked.

Rueben moved next to me and said, "We can try."

I signed into my user account, but the page came up as an error.

"Sign in with my name," Rueben said, giving me his password.

The message screen opened, and we both stared at the words on the tablet.

Abort plan. City knows all.

There was no sender's name, but Rueben and I both knew who it was from, who it *had* to be from.

Jude, Gabe, and Michel crowded around us, reading the words on the tablet. Martha was the last to join us, and she gaped as she read the message.

Jude blew out a breath and cursed. "It's from Sol, isn't it?"

Rueben gave a slow nod, but the rest of us were speechless. Then, as we watched, the words started to fade, until the message had completely disappeared.

"Has the charge run out on the tablet?" Jude asked.

"No," Rueben said. "The message was encrypted. It's meant to last for only a short time. Minutes, sometimes hours; but if we hadn't opened my message file when we did, we wouldn't have seen it."

Jude scrubbed a hand through his drying hair. "Is there a way to find out whether it was truly Sol who sent it? What if he was captured?"

"Even if someone else sent it," Gabe said, "forcing Sol to tell them the encryption to Rueben's message system, then we still have problems."

"Agreed," Michel said. "Big problems."

We all looked at one another, and I scanned their faces, from the fear in Michel's eyes to the anger in Jude's. Finally, I looked at Rueben. "What's going to happen?" I asked.

"We need to find out more," Rueben said. "We need to find out if this is a warning on a deeper level, or if . . ." He looked down at the now-blank screen. "We already have to surrender before the battle has even begun."

"Wait," Martha said. "That message could have meant a lot of things. We don't even know if it was from Sol."

But even as Martha tried to come up with other possibilities and suggestions, it was clear that there were none.

"The question is, *when* did he send it?" Rueben asked the group. "Have things changed since he sent it? And do we bring everything to a halt because of one short, encrypted message?"

"We need to assemble everyone for a meeting," Martha said. "Everyone needs to know about this, and maybe someone will know more than we do."

I could see the doubt in both Rueben's and Jude's eyes, but what else could we do at this point? As I followed the others through the corridor and into a small assembly room of about forty refurbished chairs, I wondered where Sol was and what he was doing. Had he been found out? Under what sort of duress or what circumstances would he have sent a message like that?

As we seated ourselves, Rueben sat next to me and wrapped an arm about my shoulders. "We'll figure this out," he said. "Send a message back, and we'll see if we get a reply."

"What should we say?" I asked, glad for the comfort and reassurance. But Jude watched us, his eyes narrowing. Affection was taboo in the city because the Harmony implants controlled the citizens' emotions, but from the moment I'd met Rueben in Phase Three, he'd been different. And he'd taught me that things could be different.

If it weren't for him, I wouldn't have had the courage to kiss Sol—to show him how I felt about him, no matter the trouble it could get me into.

People started to file into the room, both men and women of all ages. One man was older than any I'd ever seen in the city—probably close to eighty. I realized then that if the plan to restore humanity worked, seeing the elderly would eventually become commonplace. They wouldn't be Taken when they stopped being able to perform their assigned jobs. I had the urge to meet the elderly man. Surely he'd seen changes in civilization that I'd only heard whispered about.

Martha held her hand up for silence, and the murmuring in the room stopped. She explained to the group about the message on the tablet. Immediately, conversation started up again, and questions were fired at Rueben. He rose to his feet and walked to the front of the room, explaining the encryption process and how it worked on the tablet. Then he said, "Let's hear your ideas."

Jude was the first to raise his hand.

CHAPTER 14

Sol

The days passed in a head-pounding blur as I struggled on very little sleep to follow Dr. Wells's orders and do my work for the Faction. I had just fallen asleep after returning from compiling the list of mechanics in the city, when my cell door opened, letting in a flood of light.

I opened my eyes to see two security officers, but no Dr. Wells. I didn't know if that was a good thing or a bad thing. They hoisted me to my feet, and one of the officers said, "You're to be sentenced by the judges now."

Ah. I knew it was coming, but now that I was walking into the Legislature building that housed the courtroom, I felt as if I were dreaming somehow. Maybe I hadn't really confessed everything, and maybe Jez hadn't fled to the Lake Town with Rueben and the others. Maybe this was all a horrible nightmare, and I'd wake up in my dorm at the University, ready to face a day of science courses.

But there I was, standing again before the judges, facing the same row of faces, my hands cuffed and all eyes in the courtroom on me.

I thought of the encrypted messages I'd continued to send to Rueben, and the single message I'd received in reply. *We are all safe.*

There hadn't been any questions, or any argument. Just a simple statement. It was tearing me up to not know if they were still planning on invading the city.

I'd responded with the same message over and over. They had to know that coming to the city now was a death sentence. The Legislature's militia was ready for them.

"Solomon, we have reached a sentencing decision," the head judge said, his dark eyes focused on mine.

I held my body still as he continued to speak.

"You have been sentenced to Execution," he said.

My eyes remained open, but everything inside of me seemed to shut down, as if my body refused to comprehend the words that the judge had spoken.

But the judge continued to speak, oblivious to the shock reverberating through me. "You have been found guilty of treason to the Legislature and our city—a most grievous crime. We've taken into account Dr. Wells's petition to continue using you for information and research as we prepare for an attack from the Lake Town, but that petition has been denied."

My body felt numb, and I was surprised that I could still breathe—that my lungs were still taking in oxygen.

A commotion occurred near the door, but I was too frozen to turn my head and watch. Someone shouted, and I realized with a sudden start that it was Dr. Wells. He pointed at the judges. "I demand an appeal. I'll revise the petition if needed, but this young man is much more valuable to us alive than dead."

I couldn't agree more, but my hands were literally tied.

The head judge looked from Dr. Wells over to me. "We will consider the appeal when it's submitted. Meanwhile, the prisoner will be transferred to the Execution cell. His date of death has not been determined, but his Execution sentencing will be broadcast on the WorldNet in order to inform *all* citizens."

And suddenly I understood. I was to be used as bait for the Lake Town invasion. The Legislature was trying to take the upper hand.

I refocused on the judges sitting on the bench and let my gaze move from face to face, taking in each of their pale countenances and stiff postures. I wondered what these men and women would be doing, who they would be, if there had been no Legislature, no Harmony implant, no rain. But I couldn't blame Mother Nature for their utter lack of empathy.

"Escort the prisoner to his new cell," the head judge said.

Dr. Wells flung out another protest, but it soon died as I was escorted to the other side of the room and led through a door and into a corridor that I'd never been in before.

The walk was surprisingly short, and soon we were heading down a flight of steps and into a large office with two desks inside, as well as a row of chairs along one wall.

A man rose to his feet, and I knew I'd come face-to-face with a member of the Legislature because of the white clothing he wore. In the Before, doctors and nurses—the people who saved lives—wore white. Now, in the city, the color was reserved for the men and women who plotted repression.

The man's face was heavy, nearly jowled, and his green eyes narrowed as he studied me. I said nothing, and neither did he. If this was a dream, it was a nightmare; I was being used to entice my friends and those I loved into a trap.

The security guards moved me past the man and opened a door that led to a narrow hallway. It was brightly lit, and there was barely enough room for a grown man to walk through without turning sideways.

At the end of the hallway, the security officer unlocked a heavy bolt with his key and swung open the metal door.

Inside it was pitch black, and I knew this cell would be the last one I'd ever occupy. The next time I got out, it would be for my public Execution.

I stepped into the complete blackness, and the metal door shut with a finality that reverberated through my body. I reached out and felt along the walls. The place was about the size of two closets. The walls were cold but dry, and I couldn't help but shiver. I looked back toward the door to see if there was any light coming through, but the darkness was complete.

I wanted to pound on the door and ask them to let me out, to kill me today, to spare me from using my Execution to bait my friends.

But I knew it was already too late. No one would open the door. Dr. Wells was now my only hope.

CHAPTER 15

Jez

Jude's eyes settled on me as he stood in front of the group in the small assembly room. "If the message was from Sol, then it's a warning. Somehow we've been discovered, our plan laid bare, and the city is currently preparing for our invasion."

"Which means that we'll lose the battle before we reach the shore," Gabe said, his voice distraught.

I felt the discouragement pulsing through me.

Jude continued to speak, his gaze remaining on me, and I felt my face heat up. "If the message wasn't from Sol, then someone has discovered who Rueben really is." He looked at Rueben, much to my relief.

Rueben nodded. "If it wasn't from Sol, then how much could the city really know?"

It seemed that Jude agreed. "Right, which means we should go ahead with our original plans."

Several people started talking at once, and Martha

stepped forward and told everyone to wait their turn. "We won't accomplish anything until we hear everyone out."

Jude folded his arms as he waited for quiet. "They may or may not have Sol. Are we sending a rescue mission for him? Or do we stick to our first plan of taking over the city in its entirety and putting a stop to the Legislature's control once and for all?"

My heart swelled at his words, and I could see distinct similarities between the brothers. They were on the same side, fighting for the same thing. Sol was just doing it in the city, and Jude was working from the Lake Town.

"All in favor?" Jude asked.

"Wait a minute," Rueben said, rising to his feet. "We've only heard from you, Jude."

Jude looked annoyed but stepped back and leaned against the wall. "Anyone can speak."

"All right," Rueben said, walking to the front of the room. "There are a lot more unknowns now. We might be facing an expectant and prepared militia. I just received the final report of the status of our boats, and they are all ready to go." He glanced over at Martha, who nodded. "The question is, do we want to head into a firestorm?"

The people in the room were quiet; even Jude didn't say anything.

"And, do we stay on our original schedule?" Rueben looked over at Jude. "Or perhaps wait a couple of weeks?"

"Or change to a rescue mission for Sol," Jude added. "Once we have him, we'll know more about what's been compromised."

"That could delay us by a couple of months," Gabe offered up. "That is, if things go quickly with finding Sol."

"Or longer," Rueben added, scanning the group of people until his eyes locked with mine.

Jude must have noticed Rueben's focus, because he said, "Let's hear from Jezebel. She's spent the most time with Sol recently out of any of us."

I looked around at the group and was about to answer when the tablet chimed. A message to Rueben's account emerged on the screen. Rueben and Jude were at my side in a split second, and we all read the message together.

Too dangerous. Stay where you are.

"It has to be from Sol," Rueben said to no one in particular. Then he read the message aloud so everyone in the room could hear it.

Jude scrubbed a hand through his hair and started to pace the room. "Write him back. Ask him a question. Something that only he would know the real answer to." His eyes were back on me, both challenging and desperate.

I thought fast . . . of our whispered conversations in the rainy courtyard of our school. Of all the questions I'd asked and all the questions he'd answered, many of them about the Before.

"What color are the peonies," I said as I typed. *Red. They should be red.*

I sent the message and then waited. Everyone in the room was quiet, waiting with me.

Moments later the message came back: *Yellow.*

I stared at the word, the warmth draining from my face.

"What is it, Jez?" Rueben asked in a hushed voice.

Jude stopped his pacing and crossed to us.

"It's not him," I whispered. Then my voice grew stronger. "At least it's not him right now." My heart hurt, my pulse felt weak. What had happened to Sol? Who was sending encrypted messages?

I looked up at Jude and Rueben. "The peonies are red," I said. "Sol told me about them."

Jude tilted his head. "Do you think he forgot what color? Or do you think he's trying to tell you something?"

"No." The message had confirmed what I was starting to sense. "Something's happened to Sol. Something terrible." I grasped Rueben's arm. "We have to go after him. Send me. I'll find him somehow."

Jude scoffed. "You barely made it out of there alive," he said. "Do you think you can just run a boat back to the city and enter with a friendly wave?"

I looked over at Rueben.

"They'll be waiting for us, Jez," he said in a low voice. "They'll see our boats before we even see the city."

"A poisoned bullet will be the least of your worries," Jude said, once again agreeing with Rueben.

They were right, but the thought of Sol being held somewhere—or worse yet, sent to Phase Three to be experimented on—made my head spin.

Jude went back to his pacing, and Rueben showed his tablet to the others in the room so that they could read the messages for themselves before the encryption made them disappear.

Martha finally spoke up. "We'll take the night to consider our options, and in the morning, we'll vote on a strategy."

Everyone seemed to agree, and several people started to leave. I decided that wherever Rueben was going, I would go. I didn't want to be around Jude right now. His stormy emotions mirrored mine too closely, and it was overwhelming me.

"Come on," Rueben said, grasping my hand.

When Rueben and I were in Phase Three together, his affection had been new to me. And I still wasn't used to it. I didn't think Rueben was in love with me, because I knew the difference. When Rueben looked at me, it was in friendship. When Sol looked at me, all kinds of things happened to my heart.

Regardless, I felt Jude's hard gaze on me as I left the room with Rueben.

Rueben led me along the corridor until we reached another set of rope steps. He grabbed two wrist lights and two raincoats that hung near the steps and handed them to me. We climbed up until we came out into a light drizzle. The sky was dark with the fallen night, and I slipped on the raincoat and walked with Rueben along a path winding through the trees. He turned on his wrist light to brighten the ground before us. We were on the opposite side of the underground complex where I'd entered with Martha.

"Where are we going?" I finally asked.

"To see the boats," he said, walking slowly.

"Tell me about Jude," I pressed. "Why doesn't he like you?"

Rueben laughed, then rubbed a hand over his face. Glancing over at me in the dimness, he said, "I don't think Jude likes anyone."

"He seems to care about his brother."

"Yeah, I suppose," Rueben said. "But when they're together, they don't get along. There's a reason that I went to the city instead of Jude."

"Was Jude the one who was supposed to go?"

"Yes," Rueben answered. "But Sol routinely beat out his brother in tests, although Jude beat him out on the physical side. Martha had to make a choice, and she chose Sol, since she believed he was more levelheaded and wouldn't get into trouble."

Sol was definitely mellower than Jude, but Sol had gotten into plenty of trouble in school. Although most of it was because of me—trying to protect me. And now . . . something had happened to him, and someone was sending Rueben messages. My skin suddenly grew cold as I realized that the person who'd read my message to Sol might recognize that I was the one writing it. Why would Rueben ask Sol about flowers?

"Rueben?" I said.

He slowed and turned, his wrist light lighting the ground so that his face remained in shadow.

"What do you think really happened to Sol?" I heard my own voice tremble. "Do you think he's all right?"

Rueben stepped toward me and pulled me into his arms. I let his warmth comfort me and nestled against him. Rueben had always seemed so sure of everything, just as Sol had, but I knew we were all fragile. Life could change drastically at any moment. Mine certainly had.

"He has to be all right," Rueben said in a low voice. "We have to believe that we'll rescue him."

I drew back so that I could see Rueben's face. "Even if we have to risk our lives to do it?"

"Some things are worth the risk, Jez," he said, looking down at me. "I can tell that Sol is a risk that you're willing to take."

I nodded and released Rueben, wrapping my arms about myself. The night air had suddenly chilled. "But how can we ask the others to risk their lives, too? I mean, if the messages are true—whether they are from Sol or not—the city is expecting us."

Rueben gave a slow nod. "Everyone will have to decide for himself." The edges of his mouth lifted into a small smile.

"That's what I love about this Lake Town. No Harmony implants. Everyone can make their own decision, take their own risks."

I exhaled, thinking through everything that we knew so far about Sol—which was very little. But it was almost certain that Sol was in trouble.

Rueben started walking again, and I followed him through the copse of trees. We stepped onto the shoreline, with the ocean expanse beyond. Short docks had been built, thick and secure, and at least two dozen boats were tied around them. I worried that even that many boats would be no match for the city's militia.

"What do you think, Jez?" Rueben asked, pride in his tone. "These boats were a two-year project, and now they're complete."

At the far end of the row was the boat that we'd traveled on to the Lake Town.

As the wind coming off the ocean tugged at my rain jacket, I thought of the scenarios we might encounter taking this many boats to the city at once. Perhaps Jude and the others were right. We'd be sailing into a death trap, and then where would that leave all of the Lake Town's plans?

"I think the city is expecting us," I said. "Whether or not it's Sol who is messaging us, something serious has happened." I took a deep breath before verbalizing my next thought. "But I'm willing to go back, to fight, or do whatever it takes."

"You're not a trained fighter," Rueben said, glancing over at me. "Besides, we can't have you hurt or worse. We have many in our Lake Town who are trained in militia strategy, but our strengths will be shutting down the city in other ways."

I nodded. Martha had already told me part of their plan. "How much can be done from the water if we have to stay on the boats?"

"You mean hacking into their systems?" he said in a thoughtful voice. "We're already planning on doing that, but the true shutdown has to be done in person." He touched my shoulder. "Your Carrier key will start up the generators and enable us to have enough power to override all of the government systems. But we could delay your part. We could try to rescue Sol first, return here to strategize, then regroup and go back for the generators."

I had to return to the city. And delaying my part would only give the city more time to prepare to stop us. But if they separated the missions, then we could use Sol as part of the second mission. I'd only met a few people in the Lake Town so far, but I couldn't imagine being the one to send them to their possible deaths because I was unwilling to do my job. Martha's words came back to me—they would each get to choose.

So what would I choose?

CHAPTER 16

Sol

The Execution announcement went out the day following my sentencing. One advantage of living in a completely dark cell is that when you can't see anything, your hearing becomes very good. I could hear everything that was said and done on the other side of the metal door.

I didn't recognize the voices that were talking, but I soon began to differentiate between them. One of the men was a member of the Legislature, and he was called Officer Nathan. The other voice I heard frequently was referred to as Linus, and I assumed he was an assistant to Officer Nathan.

I was halfway between sleeping and waking when I heard footsteps echoing on the other side of the door. I moved to an upright position and scooted toward the door so that I could hear more clearly.

"Sol's sentencing has been announced," Linus said.

The next voice was Nathan's. His deep tone rumbled through the door. "Good news. Has the date been announced, too?"

"No. The board wants to keep it unknown for now, to build up speculation."

The sound of a chair scraping on the hard floor covered up Officer Nathan's next few words. Then I heard him say, "What are the estimates for the arrival of the Lake Town fleet?"

I winced. I was the one who told them about the Lake Town invasion. If only I had been somehow immune to the truth serum, I wouldn't be in this situation. At least, not in this *exact* situation. I closed my eyes—though the cell was just as dark with them open—and dreaded the answer. But I knew it already, because I had given it to them.

"Sol said in his confessions that it would be about two and a half weeks from now," Linus said. "But that could vary, and the board has already ordered the missile launches to be prepped."

My skin went cold. If I could have broken out of the cell and swam all the way to the Lake Town to warn Rueben and Jez, I would have. I covered my ears with my hands, as if that would somehow reverse or erase the words I'd just heard. I was trapped in a blacked-out cell while the people I cared about were about to be annihilated.

"Jez," I whispered, hoping that somehow she'd hear it. "Stay in the Lake Town. Stay alive. Don't come back to the city. No matter what."

I didn't know when my Execution date would be, or if they'd even wait until the Lake Town rebellion invaded. Maybe once they spotted the boats on the ocean, the Legislature would send me to my death as soon as possible.

As it was, I'd probably never see Jez again, or Rueben, or even my brother Jude.

I had been away from the Lake Town for so long that I hadn't thought a lot about my brother. He was doing his tasks for the cause, and I was doing mine, but we'd never mixed well. He never took the time to think things through before reacting, and I was all about studying out all the possibilities, then choosing the best one. I wondered if Jude would be in the same situation as me if he'd been the one to come to the city. What would his relationship be with Jez? Would he have fallen in love with her?

He'd have met Jez by now, and I could admit that I was jealous of my brother. He was in the Lake Town with the woman I loved—not in a dark cell with an Execution sentence hanging over his head. He wasn't guilty of my crimes against humanity. Crimes I didn't know if anyone could forgive me for. Crimes I didn't know if I could forgive myself for.

The voices on the other side of the door faded. I hadn't heard their final words, and I realized now that what they said no longer mattered. I had already lost.

When light flooded the cell sometime later, I awakened with a jolt. I could barely make out the features of the person silhouetted by the door, but by his build I guessed it was Dr. Wells.

"Get up," he said in a fierce whisper. "You're coming with me."

I scrambled to my feet, still reeling from the flood of light. Exiting the cell, I saw that the office was empty and that Dr. Wells was wearing all black. He removed my handcuffs and tossed them back into the cell, then closed the cell door. He handed me a dark jacket that I pulled on with trembling hands. The couple of days of inactivity had left me surprisingly weak.

Dr. Wells's grip on my arm was firm but necessary—my legs felt as if they could give out at any moment. I wanted to question him, but I sensed that I needed to be absolutely quiet. Without him telling me anything, I obediently walked with him out of the office area, away from the solitary cell, and along a dim corridor leading in the opposite direction that I'd first come.

Anything was better than sitting in that cell, awaiting Execution, but I had no idea what change of fate had been handed to me now. I didn't trust Dr. Wells, but at least with him I had a chance, albeit a seemingly impossibly small one.

We reached a door that led to a set of narrow steps, and I followed Dr. Wells up. By the time we reached the top of the flight of stairs, I was completely winded. And then we were outside. It was the first time I'd inhaled a full breath of pure air in days, and I wanted to lie on the cold, wet ground and just breathe. Even the rain was a welcome sensation. I wanted to spread my arms and rotate new life into them. I'd been in handcuffs for weeks.

"Pull up your hood," Wells said, and I obeyed.

I wasn't given the chance to revel in being outside for long. Dr. Wells prodded me forward until we had exited the University gates. We stepped onto a tram, which I was surprised was running in the middle of the night. Wells sat across from me, his arms folded.

I looked about the empty tram, then watched the dark buildings speeding past the window. We were descending toward the C Level quadrant, closer to the ocean. I felt exhausted yet exhilarated at the same time. I didn't have on handcuffs, I was out of the solitary cell, and I was sitting on a tram. What was Wells doing? What did he have in mind?

We entered a tunnel, and the tram came to a stop. Dr. Wells rose to his feet, so I followed suit, not sure why we'd stopped in the middle of a tunnel.

"We're getting off here," Wells said.

I didn't argue. I was genuinely curious to find out what his intentions were.

As soon as we stepped off the tram, it pulled away, leaving us alone in a dark tunnel. Wells switched on a wrist light, and it was then that I saw the recessed door on the other side of the tunnel. Wells headed straight for it.

We entered a narrow hallway leading away from the tunnel, somewhere deep into the earth.

"Where are we?" I finally asked, my voice hoarse from disuse.

"We're in the headquarters of the Faction," Dr. Wells said. "Come this way. We need to remove any trackers from your body."

My Harmony implant was in one shoulder, but I didn't think that was what Wells meant.

He kept a brisk pace, which I had trouble keeping up with at first. But my legs were starting to regain their strength, and I was determined to find a way to escape the Legislature. Did this mean freedom? Or was I entering a new type of prison, this one controlled by the Faction?

We passed through a series of doors, not seeing another soul, until we finally arrived at a medic room. Dr. Wells turned on the single light and led me inside, then shut the door. The place was antiquated compared to the facility that I'd stayed in when I was interrogated. A counter with a row of three cupboards was built into the far wall. Otherwise, there was only a table and two chairs in the room.

Dr. Wells shrugged off his jacket and began to riffle through a cupboard, collecting a syringe and a small knife blade. At the sight of the blade, my limbs went weak again. I sat on one of the chairs. "What trackers do I have?" I asked.

Wells glanced over at me. "That's what we're going to find out. They planted them when you were under the truth serum."

I watched him unroll a long cloth bandage. "And *you're* going to be taking them out?"

Wells shrugged. "Not my first choice, but it seems we're short on medics in the Faction." He removed an agitator rod from his jacket pocket, and I immediately straightened from my slouch. If he were a smiling man, he might have smiled. Instead, he said, "This will detect the trackers. Don't worry, I'm not going to shock you."

I felt wary, but I didn't have any reason to distrust him at this point. Wells crossed the room and held the rod a few inches away from my body as he moved it slowly around my torso, then along my arms and legs. It beeped in two places. Once on my calf, and again on my forearm.

"You have two trackers," he said, setting the agitator rod on the table. "We have to get them out, as well as your Harmony implant."

I was immune to the Harmony implant's control over emotions, but I knew that the government could still use it to track my movements if they wanted to.

Wells continued, "I wish I had a pain diffuser, but there's nothing stocked here. I'll try to be quick." He said this as he laid out the bandages on the table.

I eyed them, feeling all warmth drain from my face. I wasn't necessarily afraid of pain, or of taking a risk, but I wasn't sure I wanted Wells to be the one to cut into me. But it seemed I had little choice; this was the cost of my freedom—whatever type of freedom that might be.

I closed my eyes as Wells began the process. At least he cleaned the sites with a disinfectant first. The pain was sharp and hot, but the worst of it was when he used tweezers to dig into me, then lift away a thin metal tracker no bigger than a thumbnail. I had to close my eyes again as Wells blotted the blood with a bandage strip, then wrapped my arm tight. Next he did my leg, and finally my shoulder.

By the end of the three procedures, I was perspiring and felt like I was going to throw up. Wells gave me some stale water to drink, then said, "We can't stay here too long. I'll be back soon. I'm going to dispose of the trackers."

I leaned my head back against the wall after Wells left, wave after wave of nausea pulsing through me. I tried not to think about the amateur surgery, and focused instead on what might be going on in the Lake Town right now. It didn't make me feel much better.

Had they received any of my messages? They hadn't replied before I was confined to the Execution cell. I slowly opened my eyes and focused on the counter across the room. Wells had left his satchel, which I was pretty sure would contain a tablet.

Rising to my feet, I steadied myself against the table as lightheadedness engulfed me. Then I took several measured steps toward the counter. I opened the satchel and slid out the tablet. It powered on, and I typed out an encrypted message.

I'm safe. Don't believe the reports. Stay away from the city.

I sent the message at the same moment I heard footsteps in the corridor. Hurrying back to my chair, I sat down just as Dr. Wells opened the door.

"You don't look so well," he observed.

My heart was racing, and I hoped he didn't find out why. I wiped a hand across my forehead. "I'll be fine."

Dr. Wells gave a nod as he put away the things he'd used and picked up his satchel. "That's good, because we need to get moving."

I rose to my feet, still feeling lightheaded. But after a couple of deep breaths, I followed Wells out the door. We continued along the corridor using Wells's wrist light to see and exited through a door that looked like it hadn't been used in a long time. Climbing a flight of stairs, I tried to take my mind off the lacerations on my skin, because the thought of them still made me nauseous. And the dank smell of the underground staircase wasn't helping to ease the tightening of my stomach.

At the top of the steps, Wells opened the door to the night air. I glanced around to see that we were in a warehouse district that reminded me of the place that we'd found Jez when she and Rueben had fled Phase Three.

It was still a strange thing to be walking with my arms at my side and not handcuffed. Wells led me into a warehouse, and we were once again descending stairs. He unlocked the door at the bottom, and we stepped into a spacious room dimly lit with a few recessed bulbs against the far wall. Eight single beds ran along one side of the room, and two were occupied.

Wells motioned to one of the beds. "You'll sleep here tonight," he said, not bothering to whisper. "I'll return later. Remember, you're a fugitive now, and the city will be looking for you."

Even if he hadn't given me the warning or locked the door when he left, I was more than happy to try to get some sleep. It had been weeks since I'd slept in a bed, and weeks since I'd felt any hope.

CHAPTER 17

Jez

"Now that we're in the Lake Town, I can finally tell you our full plan," Rueben said as we stared into the night at the docked boats.

I tugged my jacket closer about my body, not because I was cold—I'd been rained on my whole life—but because Rueben's words made me both nervous and awed.

He motioned toward the boats with a wave of his hand. "These vessels will deliver us in different groups. The first group's task will be to shut down the power grid and change the sequence codes. The next group will be arresting members of the Legislature and all authorities, along with the security officials. You can probably guess that Jude is the leader of that group."

It fit Jude, I decided. Without a doubt.

"Our medic group will begin to remove Harmony implants," Rueben said. "We expect some resistance by the citizens, of course. Most of them will be loyal to the

Legislature at first—but we hope that as we educate the citizens, they will in turn join us in our mission. And then, of course, you'll be our access to the generators with your Carrier key."

"How will it work?" I asked Rueben. "Will I need to remove the key from my shoulder first?" It had been there since I was an infant, from what my caretaker Naomi had told me.

"We tried that before, with another Carrier," Rueben said in a quiet voice.

"There are other Carriers?" The information surprised me.

Rueben gave a slight nod. "Sol's grandmother was a Carrier. But once the key is outside the body, it will no longer work. It won't transfer."

I stared at Rueben, but he wouldn't meet my gaze. "Tell me how it works, Rueben. The truth."

He released a sigh, then said, "We're not exactly sure. We tried with another Carrier. But when she attempted to activate a generator, it made her very ill. So they removed the key from her body."

"But it didn't work," I said, mostly to myself.

"Jez." Rueben touched my arm. "I'm telling you this because you have a choice. I know that you think we are all depending on you, but you still have a choice."

I blinked back the stinging in my eyes. Rueben might have thought I had a choice, but I knew I didn't. "Two million citizens used to seem like such a desperately small number," I said. "How many Lake Town citizens will be part of the mission?"

"We have about two hundred who are assigned to the groups," Rueben said. "The militia is the largest group."

"What will they use to fight?"

Rueben seemed relieved at my question. "Come and see."

I followed him back into the compound and back down the rope stairs. This time we headed a different direction until we reached a large cavern. It reminded me at first of the one in the city that Sol had sent me to. This one, too, had a suspended globe on the ceiling, creating light and warmth. But instead of a nearly empty space with a few tables, this cavern was filled with men and women going about their business.

One group was working through a series of stretches and exercises. Another was firing darts at a target with what looked to be high-powered dart guns. A third group was sitting around a large table, engaged in some sort of debate.

"What are they discussing?" I asked Rueben.

"They're supposed to be strategizing, but it often gets heated," he said with a half smile. "Not everyone agrees with Jude's exact strategy of where the boats should land. Also, he wants to be the one carrying the case of chemicals on the boat to the city that will create the atomic globes. He trusts only himself with the dangerous compounds. Others want the chemicals divided into separate cases so that just one person isn't responsible for all of them."

I didn't see Jude in the room and wondered where he was. But a moment later he came striding in and, with a quick glance in our direction, continued toward the table.

The tension and energy coming off him told me that he was not about to back down based on the messages on the tablet. Rueben led me toward the conference table where Jude had seated himself. We sat in the chairs at the opposite end.

"Everyone, this is Jezebel James from the city," Jude said, waving a hand toward me.

Those around the table were already staring at me and didn't seem surprised at the introduction.

"She grew up in the city, and she's the only living Carrier," Jude continued. "As you know, we've been sent a warning—either from Sol, or from someone who has Sol in his control." He shifted in his seat and rested his elbows on his table. "What we need to do now is decide if we want to move forward with our plans despite this new risk factor."

Martha strode up to the table just then and took her own seat. "We believe that the city knows about our plans. They're waiting for us, and they'll be prepared."

I looked around the table at the innocent people. Whatever had happened with Sol in the city would affect each person in this cavern.

The other sounds from around the cavern had quieted, and several people started to drift over, listening in.

"Each person will be given a choice," Martha said. "You will not be forced to stay in your assigned group and travel to the city. Our mission has a high chance of failure."

"Should we wait?" one woman asked. Her hair was short and dark, reminding me a bit of my friend Chalice.

"We could wait," Rueben said, "but what would that look like?"

Conversation buzzed about the table. And suddenly I knew. Perhaps it was because I'd lived in the city since birth, and because I'd been brought up in their system. My heart drummed as I answered, "The city's militia would come here."

My voice had been soft, and only a few sitting close to me had heard, but Jude had been watching me. "What did you say, Jezebel?" he asked.

I cleared my throat and said louder, "The city's militia will come here." I looked around at the people sitting at the table and those who'd gathered from other areas in the room. "If the city is truly expecting our arrival, they won't wait too long for us to show up. They'll come and find us."

I knew I was right. The more I thought about it, the more sense it made. This put a new twist on Sol's message—if it had been from Sol at all. Perhaps aborting our plan was exactly what the city wanted us to do. If we didn't attack, then the city would take the initiative. They somehow had the information about our intentions, and that would be enough to declare war.

A shiver traveled up my back as Jude stood and whistled, commanding the attention of everyone in the cavern. "We need to vote. Now."

Martha clasped her hands together on top of the table. "I agree."

Next to me, Rueben exhaled. I knew that exhale. He was determined. And without speaking to each other, we both knew what the other's decision was going to be. We were going to invade the city, and I was going to do my part despite the cost to my body.

When the people had gathered around, Martha and Jude proceeded to give out instructions. Now that we knew the city was expecting us, and would go so far as to hunt us down, all emotions had heightened.

Rueben turned on his tablet, pulling up the maps of the city, and I leaned over to look at the various quadrants with him. Each area gave me a different feeling. The C Level was where I'd tried to help the women suffering from River Fever skin disease. The B Level quadrant was where I'd lived as a child and been brought up by my caretakers Naomi and David. Both had been Taken.

The A Level was where I'd met Sol, and where we'd gone to school together. And then there was the government sector, where I'd stood trial before the judges.

The tablet flashed, and a universal report popped up on the screen. Periodically, the Legislature would send out WorldNet announcements that were urgent. This one was about an Execution, which I was surprised would be considered an emergency alert. But when I saw the name of the convicted criminal, I stopped breathing.

Solomon has been sentenced to death for crimes of treason against the Legislature. Date of Execution is forthcoming.

Rueben read the report at the same time as me. "Hold on," he said.

Everyone went quiet to look at Rueben. "The Legislature has sent out an Execution notice."

"Sol?" Jude said in a near whisper.

Rueben nodded, and Jude's face went white. He rose from his seat slowly and walked around the table. Reaching for the tablet, he read the report for himself. Then Martha crowded in and read it.

I stared at the tablet, my hands clammy. But there was no doubt. Martha, Rueben, and Jude had all read the name for themselves. Sol was on the Execution list. The date of his Execution wasn't listed, but his crimes were.

Eventually, Rueben read the entire report aloud to everyone. Those in the cavern were silent as Rueben read, and when he finished, no one spoke or moved for a while. No one seemed to have answers.

A small group of people formed and talked quietly among themselves.

I looked up into Rueben's eyes; I knew I couldn't stand seeing the raw pain reflected in Jude's gaze. "How did they find out so much?" I asked in a hoarse voice.

"They had to have tortured him," Rueben said. "Or they might have altered him."

"No," Jude cut in. "Sol wouldn't give in—no matter the torture. He'd sacrifice himself before putting our Lake Town in danger." His voice was harsh, but I heard the fear and the denial behind it.

We were *all* afraid.

Jude clenched his fists. "Whatever happened, Sol will probably be Executed before we can get a single boat there, even if we left now."

"There's no date on the Execution," Martha pointed out.

Jude turned his dark eyes on Martha, and I saw Sol in Jude. Tension radiated off him, but his stance was sure and steady as he looked at Martha.

"But once they announce my brother's Execution date, it might be too late to reach him," Jude said. "We can't wait around here." He scanned the crowd. "At least if we're really going to do this. Let's vote now."

"Wait," Martha said. "We need time to process this new information."

"No," Rueben said. "I agree with Jude. We've run out of time."

Jude gave Rueben a nod.

I moved next to Jude, placing my hand on his arm. He flinched but didn't move away. His muscles were tense, his body rigid with determination. "I agree," I said, not knowing if I had any pull to persuade. "Let's vote."

CHAPTER 18

Sol

I awakened to sounds I hadn't heard in a long time. *Laughing.* At first I thought I was dreaming, or that somehow I was back in my Lake Town. But when I opened my eyes and turned toward the noise, I was still in the underground room that Dr. Wells had dumped me in the night before. Two men sat at a rickety table, passing something between them. I rose from my bed, the areas around my incisions throbbing, and my muscles aching. It had been weeks since I'd slept in a bed, and my body wasn't sure how to adjust.

A card game? The men were playing a card game. I hadn't seen cards—or any sort of paper, for that matter—since leaving the Lake Town.

Who were these men, and what were we all doing here together?

"Ah, the slumbering giant is finally awake," one of the men shot out, glancing over at me. His nearly full beard was black with some gray. He barked out a laugh when my eyes widened.

"Thought you'd died and gone to Paradise?" the other man said, this one with a slow cadence to his voice and a broken front tooth. He wore a full beard as well, and his dirty blond hair was pulled back in a tie.

"Where—what is this place?" I croaked out. I cleared my throat and added, "Who are you guys?"

"Do you want the truth, or our *stories*?"

This threw me. I realized then that these men must be like me—recruited or "saved" somehow by Wells. Had they been prisoners, too? What was their status now?

"I want both," I said, meeting the man's gaze. "I want to know everything."

"Better take a seat then," he said, scratching at his thick, black beard. "By the way, I'm Tim." He pointed to the other man. "That's Paul."

"When Dr. Wells gets back, we all shut up," Paul said, giving me a knowing look.

I crossed to them, feeling the muscles throughout my body twinge in pain.

"You look pretty roughed up," Paul continued. "We heard about your Execution sentence. We wondered how long it would take Dr. Wells to break you out."

Tim set his cards facedown on the table. "You shocked the Legislature with all of your confessions." He chuckled, and again the laughter sounded foreign.

I groaned and shook my head.

The other man smiled. "You'll get over it," Paul said, clapping me on the back.

"I don't think so," I said, my stomach roiling with both hunger and regret. "I've put my people at risk. And perhaps destroyed all hope of reclaiming humanity and restoring our world."

"Whoa," Tim said, raising his hands. "Humanity? Is that what you think you were *saving*?"

I stared at him, unsure if he knew what I had told the Legislature. "We had a plan . . . one that I divulged under the influence of a truth serum. I gave them the names of my friends and family—the names of the people who are planning to take over the Legislature. Now they're all labeled as traitors." I inhaled sharply to keep the threatening emotion from surfacing.

Tim leaned across the table and lowered his voice. "This room is full of traitors, Sol," he said. "Dr. Wells is a traitor to the Legislature. If anyone understands you, it's us. We've had to hurt our friends and family along the way, too."

Paul nodded. "My caretakers were Taken early because of something I did."

"All of us were put into prison and sentenced to Execution," Tim said, clasping his hands together. "We all have regrets. But now we can only fight for our own survival." He looked around at the others at the table. "We once thought we were 'saving humanity,' too, but now we realize we can't do anything on our own. The Legislature is too strong. That's why we agreed to join the Faction. We may not be able to save humanity, but at least we can get back at the government for what it took from us."

"We help the Faction hide people from the Legislature," Paul added. "Call us tech experts, or whatever. But if Wells gives us your name, you'll no longer exist." He let out a laugh. "At least in any records."

"You break into the record archives?" I asked. "How?"

Paul's smile was broad, and he pointed across the room

toward the tablets on the counter. "If you know how to break codes, it's all downhill from there."

I nodded, but I wanted to understand exactly. "So you break into the Legislature's records for the Faction members and erase their records?"

"Correct," Paul said. "There are some Faction members still operating in their citizen roles, like Dr. Wells. But there are many, like us, who've committed to working for the Faction and can't be found. We're doing the Faction work full-time."

I watched Paul closely. "Can you delete my records?"

"We can," Paul answered. "But not any time soon, because although we could erase all of your electronic records, it will be a while before the judges who sentenced you will forget about you."

I thought about this, and it made sense. But for everything that I'd studied about the Faction, there wasn't really anything impressive about it. Their ideals were similar to the Legislature's. If the Faction attempted a takeover, lives would be lost, and people injured. A new government would be ruling, but the Faction wouldn't necessarily be a *better* government.

"You're helping out some individuals who've had run-ins with the Legislature, but aren't you just going from one control factor to another?" I asked.

By the way the men looked at me, I could tell that they knew I was right.

"I've read the Faction's mission statement," I said. "There's no plan to remove Harmony implants or to make the society levels more equal. The citizens still won't be given many choices."

Tim was the first to speak—he seemed to be the leader

of the group. "There's not another option. Either we do as the Legislature says, or we take them down. The Faction has been preparing for years, and we can't very well go out on our own and fight. No matter what our personal ideals might be."

I didn't know these men—not yet—but a kernel of an idea was starting to grow. I was just one man, and they were right: it would be hard to accomplish what I needed to on my own. I needed help. Dr. Wells was too loyal to the Faction, probably vying for a leadership role soon. But these men were more like me. They'd been imprisoned by the government. They'd lost family members. They wanted revenge. What if . . . I still needed time to think through it all, but what if I talked them into joining me? We would find a way to send a warning to the Lake Town, and we'd find a way to stop the Legislature from destroying the island.

I'd done enough damage to my people that I now deserved to be sacrificed in the name of saving them. My life wouldn't be worth living unless I could make things right again.

"You're right," I told Tim. "None of us can do anything on our own. That's why Wells continues to recruit men like you and like me. Even the Faction needs more bodies and minds working together."

Tim and the others remained quiet, listening to me.

"What would you say if I told you that we can reverse the damage done by the Legislature?" I asked, waiting expectantly for their surprise. Nothing happened. They remained quiet, passive, and unimpressed. "What would you say if I told you that the science has been developed to reverse the flooding of the earth?"

Now Tim shifted in his seat. "We read the reports on

you, Sol," he said in a low voice. "Tell us something we don't already know about your theories."

I exhaled. This group of men had every right to be skeptical. "We've developed an atomic globe that evaporates moisture faster than it can be produced."

At this, Paul leaned forward, his eyebrows raised. At least someone seemed interested.

"The globe takes a lot of power to be produced in the first place," I continued in a hushed voice, as if there might be someone listening on the other side of the wall. "But once it's going, the atoms circulate on their own inertia." I spread my hands. "Think of it. If we could reverse the flooding or slow it down significantly, our world would change."

"Explain," Tim said, his voice tight, "*exactly* how you propose to reverse the flooding."

I let a smile slip onto my face. It had been a long time since I'd allowed any sort of emotion to show through in front of another person. "It will take years, and it will take a big effort from everyone. We need immense amounts of electrical power. If you read the report on my confessions, you'll know that there are generators that can only be started by certain keys. We call them Carrier keys."

Tim's brows lifted. "Where are these keys?"

"The only known Carrier is in the Lake Town, but part of the plan includes bringing the Carrier here," I said, not telling him that it was Jez. "Once those generators are functioning, we can install the globes around the city. And that's only the beginning."

"Do you think that the citizens will support you once the Legislature is gone?" Paul asked. "You know that most of them are loyal. They'd defend their government."

I nodded. That was part of the Lake Town's plan. We

had to get rid of the Harmony implants, and we had a team of medics who were training to physically remove the implants. But I'd come up with another idea. "I realize that. And that's where you men can help me out. We need to find a way to disable the Harmony implants, electronically, all at the same time."

"There'll be absolute chaos," Paul said, his voice hard. "The citizens will be hit with a horde of emotions and thoughts and reactions. They'll be confused. They won't be able to function. Like Adam and Eve in the Garden when they fell."

I stared at Paul. "You're religious?"

His face stained red. "I've studied religions."

Tim shoved at Paul's shoulder. "It's not like you can get into more trouble. Look at where we're living. The government doesn't even think you exist."

My eyes widened at the news. "Is that what Dr. Wells did for you?"

"Yes," Tim said. "The government thinks we were Taken. Wells removed our implants and any trackers we had when imprisoned."

I thought about this for a moment. What would the government think happened to me? If these men agreed to break from the Faction and help me with the Lake Town's infiltration of the city, we would be untraceable.

I didn't know if I could trust these men, but I did know that I couldn't help the Lake Town without them. "What keeps you in the city? You could catch a boat out of here."

"And go to your *Lake Town*?" Tim scoffed. "Even with the control of the Legislature, the citizens in the city have the best chance of survival. We work for Dr. Wells and the Faction, doing research on our tablets."

I leaned forward. "I'm focused on survival, too. Not just for today, though—for generations to come."

"It won't stop raining, you know," Paul said in a quiet voice. "The rain has been falling for nearly forty years now. The Legislature has preserved humanity despite that."

"The Legislature's idea of preservation has come at too high of a cost," I said, propping my elbows on the table. "The citizens are more like robots than humans. Our life cycles are dismal at best, serving only the government, never ourselves or our families."

Tim laughed. "You sound like me—five years ago."

"You've been here for five years?" I asked, looking around at the other men.

Tim shrugged. "We've been considered dead for five years."

I couldn't help but look past Tim at the dim room. Aside from the beds and tables, there was nothing else to the space. "Do you have to stay here all of the time? Or are you able to go outside?"

"Sometimes we'll go outside at night," Tim said. "But we've grown accustomed to our moleish existence."

I hadn't ever seen a mole, but I knew that they were critters that lived underground in the Before. Most underground animals had been flooded out years ago, the ground too saturated for them to exist. I exhaled, wondering if I'd still be in this room years from now. Would I be stuck down here while my Lake Town friends fought a losing battle? Even if my life as I'd known it was over, I couldn't give up. I had to try to open the way, to pay for some of my mistakes, even if I were recaptured in the process and Executed after all. Whatever amount of life I had left, I had to make the best of it.

The door to the room swung open, and Dr. Wells strode in.

"I see you've met our new recruit," Wells said.

All of our gazes locked on to the metal box he was carrying. He'd brought food—something smelled warm and spicy. He set the box on the table, and, without any preamble, the men started lifting out covered bowls of soup.

Wells dumped a handful of spoons on the table, and I picked one up, then waited until the other men had chosen their bowls before I lifted one from the metal box.

"Thank you," I said as my stomach practically leapt out of my body.

Wells nodded but said nothing as he walked to the long table on the other side of the room and sat down. He opened his satchel and pulled out his tablet. The same tablet I'd sent the messages to Rueben on.

I removed the lid from the soup bowl and took the first few bites almost too fast, nearly choking myself on the potato chunks.

"When you're all finished eating, we're going on a field trip," Wells said.

The men at the table stopped eating and looked over at Wells in surprise. Apparently this was an unusual announcement.

"Finish up," Wells said. "You don't want to be hungry."

CHAPTER 19

Jez

I wasn't sure how much time had passed before the cavern had filled with people. They sat on chairs, tables, even the floors. I stayed by Rueben, and he introduced me to a few of the people who came in, but, for the most part, everyone gathered in their groups.

It wasn't hard to figure out who were members of the militia with Jude. They were easily in the best physical shape out of everyone, and their gazes were intense and purposeful. Those who Rueben introduced me to were all mechanics, ready to take over the generators once I got them started.

The others I hadn't met yet must have belonged to the medic group.

"We're ready to start the voting process," Martha said into something she held in her hand. It amplified her voice throughout the entire cavern, and all conversations and whispers stopped. "We are not going for a majority, just looking at whether we have enough interest to move forward with our original plan."

She looked at me, then motioned for me to join her. My heart thudding, I walked to her side and stood before the entire cavern of people. Everyone looked at me, some with curiosity.

"Jezebel is our Carrier. She grew up in the city," Martha said. A few people started murmuring, but then quieted down. "She's the one who Sol went to train, but as you've all read in the report, the plan had to be aborted early. The Legislature imprisoned Jezebel for a time, and then Sol was forced to hide her. Rueben and the others helped her escape."

My cheeks burned hot, and I was sure that the people staring at me were silently judging me for failing, and for leaving Sol behind. Jude leaned against the large table, his muscled arms folded across his chest. His expression was unreadable. I just wanted to get the vote over with and move to the action part. Staying in this Lake Town would not reunite me with Sol.

"Let her speak." Jude's low voice echoed through the room. "We've read the reports about her life in the city, but we haven't heard from Jezebel what she thinks of our chances against the Legislature."

"All right," Martha said. "Before we vote, do you have anything you'd like to say, Jezebel?"

I looked around at everyone. I didn't know how many of them had ever been to the city, but I believed that their lives here were full of many freedoms that the citizens in the city should be able to enjoy. And if their plan with the atomic globes and removing the Harmony implants could make a better life for generations to come, my sacrifice would be well worth it. "I grew up thinking that Lake Towns were savage places."

Some people laughed; others looked like they *were* ready to turn savage.

"Rueben set me straight." My eyes caught his, and their warmth encouraged me. "Rueben was the first person I'd met, in my entire life, who seemed real. Human. He was like me, and it astonished me, but he wasn't hiding his emotions like I'd been taught to. Rueben was free like I could never imagine."

I exhaled, steadying my trembling breath. "I believe in your mission, and I would want to be a part of it even if I wasn't the Carrier." I looked over at Martha, who gave me a small nod. I raised my hand and said, "I'm voting to join the mission, and I understand the risks. I'll help in whatever way I can to restore humanity to our dying world."

A couple of people clapped, and others nodded. Some simply stared at me. Rueben came up beside me and grasped my hand as Martha stepped forward and spoke. "All those who vote in favor of the mission may remain in the cavern, and we'll start our strategy meetings right away. All those who are against the mission for whatever reason may return to their residences and submit reports with their suggestions."

Several people stood and filed out. Low conversation erupted among those who remained. A couple of guys on the far side of the cavern started arguing, but I couldn't make out exactly what they were saying. One of the men left. After a few minutes, and after about three or four dozen people had left, Martha spoke into her amplifier again.

"If you're still in the cavern, I am assuming you've voted in favor of our mission," Martha said. "If you're in any way indecisive, I'd encourage you to leave as well." Two more people left.

Jude straightened from where he was leaning against the table and walked right toward me and Rueben. "Well, Jezebel," he said in a low voice, "it looks like you got your wish. We're going to invade the city."

I raised an eyebrow. "It seems to be your wish as well."

He almost smiled at me, but instead he said, "I would never let the city get away with what they've done to my brother. I should be the one over there."

Our hearts seemed to connect. We both wanted Sol out of harm's way. We both wanted to bring down the Legislature. But there was something about Jude that I didn't trust, although I didn't entirely know what it was. In many ways, he was Sol's opposite. Sol was steady, and loyal, and I knew that he'd do everything in his power to make sure we survived. I just didn't know what had truly happened to him. And I wasn't going to find answers by staying in here.

Rueben cut in and said, "We're starting our strategy meeting. Do you want to be a part of it, Jude?"

"Yes," he said, his voice a bit softer than before. Maybe he was finally realizing that we were all on the same side. "I'll go through the militia strategy, and we can make sure our plans complement each other's."

We crowded around the largest table in the cavern. I sat between Rueben and Jude. Martha was across from us, and just as Rueben called everyone to attention, Becca walked in.

Rueben rose to his feet and crossed over to her.

She walked with a limp, but otherwise she looked healthy. She saw me and smiled. I rose, too, and found myself embracing her. Relief flooded through me to see that she was doing so well.

"I hear that I missed the voting process," she said, glancing around at those seated at the table. Her gaze landed on Jude, then flicked away. "Where do I go if I vote yes?"

Rueben chuckled. "Right here. Have a seat by Jezebel."

Becca sat by me and reached over to squeeze my arm, then smiled at everyone else. I'd forgotten how friendly she was.

Jude cleared his throat and told those with tablets to open up their maps. Rueben laid his tablet on the table so that both Becca and I could see. Jude named the quadrants of the city, all of which I knew, but then he flipped the map at an angle and showed us the underground areas that I hadn't known existed. One of them was the cavern where Sol had sent me, where I'd met Becca and the others. I was surprised to see that there were more caverns beneath the city.

"Does the Legislature know about all of these caverns?" I asked.

"If they do, they've never spoken about it to the citizens," Rueben said. He pointed to the one that I had gone to. "They were all once connected by tunnels, but most of those tunnels have caved in and flooded by now."

"Who built them?" I asked, growing more curious by the minute.

"They were built before the city was isolated from the rest of the landmasses," Jude said, sounding like an authority on the subject. The people around the table shifted their attention from Rueben to Jude now. "It was once said that the tunnels connected to other landmasses."

I hadn't ever heard of such a thing.

"The people in the Before were trying to build an entire underground city in order to escape the rain," Jude said. "It failed, of course. The tunnels collapsed, and the project was aborted." He tapped his tablet, and another map appeared on all our screens. "But two of the remaining caverns have the generators in them. With your Carrier key, we can start them up again and have enough power to run dozens of atomic globes."

Goose pimples broke out on my skin as I imagined the city a few years from now. Part of the city could be dry. The flooding would recede. Our shores would be broader. People would smile, laugh, love. They would argue, debate, cry, and feel sorrow. They would feel alive.

"Timing will be everything," Rueben added. "That's why we need full commitment from those who have voted to be a part of the mission. Every group will have a specific task, and sacrifices will need to be made." He locked eyes with Jude.

"Rueben's right," Jude conceded. "We have no room for pride or personal agendas." He noticed me watching him. "I want to get my brother to safety as much as the rest of you."

It wasn't hard to tell that he was speaking directly to me.

"But we have to follow the plan—for the good of us all." Jude tapped again on his tablet, and a third map came up—this one was made up of bold lines and shapes, and the different quadrants of the city were color coded.

"We'll start in the red zones," Jude said. "Once those are secured, we'll move to the blue zones, and finally the green zones."

"How do we know when a zone is secured?" Becca asked.

Jude nodded to Rueben, and Rueben rose to his feet.

"Everyone will have a tracking device since we don't have tablets for all of us," Rueben said. "You'll enter a number sequence into the tracking device, and it will transmit to the main tablets and update the reports. You'll also receive coded sequences on your tracker." He pushed up the sleeve of his shirt to show a flat band around his forearm. "This is what the tracker looks like."

Something inside me hardened. I was trading one tracking device for another? I understood the logistics, but I felt uncomfortable. I exhaled, telling myself to relax. These people had a lot more experience than I did.

But I couldn't stay silent. "What happens if one of us is captured . . . or . . ." I paused, not sure if I could actually say it.

"Or we fail?" Jude prompted. He didn't look offended. He reached over and snapped the band off Rueben's wrist. "The band only works with body temperature, and when you first put it on, you have to activate it with a code."

"So just take the band off if you're caught, and they can't do anything with it?" Becca asked, clearly impressed.

"Correct," Jude said, his gaze flickering to me again.

I was impressed, too. We spent the next couple of hours going over how Jude's group would start arresting the Legislature members, security officers, and any other leaders loyal to the government. The only part of the plan that I didn't like was that Jude wanted to leave the Harmony implants inside the bodies of the captured people—so we could have access to control.

I interrupted his speech. "If we don't remove their Harmony implants, then we're no better than them." Suddenly I had everyone's attention. "Think about it," I said in a slow voice. "Without emotions, the Legislature members won't be able to feel the effects of their actions. What if . . . when they do feel the effects, they realize they were wrong?"

"She has a good point," Rueben offered up.

Martha nodded, but then said, "I understand the basis for your concern, Jezebel. But how can we know for sure whether they've truly changed?"

I really didn't have an answer, and was surprised when Jude came to my rescue.

"We can never know," Jude said, "but I think we should take Jezebel's argument into consideration when we get to that point."

Everyone nodded.

"We have a lot to accomplish before we have to make those decisions," Jude continued. The next map he sent to everyone's tablets moved the conversation in another direction: where we'd keep all the prisoners.

CHAPTER 20

Sol

It felt like months since I'd seen the ocean, although I knew it hadn't been that long. Standing on the cliff above the crashing waves, knowing I didn't have any trackers or implants beneath my skin, made me feel freer than ever before. But seeing the fishing boats bobbing on the water reminded me that Jez was gone. She'd escaped the city, and I could only hope that she'd made it safely to the Lake Town.

The surf thundered below, crashing hard enough into the rocks that the spray of the ocean rose into the air and sprinkled our skin. I didn't know why we were all standing there with Dr. Wells. He'd brought me and the other men from the bunk room out through the tunnel and along several side streets until he unlocked a gate and we stepped through to this view of the dark, churning sea. It was the middle of the night, and all the citizens were asleep except for the night fishermen and the security patrol.

When you live in a dismal world of nonstop rain, the

only thing more miserable is the depth of night that makes the rain seem more endless. I thought back to the Summer Solstice several months ago and how we were able to feel the sun on our faces. Twice a year, the sun was close enough to the earth to burn through the layers of clouds and rain, and now we were just days away from the next solstice event.

But if the Lake Town plan worked, we might be able to reduce the flooding—maybe eventually stop the rain. Somehow, I had to break away from Dr. Wells and find a way to stop the Legislature's attack.

I didn't know if the men standing next to me would join me. Tim and Paul didn't know me, and I didn't know them. But I needed help; I couldn't do it alone.

"I brought you all out here so that you could see the boats," Dr. Wells said. "Which of you knows how to run a boat?"

"I can," Tim and I both offered.

"The Faction has new orders for me," Dr. Wells continued, after nodding at Tim and me. "We are going to stop the Legislature's boat attack on the Lake Town rebellion when they arrive. We want them to come into the city. They'll fight our battle for us, and while the Legislature is trying to stave off the attack, we'll come in and declare our own victory."

Dr. Wells made it sound simple, but I knew it was far from it.

Wells took a step closer to the edge of the cliff, and a wave of vertigo shot through me as I realized how close he was to the edge and how easy it would be to nudge him over it. I held my stance and didn't move. I wouldn't do anything drastic unless necessary.

"How are we supposed to overtake the boats?" Paul asked the question that I was wondering myself.

Dr. Wells looked back at us. "You will go onto the boats as crew, and then just before the battle begins, you'll take over." His gaze stopped on Paul. "Tonight, Sol and Tim will train us on how to man a boat."

I stared at him, wondering if he was serious. Dr. Wells motioned toward one of the fishing boats within our line of vision. "Come with me."

We had no choice but to follow him down a barely-there path that jutted from the cliff to the rocky shore beneath. The rain jacket that I'd been tossed in the bunk room was a size too small and did little to protect me from the growing intensity of the wind as we reached the shore. A short distance away was a smaller dock with a couple of rowboats tied to it. Just looking at the small boats in comparison to the choppy waves made me feel like I was already out at sea.

"We're going to hijack the fishing boat?" I asked as we came to a stop before the rowboats.

"Not exactly hijack," Wells answered, peering through the dark at me. "More like, commandeer."

I looked from him to the rowboat. It would be a tight fit with five men, but that didn't seem to bother Wells. He climbed in, and the other men followed him and took their seats. I untied the boat from the dock, then climbed in myself and shoved us away with one of the oars.

Paul took up the other oar, and we started to row. The water beneath us was like black ink, and the night sky didn't offer any guiding light as we rowed toward the fishing boat, which was nothing but a speck of light moving in the distance. The listless days in my cell had done nothing for my physique, and within minutes, the muscles in my arms and shoulders were burning.

As I rowed, Dr. Wells pulled something out of his pocket, and I saw that it was a government badge. "No one will speak to the captain except for me," Wells said. "I'll tell him we're on official orders and doing a training drill in preparation for the Lake Town invasion."

I winced at his words because, in fact, they weren't far from the truth. We were preparing for the Lake Town invasion. Against my friends and my family.

We reached the fishing boat before my arms completely gave out, and Wells shined his wrist light toward the vessel and called out in a loud voice, announcing our intentions.

A rope ladder was tossed over the side, and one by one, the men climbed up on deck. I was the last one up, and I tied the rowboat to the ladder before boarding. Up on deck, I looked around at the three fishermen staring at us. Their eyes were dark and fearful. I couldn't blame them.

"We're on official business," Wells said. "My men need training. In the next couple of hours, you will educate them about how to run this boat and to use it as a weapon. The Legislature doesn't want the rebellion touching land." He looked over at me and the other men. "But whatever happens tonight needs to be kept a secret. The Legislature doesn't want the citizens to panic."

The fishermen nodded, and the tallest man, who also wore a captain's cap, said, "Come with me."

The wind was bitter out on the ocean, and I wished I had something to cover my ears. The too-small raincoat barely made a difference. The fishermen showed us the boat's engine and taught us the basic mechanics of maintaining it. The captain instructed us on the boat's different speeds and how to navigate through rough waters. They showed us the depth radar and the fish finder, and how to lower and raise the nets to catch the fish. They had several metal bins already filled with squirming, silvery fish taking their last breaths.

As we moved along the deck, I peered out over the vast ocean, thinking of Jez and what she was doing. Had she and Rueben received my warnings? Would she ever return to the city? Would I ever make it back to the Lake Town? In the darkness surrounding the boat, Jez seemed far away, almost as if I'd imagined her.

But if Jez and Rueben hadn't received my warnings, then it could be only a matter of days before the rebellion arrived. The very thought of the boat I was on being used against the people I loved sent a shiver along my skin. Even if Wells's plan worked and we were able to take over the boats and keep them from attacking the rebellion, it was a victory for the Faction, not the citizens.

One of the fishermen was teaching us how to lash the ropes together into a secure knot, and I gripped the rope in my hand tightly, wishing that I didn't feel so helpless. I glanced over at Wells's other prisoners and wondered what it would take for them to turn against the Faction and join me.

A couple of hours later, we were back on the rowboat, Paul and I rowing the small vessel back to shore. The waves had calmed, and the sky had lightened from black to a deep gray. Dawn wasn't too far off—not that we'd see the sun even if we didn't return to our underground quarters—and Wells was anxious.

Once we reached the dock, he hurried everyone off the rowboat, and I tied it to the dock, using the new knot that I'd learned from the fishermen.

We climbed up the cliff's path and passed back through the same gate using Wells's key. Once inside the cavern, we shed our raincoats, and I took off my shirt as well and hung it over the back of a chair. The cavern was cold, but the shirt would dry faster off me.

Wells sat down at the table and started to review what we'd learned on the boat, to make sure we remembered everything.

"There is one thing we need to prepare for as well," Dr. Wells said, spreading his hands on the table. "If the rebellion doesn't arrive within the week, the government is planning on going on the offensive."

"What do you mean?" Paul asked.

I didn't have to ask, because suddenly I knew. The government would go after Lake Town. They'd launch their own fleet of boats. The thought made my head pound.

"The Legislature isn't going to sit around and wait for Lake Town rebellion to make more preparations," Wells said. "They used the announcement of Sol's Execution to try to speed up the Lake Town attack. But they won't wait much longer."

My throat thickened.

"What does this mean for us?" Tim asked, and I wasn't sure I wanted to hear the answer.

"It means that we'll have to be on those boats," Wells said. "There are four of you here, and the Faction will be training other men as well. We hope to have three dozen of you ready before the week is out. You'll have to get on the Legislature's boats, and then just before you reach Lake Town, you'll take charge of them."

Wells's expression was hard and left no doubt. We'd be expected to use whatever force was necessary to commandeer the boats. I looked around the table at the other men. Their gazes were equally hard. These men would be ready, for better or worse. A battle was imminent, and I'd be in the middle of it with these men. The question was who we would each be fighting for.

Finally, Wells left, and I hoped he wouldn't hurry back. The men moved to their beds and climbed beneath their covers, but I wasn't ready to let them sleep yet. I had to use this opportunity to talk to them privately, to see if they'd help me disable the Harmony implants electronically. I could wait until the rebellion invaded, but there were too many ifs—too many things that would have to fall into place. If I could find a way to disable the implants by the time the rebellion arrived, it would be an entirely different battle than the Legislature was preparing for.

The chaos of the Lake Town invasion coupled with the Faction overtaking the boats would present a perfect time to act. If the Harmony implants suddenly went dormant in every citizen, emotions would flood their minds and bodies, and the rebellion could take advantage of that—they just didn't know it yet. It was another message I'd have to send.

My plan wouldn't work very well, however, if we ended up having to sail toward Lake Town. It was crazy, I knew, but I was hoping that Rueben and the others had decided to ignore my warnings. I hoped that they were coming to the city.

"I know we're all tired," I said into the quiet room as I sat on my bed.

Tim groaned. "I hope you're going to shut up now. Wells could be back any time, and we'll be back on a boat when night comes again."

But I kept talking, fast and smooth, before anyone could tell me to stop. "We've all been rejected by the Legislature. We've all been recruited by the Faction with the promise of avenging ourselves and our grievances against the government. We've all chosen a different life over our former lives. But I want you to consider joining me in a new plan."

Tim groaned, but didn't protest further. Paul was lying on his back, his eyes open. I waited a beat, and then I said, "If you can make records disappear, do you think you can break into the system and disable the Harmony implants?"

Tim snapped his head in my direction. Paul laughed.

"I've thought about it since you first suggested it. It will only create mayhem," Tim answered. "Do you know what it would be like to have two million people all of a sudden experience a high-voltage emotional download?"

I nodded. "I can't imagine exactly what might happen, but I do know that it might be our best weapon against the Legislature. Think of all the people who might side with us."

Paul sat up, scrubbing his fingers through his beard. "The Faction might actually like the idea," he mused. "It might create enough chaos to give the Faction the advantage in taking over the Legislature, and then we could re-enable the implants and calm everything back down."

"No," I said quietly. "Here's the thing. We wouldn't be doing it for the Faction. We'd be doing it for Lake Town. And we wouldn't be enabling the Harmony implants again. It would just be a temporary measure until they can be removed."

"Permanently?" Paul said, his eyes intent on me.

I nodded. "Do you think it's possible to disable the implants?"

Tim blew out a breath. "You're assuming a lot, Sol, by asking that."

I didn't let my gaze waver from his. "I know. But I also know that you're all just pawns to Dr. Wells and the Faction. Aren't you tired of being used?"

"And your plan isn't *you* using us again?" Tim asked.

I didn't hesitate. "You'll always have a choice." I looked at the other men. "Just think of a world where you'll always have a choice."

"Freedom?" Tim suggested.

For the first time in a long while, I felt like smiling. So I did. "Yes."

"Wars used to be fought in the Before for things like freedom," Paul said in a quiet voice. A quiet and warm voice. I could sense his interest increasing.

"And religion," Tim added. "Will the citizens want that sort of freedom again? What will they do with it?"

"They'll learn to live a life that's worth something," I said, and this time no one disagreed with me.

CHAPTER 21

Jez

"What are you thinking about?" The voice behind me startled me.

I'd taken a break from the meetings and combat training to climb back up the rope steps and watch the preparations on the boats. My mind was exhausted from being questioned about every detail of the city—the schedules, the government restrictions, how I thought the citizens would act when under attack, the strength of the militia, the locations of any weaponry they had, what they valued most, and what they were willing to give up. I realized that the mundane facts I'd been made to memorize in A Level classrooms were actually details that were becoming increasingly important. Rueben, Jude, Martha, and the others had soaked in every word I'd spoken, appearing almost reverent with gratitude at everything I shared.

The mechanics had also spent hours with members of the militia, learning knife combat. I'd been given my own knife to keep strapped to my thigh, and now my hands—as well as other muscles—ached from the lunges and leaps we'd been practicing. We'd also practiced knife throwing, and I found that I was decent at it. Jude said that if we could aim well and throw hard enough, we would do enough damage to an opponent that we wouldn't have to risk our own injuries by entering into a hand-to-hand fight.

Even after the main training ended, I spent a couple more hours throwing my knife at the stuffed canvas bag. Only when I could hit the target ten times in a row without missing did I allow myself a break.

I'd come above ground to cool off and to let my mind and body rest, if only for a moment. The sun was out behind the rain clouds somewhere, and there was enough light to watch the men scurrying about the decks. Since the votes were cast to continue with the invasion of the city, everyone had jumped into full work mode.

Jude came out of the jungle of trees that led to the entrance of the underground training cavern and walked toward me. His dark hair was damp against his forehead—not from the rain that was barely falling now, but from the training exercises he'd been leading the militia through.

The militia members were impressive: men and women conditioning their bodies and minds for all instances of combat, both physical and mental. They were like soldiers and security officers rolled into one.

Jude's dark eyes were on me now, making my heart rate quicken. Not like his brother Sol's did; Jude just made me feel unsettled and nervous. I knew I should trust him, but I couldn't quite bring myself to.

His presence threw me off, and I didn't know how to answer when he asked what I was thinking about. I'd been thinking of Sol and whether or not I'd ever see him again. But I knew if I said that, the tears would start, and once the tears started I feared they'd never stop.

"I was just watching the boats," I said. "And realizing how little I know about boats, even though I've been surrounded by an ocean my whole life."

Jude didn't say anything. He stood by me, his hands in his jacket pockets, as he looked out at the boats alongside me. "Today might be the last day of peace that we have in a long time."

I looked over at him. "We're leaving tomorrow?"

"Tonight," Jude said. "If the city knows our plans, they'll be expecting us next week. So we're going to surprise them." His gaze slid to me. "It might be the only advantage we have."

I swallowed against the hard lump that had formed in my throat. I had no intention of backing out, but it was surreal to think that the time had actually arrived. "Everyone is ready?"

"They'll have to be," Jude said, studying me now and making me blush. "You aren't going to change your mind, are you?"

"Of course not," I said quickly. Perhaps too quickly, because Jude's dark brows pulled together, and he looked back toward the boats.

"I haven't seen my brother for almost two years," Jude said. "After Sol left Lake Town, I wondered if I'd ever see him again, if his mission would be successful. So many had gone before him and tried and failed, including our parents."

I just listened, not knowing what to say. It seemed as if Jude were talking more to himself anyway.

"But here you are," he continued. "With Rueben and the

others. They all made it back—except for Sol." His eyes were on me again. "Do you think Sol intended to stay behind? Or . . ." He lowered his voice, though no one was near enough to overhear. "Do you think Rueben intentionally left him?"

"I don't think either of those things happened," I said, remembering the message Sol had sent urging the others to get me out of the city as soon as possible. We had hurried, and we didn't slow to wait for Sol. Who knew how far he'd been behind us? He could have missed us by moments or by hours. My throat was now dry. "He said he'd try to meet us, but for us not to wait."

Jude nodded. He knew all of this; we'd reported it all when we arrived in Lake Town. I touched his arm, wanting Jude to hear the truth in my words. He looked down at where my hand rested on his jacket sleeve. "Sol is the smartest person I know," I said. "He knew what he was doing when he warned us. He also . . ." I paused, my voice trembling. "He also made more than one sacrifice in order to protect me." I dropped my hand from Jude's sleeve. "I don't know why he singled me out."

"Because you're a Carrier living in the city," Jude said. "You were our only link inside."

I knew that, but what I didn't understand was why the Lake Town people would go to such risks to get me out of the city, and then just leave their best man behind.

"Sol sent us messages about you," Jude said. "It was clear that he cares for you, as more than just a part of our invasion plan."

My eyes stung with tears. Hearing Jude talk openly about Sol's feelings for me made me miss him even more.

"That's why I want you on my boat," Jude said. "I don't

know what will happen to Sol, or what might have already happened, but I do know he'd never forgive me if something happened to you."

My breath felt thin. "We're going to invade the city. You can't protect me from everything. No one can. Rueben told me what happened to your grandmother when she used the Carrier key." Jude didn't react, and I tried to read his face, but he kept his true thoughts well hidden. I still couldn't shake off my bad feeling about him—especially since I knew that he and Sol had clashed before Sol had left Lake Town for the city.

"You'll be safer with me than with Rueben or the others," Jude said.

It didn't make sense. Jude was leading the militia on an offensive attack, and I was supposed to try to sneak past the city's defenses with the mechanics to get to the cavern rooms with the generators.

I took a small step away from Jude. "Rueben already expects me to go with him. I don't want to be separated from the mechanics, since I'll need to work hand in hand with them."

Jude's jaw tightened, but he didn't argue further. He turned back toward the ocean as another person approached. I looked over to see Rueben, and was filled with relief. He barely offered Jude a glance before turning to me. "We're loading the boats now so that we can leave at twilight. Did Jude fill you in?"

So Rueben knew that Jude was coming to talk to me. But what was he supposed to tell me? Surely Rueben didn't know that Jude had tried to talk me into going on Jude's boat.

"He told me we were leaving tonight, to throw off the

Legislature," I said, glancing over at Jude. Again, his face was unreadable.

"Exactly," Rueben said, tilting his head. "Come on, we have a lot of work to do." Finally, his eyes shifted to Jude's, and something passed between them that I couldn't identify—like a silent argument.

I followed Rueben to the boats, and the tension that always seemed to creep up when Jude was near eased from my shoulders. We reached one of the midsize boats, and although it was built of old scraps of metal and wood, it was newly constructed. Rueben extended his hand and helped me make the small leap from the dock onto the deck.

As I landed, the gentle sway of the boat knotted my stomach, and I remembered our tumultuous voyage over to Lake Town. Rueben showed me around the boat, and showed me the sails that they'd created to save on using the motor. "If we have to, we can navigate with just the sails," he said.

I was impressed that anyone could master the wind like that—it hadn't been done that way since the Before.

Then we started loading supplies. Soon most of the mechanics were there helping us. Once we finished with our boat, we started on the others. I saw Jude's eyes on me a time or two, but he didn't approach me again.

The rain was barely a drizzle as Rueben and Michel started the engine—the heavens were on our side. We were about the twelfth boat to pull out of the harbor—Jude's three boats of militia having been the first group. Night had fallen, and Rueben made good use of the boat lights. I sat next to Becca as the wind tugged at our hair and clothing. The temperature was cold, but I didn't feel it. My heart was pumping plenty of blood through my body, keeping me almost too warm.

Becca gripped my hand in excitement, and I squeezed back.

"Can you believe it?" she enthused. "We're finally doing this—after years of planning."

I smiled at her, but my throat was too tight to speak, both from excitement and fear. What would we find when we got to the city? Jude's boats would be there first. What would he find? There had been no additional reports by the city, and similarly no message from Sol on Rueben's tablet. I didn't know if that was good news or bad news, but we would soon find out. We'd be at the city before the morning broke, with Jude paving the way. Anticipation tingled through me, and I didn't realize that the wind had picked up until I heard shouts from across the deck.

Rueben and Michel were closing down the sails, and Gabe hurried toward us. "Go below deck with the others. The wind is getting stronger."

I scanned the sky to see the low clouds darkening, and a flash of light shot overhead, so close that I ducked. The lightning briefly lit everything on the boat. Becca grabbed my arm. "Come on," she shouted, just as we were both thrown to the deck by the impact of a huge wave.

I grabbed for purchase, but my hands found nothing, and I started to slide toward the railing. People around me were shouting, but I could only focus on trying to stop myself. My hand finally touched something, and I hung on. Something or someone slammed into me, nearly making me lose my grip, and then the person slid past me.

I watched with horror as he was pitched off the edge of the boat, but my mourning was cut short by another person crashing into me. I grabbed at them to stop them from sliding off the deck.

"Becca!"

She looked up at me, her eyes round with fear. "Jez! We've got to get below deck!"

But both of us were stuck, and we knew it. The boat tilted at a steep angle, and when the wave beneath it moved, the boat seemed to fall a dozen feet, only to start tilting again, moving as if it were a living thing.

I realized that I was holding onto a fallen mast pole that must have been cracked by the lightning. Above the wind, I could hear people shouting, screaming, but the words were indecipherable.

Becca's eyes met mine, and although it was nearly impossible to talk, it was obvious we both knew we might not survive this storm. The rain continued to drive against us, and the wind somehow blew even stronger. The boat lifted again, tilting until Becca and I were almost dangling from the mast pole. More people slid past us, and I reached desperately for a young man. He grabbed onto my leg, but as the boat crashed back to its ocean bed, he lost his slippery hold.

As the boat was tossed about like a leaf in a breeze, I marveled that we hadn't yet sunk, and I knew that those below deck couldn't be much better off. Suddenly the deck groaned beneath me and completely shifted. Becca and I were both moving, sliding with the mast pole that had broken free of its base.

"Hang on!" I screamed at Becca. Her face was white and her eyes huge as she stared back at me. I looped our arms together, and we slid straight toward the boat's broken rail. We slammed into the rail together and came to a miraculous stop against it.

I don't know how long we clung to the mast pole,

sliding back and forth across the deck, only to slam into the railing over and over, but it seemed hours had passed before I finally opened my eyes, not having realized that I'd been squeezing them shut and burying my head against my shoulder. The first thing I saw was Becca next to me, her pale hair like strands of string across her face and the delicate skin around her eyes looking bruised.

"Becca," I said, but it came out a whisper. My throat burned from swallowing seawater and from screaming during the storm. The boat was rocking gently now, up and down in long, stretched-out motions. I couldn't turn my head—something in my neck ached fiercely—so my only view was of Becca and the gray sky beyond. The storm had abated, but the rain still fell all around.

Becca's eyes fluttered open.

"Are you all right?" she whispered.

I would have nodded, but I still couldn't move. Gradually I became aware of other parts of my body, and the pain started to pound through me. I was certain I'd been bruised over and over by the mast pole and the deck railing.

Other sounds reached my ears. Someone's low tones as they talked, another person . . . crying?

Becca released the mast pole we were both clinging to and rose to a sitting position. Her face pinked as she squeezed her eyes shut. "Is it your leg?" I managed to say.

She nodded, then opened her eyes. "I'm better off than most, though."

Her gaze moved past me to whatever was beyond, and horror dawned in her expression. I struggled to lift my head, and a sharp pain twinged in my neck. Then Becca was scooting close and reaching over me.

"Hold still," she said, and I winced as she lifted something off my neck, or pulled it out—I wasn't sure.

She placed her hand on my neck, and the pain was sharp, yet better than it had been before.

"What is it?" I whispered.

She glanced down at me. "A splintered piece of wood was in your neck. It's bleeding a little, but you should be fine." When Becca lifted her hand, I saw the blood on her fingers. "We need to find something to wrap it with," she said. She moved to her knees and then stood, holding onto the still-intact rail.

I wrapped my hand on my neck where it throbbed and sat up. Nausea rolled through me, making it hard to focus. Becca stepped carefully around the debris, limping on her bad leg. The deck was in chaos. Broken bits of wood were everywhere, and there were several gaping holes in the deck. A few people were sitting up as if they'd awakened about the same time Becca and I did. A couple of people were lying motionless, and I feared the worst.

I searched for Rueben or Michel or Gabe, but I didn't see their familiar forms. Bile burned my throat and my neck throbbed, but the destruction of the boat was worse. Was our mission at an end? I wondered how the other boats had fared.

Becca returned and knelt next to me, wincing at the movement. "Here," she said, handing me what looked to be a shirt. I pressed it against my neck without asking her where she got it from. She helped me secure it tightly so that I didn't have to keep holding it.

"Have you seen Rueben?" I asked.

"Not yet," she said, looking about the deck. Broken masts and torn sails littered the deck, when just hours before it had been in pristine condition.

And then we both heard a shout from below. Becca rose

to her feet, and I grasped her hand, and she helped me stand as well. We started toward the entrance to the lower deck.

When we reached the opening, Rueben was coming up the stairs. I was so relieved to see him, and to see him alive, that tears formed in my eyes.

"Bad news," he said in a raspy voice, as if the lives lost and the boat's destruction hadn't been enough. "The engine is completely inoperable."

CHAPTER 22

Sol

Another sleepless night spent on a boat had left me exhausted, but we had to start decoding the system set up by the Legislature to monitor the Harmony implants.

Tim yawned as he settled in front of a tablet. Paul sat across from Tim with a grudging resignation and turned on another tablet and started to research.

I watched Tim work, marveling at his agility on the tablet. He stopped on a government page that I'd never seen before.

"This is a portal," Tim said. "Once I access it, this tablet and all my movements on it can be traced."

"How close do they monitor the portal visitors?" I asked.

"It's hard to say," Tim answered. "Dr. Wells might know, but since we can't ask him, we'll just have to take the risk."

"You'll just have to create new logins each time you go into the portal," Paul said without looking up from his own tablet.

"Or," Tim added, "they could lock the entire system if they think there's a threat."

Paul looked up. "How long do you think that would take them to do?"

"A couple of hours," Tim said, "maybe sooner if their technicians are paying attention this early in the morning."

And it was very early in the morning. Dawn was about an hour away—not that we'd see the changing of the sky from black to gray down here in the underground room.

Paul spoke next. "We don't know enough to navigate the portal quickly. We'd get in, then probably get booted out before we can even figure anything out."

Perhaps he was right. We needed to do more research. I was out of my element, and that's why I needed these two men to work together.

"Show me what you're thinking," I told Tim.

Tim tapped on the portal login, entering as a guest. "I'm in," he said, his voice triumphant.

Paul groaned. "It's too soon. You'll get locked out before you can start anything."

"Let me show you something," Tim said. We all watched as Tim navigated the site, clicking on the different menu selections, then exiting out of each one.

"Go back," said Paul, who'd abandoned his own research to watch Tim's progress. "Open up the 'Harmony Implant Mandate.'"

"It's just the history of it," Tim said and opened the document.

Paul scanned it, then said, "It's a dummy link." He

pointed to the top of the screen. The link address was a couple dozen characters long. Then he quickly tapped something onto his tablet. Just as he did, Tim's tablet shut off.

"What happened?" I asked, staring at the blank screen.

"That was fast," Tim said. "Someone's awake."

"Hopefully we're faster, though," Paul said. "Got it."

Paul continued typing a long list of commands.

"What's he doing?" I whispered to Tim.

With a grin, Tim said, "I think we have our first victims."

"Victims?" I asked. I didn't know why Tim was smiling, but I hoped it was good news.

I watched as Paul selected a list of number chains, all of them starting with the letter C. "Let's see if this works," he said, then he deleted the chains. He clicked on "Save Adjustments" just before his own tablet's screen went black.

"What just happened?" I asked as we all stared at the dark tablet.

"I'm not exactly sure," Paul said. "I mean, I know what I did—I deleted about a hundred Harmony implant codes—but I'm not sure what the effect will be."

I looked at Tim, but he shrugged.

Paul flipped over his tablet and opened up the battery compartment. The batteries inside were supposed to last years. He popped out the thin disc, then popped it back in. Remarkably, his tablet turned back on within seconds.

Tim picked up his tablet and did the same thing.

"It's a hard restart," Paul told me when he saw me watching. "For now, our tablets are on, but I wouldn't be surprised if a Legislature technician disables them permanently. Especially mine.

"Let's go see what's happened," Tim said.

"How do we see that?" I asked.

"Well," Tim continued. "The Harmony implant codes that Paul deleted were all from C Level, right?"

Paul nodded, hardly seeming to be paying attention to us as he focused on his activated tablet.

Tim rested his elbows on the table. "So we visit the C Level as they show up for work."

Paul smiled. "That's as good a guess as any."

"Really?" I said. "It was just that easy?"

"Not easy," Tim said.

"The technicians will be on high alert for any other security breaches," Paul added. He rose from his chair. "Let's go. I can't wait to see what we just did."

Tim laughed, but my stomach roiled. There was a chance that nothing had happened to those whose Harmony implants we'd disabled, but there was a greater chance that something had. Paul had completely deleted the tracking, and none of us quite understood what that might mean.

I pulled on my too-small jacket that was still damp from our boat excursion, and the group of us left the bunk room. Out in the corridor, my excitement overtook any exhaustion I might have felt from not sleeping all night. We hurried into the tunnel and made our way to the main street. The trams were just starting their first runs, and we caught one to the C Level, ready to get off if an official came on to check our IDs.

We climbed off the tram at the first stop and then hurried through the rain toward a row of C Level warehouses.

"We have no way to know which people have had their implants deactivated," Tim said.

"They all enter through the same tunnel into the warehouses," Paul said.

I knew that tunnel from the time I'd spent in C Level. And now I was remembering the scanning process, and my cold skin grew colder. Would the people with deactivated implants even register in the scanners?

Paul led us toward the tunnel, but then once inside, he detoured us through another door. It seemed that Paul was well familiar with the C Level areas. We followed him up a set of metal stairs that rang out with our footsteps. Once we reached the top, I realized we were overlooking the inside of one of the warehouses. We stood on a platform secluded in shadow. A wire mesh was the only thing separating us from a two-story fall.

"Now what?" Tim asked.

"Now we wait," Paul said.

The warehouse was empty for now. And we waited about a half hour before the lights switched on. The first workers came in shortly after, and we could see each one scanning themselves in. We had no idea if the workers in this particular warehouse were even the ones with the IDs that Paul had deleted.

And then something happened. We all leaned closer, holding our breath. It seemed that one of the scans hadn't processed. A young woman had been moved to stand by a wall with a security officer.

She didn't seem particularly calm about it, either. Even from our distance, I could see that her face was flushed.

"Is she crying?" Tim whispered.

"Shh," Paul warned.

Tim ignored him. "She is crying. And look, there's another guy who's been singled out."

We stared in fascination at the woman who was crying against the wall. Others in the warehouse had slowed their work to watch the woman as well. It was a new experience for everyone—both the woman crying and those seeing her cry. The man standing next to her had a pale face, and he fidgeted as if he didn't know how to react.

The next person who was led to wait by the wall was an older woman. She appeared to be quite agitated.

"Let's go," Tim said.

We all looked at him, surprised at the intensity in his voice. He motioned with his head, and we glanced down to see a security officer looking up, right at us. If we hadn't been in the shadows, he could have potentially identified us.

"I hope he thinks we're maintenance workers," Paul said, but I could tell by his tone that he was worried as well.

As the closest one to the stairs, I led the way, hurrying down the metal steps and wincing at the sound my footsteps made. We made it to the bottom and out into the tunnel. Then we started to run. If we were caught, I knew there'd be no chance for any of us. I was already sentenced to Execution, and this time the Legislature wouldn't consider delaying it, even if they were trying to bait the Lake Town invasion.

We caught a tram back, and as we piled into the bunk house, Paul shut and locked the door behind us.

"We can't go back there," Tim said. "They'll be watching all of the entrances now."

Paul didn't say anything but crossed to the table with the tablets.

"What are you doing?" I asked, as he booted up the two tablets, then fetched the other two from the counter.

"We're all going to hack into the system at once," Paul said. "Our decoding worked, and we're going to do as much damage as we can."

I didn't want to think of it as *damage*, and I especially didn't like the wild look in Paul's eyes.

Tim met my gaze, his concern matching mine. But Paul only grinned, pulled out a chair, and picked up a tablet. "Let's do this," he said.

My mind was spinning. This was what I wanted, but I was suddenly overwhelmed by the magnitude of what we'd done. I hadn't thought through how it might affect someone, like the crying woman, to have emotions suddenly crashing in on her. She must be scared and confused, and now there was a possibility that she'd be punished for something that she had no control over.

The crying woman hadn't been trained by her caretakers, like Jez had, to hide her emotions in a world forbidding them.

"We need to help them," I said, mostly to myself, as I tried to grasp the full consequences of what we were doing.

"We are helping them," Paul said with a grunt, tapping on his tablet. The two tablets that had gone inert were now powered up and working, although I had no doubt that they were now being tracked.

"We'll have to get out of here once this is done," I said to no one in particular.

Tim's head popped up from his perusal of the tablet he held. "Yeah, there's probably security on their way right now—as soon as they locate the signals of the tracked tablets."

"So, let's hurry," Paul said, his tone leaving no room for argument. He looked at me from across the table. "Be careful what you wish for."

I swallowed. He was right. I had brought them into this, insisted that we needed to work together in order to make something happen. And something was happening now.

I picked up the tablet in front of me and powered it on. Following Tim's instructions, I got into the portal. For the next twenty minutes, we deleted as many Harmony ID numbers as we could pull up.

CHAPTER 23

Jez

Day after day, we drifted on the open sea. Rueben had made it below deck in the worst of the storm, helping a couple of people down there. Michel and Gabe had some superficial injuries, but had managed to hang on to the railings.

Rueben estimated that we were too far off course to return to Lake Town, and that we needed to continue toward the city.

"But we'll be completely at the mercy of the citizens," Becca had argued.

She was right. We had no way of knowing how the other boats had fared in the storm, or if Jude's militia had reached the city by now. Maybe they were making progress, or maybe they'd been defeated.

I sat on the deck that we'd recently cleaned of blood and dead bodies. Four people were missing—drowned, no doubt—and another eight had died. We'd given them sea burials and then spent three days making repairs as best we could. We had one full sail, pieced together from the other sails, and each day Rueben and Gabe worked on the engine, but it still wasn't running.

I pulled my knees up to my chest and wrapped my arms about my legs as the mild wind tugged at my torn clothing. My neck was healing, and probably should have been sutured, but we had no real medical supplies available. It had all been with the medic boats. I wondered what Sol was doing right then. Was he still alive? How had the invasion gone? Had it even happened? Had Jude been able to get his militia into the city?

I felt helpless, like a bird floating on the sea, being moved whichever direction a wave took me.

"Hey," a voice said above me.

I looked up to see Rueben.

"How's your neck doing?" he asked.

I reached up to touch the new wrapping that I'd tied on that morning. "Much better," I said quietly. "Many are worse off than me."

Rueben settled next to me.

"Any luck on the engine?" I asked, looking over at him.

His eyes were warm and brown. Something inside me warmed as well. Rueben had that talent—to make me feel better just with his presence. "Nothing yet, but we're not giving up,"

Of course he wasn't.

"But our boat is severely disabled," he said. "Even when we reach the city, we'll be more of a burden than a help to the militia."

I nodded, and found myself leaning my head against his shoulder. I had been exhausted for days, weeks . . . months, even. "Do you think they've invaded the city yet?"

"I don't know," Rueben said. "Maybe they returned to Lake Town to try to meet up with us." He blew out a breath of frustration—one that we all felt. "The tablets still aren't syncing up, so I can't scan for any news."

"So we still wait," I said, knowing I sounded dejected. Ironically, the wind had been more mild than usual the past few days, so short of fixing the engine, our progress would continue to be slow. It seemed the storm had worn itself out.

"There's another option I wanted to tell you about," Rueben said.

I lifted my head, interested. I hadn't known we had options.

"We're not far from another island," Rueben said. "At least according to Gabe."

"Which island?" I knew there were other civilizations that existed in the form of small island communities. But the city never interacted with them. If someone from another island tried to enter the city, they were turned away—the possibility of a foreign disease was too high.

"We call it the Exile island," Rueben said. "It's where a lot of the Banished go. I've never been to it, but Gabe seems sure he knows what he's talking about."

I felt both dismayed and hopeful at the same time. "Can we repair the boat there?" I asked.

"That's what we're hoping," Rueben said, grasping my hand and squeezing it.

That bit of comfort sent warmth through me.

"But I have to warn you about something," he said, and my body tensed. "We'll need all the women to stay out of sight on the boat."

"Why?" I asked.

"Gabe said that the people on this island are pretty barbaric."

I raised my eyebrows at that. In the city we were led to believe that Lake Town people were uneducated and uncivilized. Rueben had been quick to set me straight, so it was odd that he was now calling another island culture savage.

"The population is small," Rueben said, "and they are in need of women. They've been known to kidnap women from neighboring islands. Like pirates—except they steal people instead of treasures."

"What do they need women for?"

"Babies," Rueben said. "They need to replenish their population."

I felt cold all over. There were nearly a dozen women on our boat, including Becca and me.

"But there could be good news," Rueben said. "We might be able to recruit some of them to help us with the invasion, be a part of the militia."

I thought about this, and it seemed like a long shot. We didn't even know where Jude was. As if he could read my mind, Rueben said, "We'll find Jude."

It wasn't exactly what I was thinking—it was the invasion as a whole that I worried about, and Sol. Always Sol.

I peered over at Rueben. "Do you think the others returned to Lake Town?"

Rueben studied the gray waters. "If I know Jude, he would have continued on, as long as his boat made it through the storm. He wanted to invade much sooner than everyone else. If he has his way, we'll arrive to a newly conquered city."

"There are two million people in the city," I reminded him.

"Two million controlled people," Rueben said. "Once that control is vanquished, anything can happen."

He was right, and that's what I feared.

Footsteps approached from behind, and I turned to see Gabe walking toward us. He sat down on the other side of me, and said, "Did Rueben tell you our plans yet?"

"Yes," I said. "Are you sure we can get the boat repaired if the island is hostile?"

"We'll have to barter with them." His gaze flicked from me to Rueben. "We just can't let them know we have women on board."

A chill moved along my back, and it wasn't from the cold rain.

Gabe pulled out a piece of what looked like leather from his jacket pocket. "Here," he said, and I saw that a map had been carved into the leather. He pointed to a jagged circle. "This is the island, and this is where we are."

"So close?" I asked, surprised when he pointed about an inch from the circle.

"We'll be there within the hour," Gabe said, looking at me. "Becca's leg is still hurting her even though her bullet wound is almost healed. I think she twisted her ankle during the storm. We need you to keep the women sequestered."

I saw something like fear in his eyes, and it seemed to reach out to me. "I'll keep everyone below deck. How long do you think the repairs will take?"

"Two or three days, depending on what kind of supplies are available," Rueben answered.

Gabe scrubbed his hand through his hair and still seemed agitated. "Jezebel," he started in a hesitant voice. "No matter what might happen above deck, you must stay below deck with the women."

I looked at him sharply. "Do you think the islanders will fight you?"

"We don't know," Rueben hurried to say, throwing a warning glance at Gabe. "We need to be prepared for anything."

What weren't they telling me? "We can fight with you," I said. "Becca told me all the female mechanics have been trained to fight."

"You don't understand," Rueben said. "We can't afford to lose any more mechanics. The storm already took too many." He lowered his voice. "If something happens to us—to the men—then the women will need to find a way back to Lake Town or even to the city. Protecting you is the priority. If all of us die, then the entire world will continue to die."

I was silent, then said, "Maybe we can explain that to the islanders."

Gabe released a short laugh. "My family came to this island when I was a young child," he said. "We only stayed for a few minutes before we were driven off. There's no reasoning with the islanders. They aren't even loyal to one another. Most of them were Banished from the city or other locations, and it was probably for a good reason. There are some who were born on the island, of course, but they've grown up in a savage environment."

"Gabe! Rueben!" Someone called out.

Michel hurried toward us. "Land's been spotted."

We all scrambled to our feet.

"We're closer than I thought," Gabe said in a panicked voice. "Hurry below," he told me. "Keep the women quiet."

I had more questions, but Gabe was already giving out orders, Rueben at his side, as they moved about the deck. I saw a couple of women on the far side of the deck and ushered them to the door that led below. I followed them down and saw that most of the women had already gathered,

Becca among them. She sat on a wooden crate, burrowed beneath a blanket.

I crossed to her. "How many women should there be?"

"Fourteen," she said. "Plus the two of us."

I began counting heads and was relieved when I reached fourteen. "I'll be right back," I told Becca, and hurried to the steps before she could protest.

I opened the door to the deck and peered out at the activity. A dark shape stood out in the water—the island was in sight. My pulse raced as I made out forms standing on the shore of the island. The islanders had already seen our boat and were waiting. From this distance, I hoped they wouldn't be able to tell that I was a woman, but then Rueben saw me and motioned for me to get back down.

I moved more fully behind the door and continued watching. The islanders looked to be wearing clothing of thick leather and shawls of animal fur. Many of them had shaved heads, but some of them had long hair threaded into thick braids. I wasn't sure if the women had the long hair and the men were shaved, because all of their clothing looked similar. I didn't see any children—just a couple dozen adults.

And then I noticed the smoke. Behind the gathered people was a bonfire of sorts. Were they cooking? Burning something? Or is that how they stayed warm? I couldn't see any huts or houses, but behind the islanders rose a thick tangle of trees. Perhaps they had underground housing like Lake Town?

I pulled the door so that there was only a small slit to peer through. A new sound resonated through the air—a deep chanting of words that I couldn't understand. Behind the row of people were others in a circle around the fire. They were moving, or even dancing, and they were chanting.

My breath caught as I remembered stories about the Before and the religious zealots who'd tried to stop the rain, believing it was the Great Flood returning to the earth. The early members of the Legislature had put as many zealots to death as they could capture, and burned all religious books. Those that escaped death created hidden communities where they could perform their rites and sacrifices.

Fear pulsed through me. I felt like I'd just reentered the Before, where chaos, death, and crime ruled the world.

CHAPTER 24

Sol

We ran, wearing only our raincoats, and carrying nothing. We'd left the tablets in the bunk room since they were like tracers now, and we left the bedding, clothing, and food behind. Paul was leading our group, and I had no idea where we were going. All I knew was that we couldn't remain in the bunk house. Dr. Wells would figure out that we ran, especially when the security officers arrived to arrest whoever had broken into the security portal.

We exited the tunnel and stepped out into an unusually warm day. The rain was more of a mist, and if the bank of clouds hadn't been obscuring the sun overhead, we would actually have been too hot. I stopped short as I noticed a commotion across the street. Commotions were very rare in the city, and were usually quelled immediately with the help of agitator rods.

Several people were on the wet ground, their hands

cuffed behind their backs. But no security officers were nearby. The ones I could see were down the street a ways, in some sort of fight with about a half dozen men.

"What's happening?" Tim said, gaping.

"Beautiful chaos," Paul said, pointing down the opposite side of the street. "We need to take cover. Look who's coming."

A tram approached, and through the long windows, I spotted more uniform-wearing men. I didn't know if they were coming to help with the problems among the citizens or if they were following the tablets' locations.

This time Paul looked to me, and I saw something I hadn't seen before in his eyes. Desperation. "We can't return to the bunk house," Paul said. "And we can't take refuge with the Faction. They won't be pleased with what we've done."

"That won't stop the Faction from taking advantage of what we've done," Tim countered.

Paul took a few steps back, toward a corner of a building. "We need to get out of sight."

We followed Paul, and I looked for somewhere we could go without the officers noticing us. Chances were that we wouldn't be recognized, but I didn't know what kind of luck we could expect.

"I know a place," I said, thinking of the cavern I'd sent Jez down into. "We can stay there for a while, until we see the fallout." I also hoped there might be tablets down there, but I wasn't sure what Rueben had stripped before he'd left.

"Where?" Paul said.

"Near the University," I answered, which meant that we'd have to make our way across half the city. The B Level district was above the C Level. And the A Level and University beyond that.

I could tell the distance made the other men nervous, but that was my only solution. Paul looked to the others, and each nodded.

"Let's go, then," Paul said, turning back to me. "We'll have to catch a tram at some point. Let's wait until we're out of this neighborhood." He peered around the corner of the building.

I joined him to see the officers apprehending more people, cuffing them, and corralling them into panicked groups. A couple of people lay on the ground, most likely shocked by the agitators.

"Let's go around this building and cross the street farther down," Paul said.

We all agreed and made our way around the warehouse we'd stopped near. The alley behind the building was lined by a high wall separating us from the ocean. As we hurried along, I wondered how close the Lake Town boats were, or if they were even coming. I wondered if the deactivated Harmony implants would help or hurt their cause.

If the Legislature had enough time before the Lake Town invasion, my activities might only result in fuller prisons. We'd deleted hundreds of IDs, but in a city of two million, we'd barely stirred things up.

We exited on the other side of the building, crossed the street, and started walking toward the B Level neighborhoods. We moved quickly, and I focused on not paying attention to the skirmish behind us.

"Let's take that tram," Paul whispered as we neared a tram stop.

I scanned the windows to see what type of passengers it carried. The tram looked about half full of B Level workers, which was probably a good thing—we needed to blend in.

We hurried to catch the tram before it pulled away, and I sat on a bench next to Paul and across from Tim. We said nothing as the tram moved, but I looked around at the people, wondering if any of them had been affected by our deactivating.

Two women sat not too far from me. One of them kept her head bowed, while the other was staring at the tram door with wide eyes. She looked afraid, or perhaps overwhelmed. It didn't take much deduction to see that something was going on with her. I rose from my seat and crossed over to her.

"Are you all right?" I asked her in a low voice, hoping not to draw attention from the others nearby.

She looked up at me, and her eyes seemed out of focus. Then she said, "I am fine, sir." Her voice was flat, but I knew the signs. It reminded me of Jez and how she carefully schooled her emotions.

"Changes are happening in the city," I said. "You're not alone."

Her eyes widened slightly, but she pressed her lips together, and I could see that she was determined to keep whatever was swirling inside her mind to herself.

I went back to my seat. Paul had seen the exchange, and although he hadn't heard my short conversation with the woman, it was like he understood my thoughts. How many of the citizens would pretend like nothing had changed with their implants? How many would continue in their daily tasks as before, all the while hiding their new emotions?

At the next tram stop, Paul stood, and without a word or signal, the rest of us followed him off. We weren't even close to the University.

As the tram pulled away, Paul said, "Let's walk to the

next stop and take another tram the rest of the way." Then he looked at me. "Don't question any more citizens."

I wanted to argue, but now wasn't the time. We had to get to a secure place, and we had to find out how widespread our deactivation was. So I nodded my agreement, and we set off.

"Oh no," Tim said suddenly.

Through the gray mist of the morning, I saw a thick cloud hovering in the distance. But it wasn't a cloud at all. It was smoke, and it wasn't over a building, but out over the ocean, which meant it was a boat.

My heart hitched. And even though I might have been able to come up with other explanations, I knew it could only be one thing. The Lake Town invasion had started.

CHAPTER 25

Jez

Rueben's hand came around the edge of the door, and he hissed, "What are you doing, Jez? I told you to stay below."

"I don't think we should try to land here," I said, my voice raw with fear. "Look at them. They're . . . like warriors."

The chanting was louder now, and I could smell the smoke from the islanders' bonfire. We were less than a hundred yards away from the shore line, and although I'd kept myself hidden behind the door separating the stairs from the deck, I could see the islanders clearly.

Women and men were intermixed, their clothing a mishmash of fitted leather wrapped around their bodies like armor. I could imagine that at night, the people could easily disappear behind a bush or tree. Many of the men—I assumed they were men—were bald, or shaved. Their scalps were wet with rain and reflected the light of their fire.

But it was their eyes that sent a shiver throughout my entire body. Dark and wide, and . . . hungry? I couldn't explain it—not even to myself.

A series of tall, wooden towers lined the beach. I could see that they were manned by men or boys who stood at attention with bows and arrows. From the boat, it was clear that the bows and arrows weren't of primitive wood, but of advanced metals. The silver gleamed even from a distance.

"If we can't repair our boat here," Rueben was whispering from the other side to the door, "we'll probably have to return to Lake Town. Although the distance to the city is about the same."

"So then, we'll just continue to the city," I said, although a part of me knew it was impossible. If we showed up at the city without any way to escape, we'd be captured and likely Executed. The thought of Execution sent Sol's face flashing through my mind, and I wondered if he was still alive.

The chanting changed then, growing lower and more frantic. The islanders danced around the bonfire with exaggerated movements, raising their arms to the sky, then dipping down to the wet earth. They appeared to be synchronized, but then one individual moved in the opposite way, and the rhythm fell apart. It was fascinating, yet terrible, to watch.

The people stood crowded together on the shore, watching our boat approach. I had been so focused on their wild eyes and skin-tight clothing that I hadn't noticed the metal spears many of them carried. Others held what looked to be knives in their hands. They were armed and waiting.

Gabe rushed over to Rueben. He looked shaken up, and he didn't even seem to see me standing behind the door. "That bonfire wasn't burning when we first spotted the island."

Rueben's brows drew together. "Is that significant?"

"Yes," Gabe said. "They might be performing a sacrificial dance."

I was about to ask what that was when Gabe continued. "One of the mechanics had a breakdown when he saw the bonfire. Like me, his family crossed paths with these islanders once before. He says that a sacrificial dance means that the islanders are anticipating a meal." He looked back to the island, then at Rueben. "He says they're cannibals."

The breath left my body, and I couldn't think. The thought of them kidnapping some of the women for childbearing was nothing compared to this new information. None of us were safe.

"We have to get out of here," Gabe said, "and turn the boat around." He hurried away then, shouting commands about reversing the single sail.

"Jezebel," Rueben said, turning to me, panic in his expression. "Shut this door and barricade it." He started to push the door closed, but I pushed back.

"I can help you," I said. "*We* can help you."

Rueben was stronger than me, and he was winning the battle over the door. "There may not be enough time to reverse the sail," he said in a fierce voice. "Some of the men can go ashore and be a distraction while the rest of us reverse the direction of the boat."

I grabbed his arm. I couldn't stand the thought of Rueben leaving the boat to sacrifice himself in that way. But then I froze. Beyond the boat, I saw that the men and women who were waiting on shore were now moving. Toward us. And two of them were carrying a sort of raft between them made of wooden planks lashed together.

"Rueben, look," I said.

He turned his head, and the color drained from his face. When he looked back at me, his eyes seemed suddenly blank. "Get below, Jez."

I shook my head. "I'm not going to sit below deck while you fight. You need us."

"Please," he said, shoving the door closed. He must have been leaning against it, because I couldn't push it open again.

"Rueben!" I called out, pounding on the door, but he didn't respond.

I pushed at the door again. It was locked.

I wasn't going to be able to break it down on my own, so I started down the steps to recruit help. It took me a moment to get used to the low light, and when I reached the bottom of the stairs, Becca met me.

"What's going on?" she asked.

Other women gathered around us as I told them everything I'd seen and how Rueben and Gabe wanted us to stay below. "The islanders are rowing out to the boat," I finished. "I don't know if we can get the boat redirected in time."

Just then, there was a loud thump overhead as if something hard and heavy had fallen onto the deck.

We all froze, none of us daring to say a word. But as I met the wide eyes of the other women, I saw fierceness and determination instead of fear.

Another thump sounded, this one not as loud. I imagined one of those metal arrows or spears embedded into the boat's deck. Then a series of thumps erupted, and I knew the islanders had reached the boat and were fighting our men.

Becca moved closer to me. "I can't stay down here and do nothing."

"I can't, either," I said, looking from Becca to the other women.

Slowly, they started to nod, and one by one they stepped forward until we formed a tight circle. Becca reached for my hand and squeezed tightly, and I did the same with the woman on my other side, and soon the group of us were holding hands.

"Whatever happens," I said as another thump on the deck shook the ceiling above us, "we will fight for our own freedom so that we might restore it to others."

"Let's go," one woman said, and the rest of us echoed, "Let's go."

It was a simple phrase, but in our situation, it meant so much. We were all committed to fight together for what we believed in. I slid the knife I'd trained with from the strap around my thigh. Even during training at Lake Town, I had never thought I'd be actually fighting face-to-face with someone. I swallowed hard and started up the stairs.

The sound of footsteps following me urged me on, and when I reached the door, I tried to push it open. It was still locked, but I could hear the sounds of fighting more clearly now. Thumps, shouts, cries of pain. My blood chilled at the images that leapt into my mind, but I wedged my shoulder against the door, motioning for a couple of the women to join me. Three of us crowded on the top step and, at my command, we threw our weight against the door.

The door gave way on our first attempt, and I stumbled sideways into the cold rain as the door crashed to the deck. I had to orient myself, and when I did, my heart seemed to leap into my throat. Several islanders were aboard and were fighting ferociously. It seemed that our men were holding them back, and as I watched, one of the islanders was pitched over the side of the boat, pushed by a mechanic.

But more were coming.

"Watch out!" I screamed as I spotted an islander, fresh out of the rowboat, run at Rueben with a spear. Rueben's back was turned because he was fighting another man.

At the sound of my scream, several of the islanders, as well as the Lake Town men, looked in my direction. It was like they'd frozen midfight. Only men had invaded our boat, and I suddenly felt very exposed. Rueben's warnings about being abducted echoed through my mind, but Gabe's caution about the islanders being cannibals drowned out all concern for myself.

Rueben caught the movement of the charging islander in time to move out of the way, and then he was running toward me, yelling at us to get below deck.

The women behind me continued to come up the stairs, their knives in hand.

"What are you doing?" Rueben shouted. "Get back!"

Even if I had tried to barricade myself behind the door, it was too late now. The nearest islander was already grabbing one of the women. She lashed out and sliced his arm with her knife. He yelled in pain, and they wrestled over the knife in her hand. Another woman joined in, and together, the two were able to wrest the islander to his knees.

Rueben looked from the scuffle to me, and I could see that he was torn about who to protect first.

But his decision was made for him as an islander lunged toward him, spear in hand. Rueben had no choice but to turn and fight the man off. I moved to help him, and dove at the islander's knees to throw him off balance. The man tumbled against me, and we landed in a hard heap. Rueben was in the mix in a second, pulling the islander off me.

But the man had already wrapped his bare hands

around my neck, squeezing the breath out of me. I had dropped my knife, so I clawed at his hands, trying to create space enough to breathe. My body started to quiver as my oxygen was quickly depleted. And then suddenly the islander slumped, releasing his grip. The pressure on my neck was gone, although the pain was still there.

The islander was lying inert on top of my body, his weight preventing me from taking a full breath.

"Jezebel!" Rueben said somewhere above me.

But I'd closed my eyes to focus on breathing and forcing my heart to beat. I wondered how this would end for me—if my life would be over at any moment.

Then the weight shifted, then lifted, and my body gasped for air. I opened my eyes to see Rueben above me, lifting me up. I tried to wrap my arms around him to hold on, but the strangling had taken all my strength.

"Jez, stay with me," Rueben said.

I blinked up at him, and the sounds of the fight came back in full force. Yelling, screaming, thuds, and thumps. I tried to turn my head, but my neck injury from the storm seemed to have reopened.

Rueben stumbled, and I grasped his shirt with my hands, clinging to him as he regained his balance.

He set me down near the captain's wheel, and Gabe appeared, asking me questions.

But my voice didn't seem to work—I couldn't answer him.

I was leaning against some sort of crate when an islander charged toward us. Together, Rueben and Gabe were able to deflect him, but then two more islanders joined in the fray.

They were positively wild looking. Their eyes didn't

seem human, but feral, and their bodies were strong and wiry as if every calorie they consumed were put to extreme use. But I didn't want to think about their eating habits.

The two islanders were fighting Rueben and Gabe, one on one. I had long lost my knife, but I searched around for something else to use as a weapon. And then I saw the inert body of an islander lying a few feet away, a short spear at his side. I crawled toward him and grabbed the spear.

I inhaled and rose to my feet. I was still dizzy, but I felt stronger now, despite the fear coursing through me. I didn't like the number of people I saw lying motionless on the deck. Rueben and Gabe had both overpowered the islanders they'd been fighting, but the battle was far from over. More shouting came from the shore, and I saw that more rowboats were on their way toward us. Once those islanders climbed onto our boat, we would be far outnumbered.

And then I saw two islanders fighting each other—one a man, the other a woman. I stared at the woman, who was crouching low, deftly wielding a short spear like the one in my hand. *Chalice.* I shook my head, disbelieving. Chalice was dressed in dark leather like an islander, yet she was fighting against them. Her hair was blacker than night and was still cut short with silver streaks running through it.

"Chalice!" I yelled as the man she was fighting fell to his knees in defeat.

It took only a moment for Chalice to see me.

I didn't know if I was making a mistake by singling her out. Perhaps she was still fighting against the Lake Town people, but she'd had a personal vendetta against a fellow islander.

"Jez," she said, her low voice cracked with exertion.

Her deep-blue gaze met mine, and I knew she was on

our side. She had been Banished, and this island must have been where she ended up. Chalice ran over to me, but before I could say anything to Rueben, he blocked her advance.

Rueben struck out and sent her short spear to the floor. Chalice took a step back, raising her hands.

"She's a friend," I called out. "Chalice is a friend."

Rueben looked from Chalice over to me. "Are you sure?"

This was not the time to explain—not with the fight still raging around us. "I trust her." And I hoped I was right. It had been months since she'd been led away from the University assembly, accused of joining a religious cult.

Rueben lowered his knife and nodded at Chalice. "Can you help us?"

Chalice stared at him, then stepped closer. "I can. You must all start to act as if you have the fever. Tell your people. I'll send out the alarm."

I stared at her, not fully understanding. Rueben seemed to understand, though, and he and Gabe fell to the deck and started to writhe and moan.

"The fever!" Chalice yelled. Then she ran to the railing and screamed at the approaching rowers. "The fever! They have the fever!"

The rowers continued their forward motion, but then another islander started to yell, "The fever!"

A couple of islanders jumped overboard and swam toward the rowboats. It was only then that the rowers seemed to comprehend what was going on. They reversed their direction and allowed the swimming islanders to climb aboard.

Chalice continued to run around the boat, screaming out, "The fever!"

Our people caught on quickly and started to mimic Rueben and Gabe's writhing. We'd become a boat of miserable, moaning people.

Chalice staggered about, moaning herself. "I have the fever now!" she shouted. "Jump off the boat and save yourselves. Don't let these foreigners touch you, or you'll get it, too."

When the last living islanders had jumped off the boat, only then did Rueben and Gabe stop their moaning. The boat had changed direction, but it would be a while before we were far enough from the shore to feel safe again.

I sat up, my body feeling bruised all over, but I was alive. "Chalice," I said, as she continued to yell toward the island about the fever and how she was now dying.

I rose and walked toward the rail where she stood. "Chalice," I said again. "We're safe now. Thank you. Whatever the fever is that you were screaming about, it seems that we're saved."

She turned to me, her hair and clothing just as wild as the island she'd come from. But her eyes didn't have the empty, dead look in them, and for that I was grateful. "The fever is the rotting disease from the Before—similar to Leprosy—but the effects are immediate. At least according to island legend."

I nodded, my mind and thoughts a numbing whirlwind. "Thank you," I said again, my voice raw with emotion.

And then she smiled the first smile I'd ever seen her give.

CHAPTER 26

Sol

Horror pulsed through me as I stood with Paul and Tim, watching the smoke coming from somewhere over the ocean. A boat was on fire, and the only explanation I could come up with was that the Legislature had fired a missile at a Lake Town boat.

"Come on," Paul said, tugging my arm when I didn't move with him and Tim. "We need to get to your secure hiding place.

But I knew now that I couldn't take them to the cavern. We'd be blocked off from all the happenings in the city, and I couldn't just sit there and do nothing, not knowing what was happening above ground.

I turned to explain this to Paul, but he'd dropped my arm and was staring at another cloud of smoke, this one about a half mile from the first.

"We've got to help the Faction," Tim said, speaking fast.

"We've got to stop the city from taking out the Lake Town boats."

"What if Dr. Wells knows what we've done?" Paul asked. "He'll turn against *us*."

I didn't care about Wells and his power over us. If we couldn't stop the attack on the Lake Town boats, then our efforts would come to nothing. I met Paul's gaze and knew that he felt the same.

"I'm going to the ocean," Paul said.

"Me, too," I echoed, and Tim agreed.

"We need weapons," Paul said, giving me a pointed look.

There was a chance that Rueben had left things behind in the cavern. He would have been able to carry only so much out with him. "We'll go to the cavern and see what we can find."

We spent the next thirty minutes hopping from one tram to the other until we'd reached the University. Nearly every street we passed had security officers and citizens on it, all in some sort of skirmish. It was an odd scene, but we didn't ask any questions, taking advantage of the fact that the security officers were too distracted to pay us any mind.

I led the men down a side street and into a small park between two residential buildings—the place I'd last seen Jez. Memories of our last moments together washed over me as I opened the park gate. Her fervent kiss, the look of fear in her eyes, and how she climbed down the ladder rungs, disappearing into the thick darkness.

I brushed away the wet leaves and lifted the metal grate. Paul peered into the blackness. "How far does this go down?"

I thought I detected wariness in his tone, so I said, "I'll lead the way. You bring up the rear and replace the grate.

There's another way out of the cavern that will take us to the ocean."

Paul's eyebrows lifted at this, but he didn't question me, just nodded.

I started down the ladder, my hands gripping the metal rungs as I thought of Jez and her descent. The quiet surrounded me, broken only by the footsteps of the other men as they descended after me. A dank smell permeated the narrow chute of earth and roots, and below, I could hear the sound of trickling water.

Soon, the sound of the grate being slid into place screeched through the narrow space, and then I knew we were committed. I continued to descend, and when my feet hit the ground at last, I called up to the others. "I'm at the bottom." I scooted back while the others joined me. "We all need to hold onto one another so that we don't become separated," I instructed.

With no tablets or other sources of light, the tunnel was pitch black. I remembered enough about the cavern to know that we needed to follow the sound of the water until we reached the division of the tunnel, and then we'd go right.

The progress was slow, but steady, and I kept hoping that I hadn't forgotten my way. But as we moved deeper into the tunnel, a distinct smell of smoke arose. Something was burning.

"Do you smell that?" Paul asked.

I did, and I didn't like it. My eyes started to water, but I pressed on. When the sound of the water dropped off, I knew it was going into a rock cavity, and to my surprise, I could see a thread of light coming from the tunnel on the right. I might have been relieved, but the air had changed as well, heating up like we were approaching a bonfire. Had there been a fire down here somewhere? Was there still a fire?

I blinked a few times to adjust my eyes against the dingy smoke that now hung in the air, and, sure enough, there was a horizontal strip of light in the distance, running along the ground like it was coming from underneath a door. I knew it was the light from the atomic globe, but what I didn't understand was the intensity of the heat in the tunnel.

"Is that where we're going?" Paul whispered.

I started to nod, and then realizing he couldn't see me, I said, "Yes, but I don't understand the heat and smoke. There's an atomic globe in the cavern, but the heat hasn't reached this far before."

"What if the Legislature found out about this place?" Paul asked, echoing the fear that was nagging at my own mind. "Maybe they destroyed it?"

"It's a possibility," I whispered, wishing that it weren't. "Let's go." I continued leading the others. We still needed weapons, and we'd come too far to turn around now. I pulled the collar of my shirt over my mouth and tried not to inhale too deeply.

I continued down the tunnel with more confidence than I felt. All I knew was that the unexpected lay on the other side of that door.

We halted just before the door, and I listened. The smoke was definitely thicker here, and I didn't hear any voices or other commotion, so I opened the code reader near the bottom of the door and put in the code. It hadn't been changed, and the door slowly slid open.

The brightness of the interior momentarily blinded me, and I blinked against the flood of yellow light from the globe. But that wasn't where all the light was coming from. Someone had set the cavern on fire, and it was still smoldering . . . I didn't know if it had been Rueben trying to destroy evidence or if officials had discovered it and torched the place. Opening the door released all of the heat and smoke from the fire, and now it funneled out around and through us, causing us to literally fall back with the pressure of the hot air.

The other men cried out as they landed on the ground, but I was too stunned to make a sound. My eyes burned now from the intensity of the heat, and my throat felt like it had been scorched dry. I scrambled backward, rising to my feet, and pressing myself against the cool tunnel wall. But even the wall was nearly too hot to touch. We'd come to the cavern expecting to find some weapons and escape to the ocean to help defeat the Legislature. Instead, we'd walked right into an unmerciful oven.

The cavern walls were scorched black, and everywhere metal objects that had once been tables and chairs and weapons had melted into disfigured shapes. There were supply packs near one wall that were singed, but not burned. I closed my eyes against the heat and smoke as the perspiration prickled across my entire body.

"Can we make it through the heat?" Paul asked hoarsely, nudging me.

We couldn't stand here much longer. The cavern's shape was acting like a radiant oven, and in a few minutes, we'd be overcome with heat exhaustion. "I don't know," I said truthfully. I peered across the cavern to where the other exit was. We'd have to pass the cavern to reach the exit.

"Are those tablets on the ground?" he asked.

There was no guarantee that the heat hadn't rendered the tablets useless, but a new rush of resolve shot through me. Just beyond the fallen tablets was the exit.

I met the wide-eyed gazes of the other men. "Let's grab

the tablets and those packs, and I'll lead you to the other exit. We need to hurry before the heat knocks us out."

The men nodded, and we moved inside the cavern. The heat was even fiercer than I expected. My eyes stung, and my skin felt like paper. We picked up the tablets on the ground using our sleeves, and I motioned to a couple of packs by the far wall, hoping there would be something of use inside that wasn't damaged. Tim and Paul picked them up, and then we hurried toward the door.

I entered the code into the reader on the door on the far side of the cavern. Nothing happened. The heat from the fire must have damaged it. I searched through Tim's bag for something to pry open the door.

Paul rammed his shoulder against the door, then was joined by Tim, and together they slammed into the door, causing it to shift. It still didn't open. "Try your code again," Paul called out.

I tried the code again. The door slid open, and hot air whooshed past us and poured into the narrow tunnel leading out of the cavern.

"Let's go," I said, leading the way. The light from the globe bounced off the walls, and our progress was swift until the light behind us dimmed. The air gradually became cooler, and cleaner, but not much. The heat and smoke had done a good job of racing ahead of us.

I didn't exactly remember how long this part of the tunnel was, but by the time the dark ebbed to gray, I knew we were getting close. And it wasn't a moment too soon. We'd slowed down considerably, our bodies sweating more than I'd thought possible without actually passing out.

Two sharp turns in the carved rock tunnel later, I practically stumbled onto the shore. The cool rain upon my face and pure air was the most beautiful thing I'd ever felt. I collapsed to my knees and braced myself with my hands against the rocks and dirt, taking several deep breaths. The other men fell beside me, equally exhausted and grateful.

My throat screamed for water, but I rose to my haunches and looked out over the ocean from our place against the cliffs.

Two boats near the shore were encased in flames and smoke. I didn't need to move one step closer to know that both of the burning boats were from Lake Town.

CHAPTER 27

Jez

Chalice wrapped her arms around me, hugging me as we were never allowed to in the city. Showing affection would have demonstrated emotion, and that was against the city laws.

I leaned against my former roommate—I had thought I'd never see her again.

Behind us, the Lake Town people had finished cleaning up the deck as best they could. They'd already pushed off all the dead bodies, speaking words over each of our own. Most of us were still in shock, and no one was really talking—just watching the island as we drifted farther and farther away from it.

I grasped Chalice's hand and looked at her fingers. Three of them had metal rings on them, one in the form of a religious emblem called a crucifix from the Before. Another was shaped into a large open-lidded eye.

I laughed, a real laugh, despite all that had just happened. I was so thrilled to be reunited with Chalice and to see that, even living in Banishment, she hadn't changed. Her stubbornness sent comfort straight through my body.

"I can make you some rings," Chalice said, turning her hand over so that I could inspect the handiwork better.

"I'd love that," I said, in true sincerity. Even if, for some reason, I ended up living the rest of my life in a city prison, I'd wear one of Chalice's religious emblems with honor. I hadn't been allowed to consider the possibility of a deity in my life—religious beliefs were forbidden after they'd caused many devastating wars in the Before. But something—or someone—had reunited me with Chalice again.

The storm, the islanders, Chalice's stroke of genius with the fake fevers . . . it was just too many coincidences for them not to have a higher being orchestrating it all.

And for what? I hoped it was because Lake Town would prevail over the city.

Together, Chalice and I watched the shores of the island grow more and more distant. The bonfire still raged, even higher now, and dark, dancing figures were silhouetted against the bright orange light. Standing near the broken ship railing, with the wind and rain pelting my back, the island scene seemed unreal somehow, like I was watching a picture come to life.

"What was it like?" I half spoke, half whispered.

"Brutal."

Knowing what Chalice had been through in the city, and that she'd been altered and then Banished, I shivered to think that the island had been worse.

I released Chalice's hand and faced her. Her expression was closed and hard to read, even with the orange flames on the island providing more light than usual against the rainy day.

"Are you all right?" I asked. I didn't know if I could bear to hear her story, but I couldn't stop myself from asking.

Chalice's gaze shifted away from mine, and when she spoke again, I had to lean close to hear.

"I had no idea how the others outside the city lived," Chalice said, her dark eyes seeming to grow even darker. "I'd heard stories like we all did, about savages and cannibals. But I never quite believed them."

She paused so long that I finally said, "You don't have to tell me."

Her head snapped up. "It's just hard to sum it into neat words, you know? I mean, they are savages, and they are cannibals, but they are also surviving in desperate circumstances." A tear welled in her eye, and she brushed it away.

"Were they cruel to you?"

"Not cruel in the way that you might think," Chalice said, her gaze moving across the ocean as if searching for something. "They live the most basic and primitive laws of survival. Remember when I told you about Darwin one night?"

I nodded. Chalice had done some illegal research when we were first assigned as roommates over a year ago. She'd told me about an ancient scientist from the Before and his theories about the human race. I hadn't wanted to hear illegal information, but I was also fascinated and couldn't bring myself to tell her to stop. "Survival of the fittest?" I asked.

Now it was her turn to nod. When she didn't speak for a while, I didn't push her. She finally said, "When you read something from a school lesson, it doesn't give any credit to what the true lives would have been like of the people in that situation. You can't even try to understand until you're faced with the same desperation and therefore the same decisions."

My mind was spinning as I tried to comprehend. Did she mean that she'd been living as a savage these past months and had been a cannibal, too? I must have shuddered without realizing it, because her expression closed off again, and she shut her eyes.

But she continued to speak. "When you're faced with a choice between life and death, it's remarkable how many people will truly choose life. They will do things in order to survive that they might not have ever thought themselves capable of." Her eyes opened, and this time they were clear, confident. "There's the pain of hunger and the weakness that accompanies it, and then it turns into something deeper, more base, almost animalistic, until you are no longer your former self."

I felt cold all over, and it was hard for me to imagine the desperation she was speaking about. But I had seen cruelty, and I had known sorrow.

Chalice touched my arm. "When the island disappears from sight, I want to put it completely behind me. Do you understand?"

I nodded, knowing that she must have endured experiences too difficult to speak about.

Dark figures continued dancing around the bonfire on the diminishing island.

"They're not dancing to celebrate any longer," Chalice said in a quiet voice. "They're dancing to ward off the fever plague. Look." She pointed at a group of people still close to the shore. Some of the rowboats were just reaching land.

I watched as a fight broke out between the people still in the rowboat and those on the shore. One man was trying to push the rowboat back into the ocean. A couple of people in the rowboat jumped out and started swimming to the shore.

"What's going on?" I asked.

"They're afraid that some of the islanders have already caught the fever," Chalice said. "They don't want to let them back onto the island."

Then, to my horror, one of the fights escalated, and one of the men collapsed to the ground. Two others rolled him into the water, and the waves closed over him. "They're killing their own people?"

Chalice released a short, bitter laugh. "They do not consider themselves a tribe, or family, or unit, or anything of that sort. On the island, every single person is out for himself. It's you against everyone."

I wanted to turn away, but I couldn't stop watching. A couple of the islanders were forcing the swimmers back, pushing them under water. I clenched my hands as I watched them flailing in the water—drowning.

"No one is safe," Chalice continued. "No woman, man, or child."

I hadn't seen any children, and I wondered how they survived if they were always on their own. "Where are the children?"

"They're kept in a fenced area and watched over by guards until they're six years old," Chalice said. "After that, they're considered old enough to protect themselves."

I watched Chalice as she spoke since I couldn't bear to watch the islanders turning on one another. Her eyes were dark and haunted.

"When I first arrived at the island, I quickly learned that

I couldn't trust anyone," she continued. "I banded with a few children and became their caretaker. But when two of them were abducted, I couldn't handle it anymore. I built my own shelter in a tree and scavenged for food on my own." She nodded toward the island.

I couldn't see the islanders who'd been swimming or the ones in the rowboat, and I had a feeling that they were now floating beneath the surface of the ocean.

"The only time it's safe to come out of hiding is when there's a bonfire at night," she said. "The islanders drink a root juice that makes them act differently—friendly and happy. But too much of the root juice, and some of them will get even more angry, and that's when they'll go after children."

My stomach lurched, and I gripped a broken rail in front of me.

Chalice shook her head. "When I saw your boat, I was going to stay hidden, until I realized that if I could create some sort of disturbance, maybe I could escape." She ran a hand over her hair, which had grown nearly to her shoulders from the cropped style that she'd worn in the city. A smile lifted the corner of her lips. "I couldn't believe it when I saw you, and I had to act fast before your boat got too close to the shore. Or it would have been too late for everyone."

"You saved my life, Chalice," I said. "You saved *all* of our lives." I looked about the boat. Rueben was with Gabe by the captain's wheel, but I didn't see Becca anywhere. I knew she'd been injured again, but she had been up and walking soon after the islanders fled the boat.

Chalice blinked back the tears forming in her eyes, and I realized it was the first time I'd ever seen her cry. "You saved *my* life, Jez." She looped her arm through mine, and her thinness startled me. She'd always been petite, but now she seemed positively waiflike. "Now, where are we going?"

It was my turn for a bitter laugh. "We were on our way to invade the city," I said, "with an entire fleet of boats from Lake Town. But we were caught in a storm and lost most of the sails."

She didn't seem surprised at the news. A woman living on a Banished island was certainly no stranger to bad luck. "And then you encountered us?"

"Gabe," I said, nodding in his direction, "thought we might be able to do some repairs on your island. His family was here when he was young, so he knew of some of the dangers. All the women were expected to stay below deck."

Chalice peered over at Gabe. The rain had kicked up, and everyone on the boat appeared as muted gray shapes. "If it was more than ten years ago, then maybe Gabe would have been right. But it seems that life deteriorated on the island more and more." Her eyes were back on me. "Food sources deteriorated, and a new leadership took over."

"So there is a leadership?" I asked, curious.

"Of course," Chalice said. "We call them chiefs, and they start the bonfires each night and decide who hunts and who builds and who guards the children."

And who is killed? I wondered.

"I wouldn't exactly call it an organized government, though," Chalice said. "There are frequent changes in leadership when someone is . . . killed."

The rain and clouds had made the island almost impossible to see.

"I won't miss it for a single moment," Chalice finished. She fell quiet then, and I watched the last evidence of the island disappear in the driving rain.

She might have finished telling her story, but I knew she'd never forget it.

CHAPTER 28

Sol

I stared at the burning boats, feeling as if I were replaying a nightmare in my head. But there was no mistaking that the boats were from Lake Town. I'd worked on enough of them to recognize the black-stitched sails and the rough-hewn fitted planks that made up the sides and the decks.

I watched as people jumped off the sides of the burning boats, and I heard their screams reverberating across the ocean.

"They've fired missiles at them," Paul said, pulling me out of my shock.

Just then another missile screeched through the air, striking one of the burning boats. There was an explosion an instant later, and I could only hope that Jez, Rueben, and Jude weren't on that boat. But as it was, I knew most of the Lake Town people, and now I was a witness to their deaths.

Tim knelt on the ground and sifted through the bag

we'd brought from the cavern. A glint of metal caught my eye, and I knelt beside him, digging through as well.

"There are firing guns in here," Tim said. "Do you know how to use them?" he asked me.

I pulled out a gun that had a wide barrel. It shot flares that might mimic a missile, but wouldn't do much damage. They were for distress signals. I set the flare gun down and pulled out several short knives. They'd once been food implements, but Rueben had retrofitted them into strong weapons by sharpening the blades and wrapping the hilts with leather for a stronger grip. I handed the knives one by one over to the men. With grim faces, they each took one.

I hid my knife in the pocket of my jacket, then rose to my feet. "The flare guns will only attract attention to us. We've got to get on the Legislature's boats to stop the firing."

"That's only the short-term solution, you know," Paul said. He looked at me and Tim. "Can either of you break into the Legislature's control rooms?"

Tim lifted a hand. "I've done it before. In fact, that's why Wells saved, and then recruited, me."

We both stared at him.

"You never told us that," Paul said. "That might have been useful information."

Tim lifted a shoulder. "I wasn't ready to share it until now."

"Until we're crouching on a beach in the middle of a battle?" Paul asked.

"Should we split up?" Tim asked.

"Not yet," Paul said, and looked at me for confirmation.

I wavered. I could hardly stand seeing the Lake Town boats being fired upon, but if Tim could break into the control room, we could disable the entire city's Harmony implants.

Paul's eyebrow lifted at my indecision. "Let's vote."

Tim hesitated. "Boats, and then we'll see what we can do in the control room."

"All right," I said. "Boats."

Paul nodded, and we started to run toward the docks. Another missile was fired, and my knees nearly gave out as it hit its target. I could only see two boats from Lake Town, but I was sure more were coming. The Lake Town invasion was supposed to include the entire fleet, built over the past few years. They wouldn't have just sent a couple of boats.

"Watch out!" Tim yelled.

I stumbled at his shout, and we all dove to the ground as a series of bullets was fired in our direction. I looked about wildly for our assailants. A group of militia men were coming down the cliff's path near where we'd exited from the tunnel. They were armed, and several of them had their guns pointed at us.

We had no choice but to raise our hands in surrender. All our work, all our subterfuge, and now we'd been randomly caught by the government's militia. These were no average security officers, but the official army of the Legislature. As they grew closer, I noticed something wasn't quite right. They didn't wear the black caps.

I recognized Dr. Wells leading the group.

I almost smiled, but then remembered that I was his enemy, too, and it was likely he knew it.

"I thought you'd been captured," Wells called out, signaling for his men to lower their guns. "Where have you been?"

Paul scrambled to his feet, and the rest of us followed. "We barely escaped," Paul said, and I could practically hear him telling me to keep silent.

Our knives were hidden, and we'd left the pack from the cavern back among the rocks. It would be a small miracle if Wells believed us.

"Right," Wells said, looking from Paul and scanning the rest of us. We probably appeared roughed up from our travels through the tunnels and the cavern. "We have a lot of boats to take over," Wells continued. "The two Lake Town boats are a lost cause now, but more are coming."

I looked out to the horizon where Wells was staring, and he was right.

My heart equally soared and plummeted. At least three more boats were approaching from the far north side, and it seemed that the city's boats had just spotted them as well.

We joined in with Wells's men and hurried toward the docks. There were three boats that looked about ready to take off, and Wells divided us into four groups, leaving one group on shore. Paul, Tim, and I were put together in one group.

None of us had guns, and we didn't reveal that we carried knives. I was grateful that Wells stayed on shore and didn't accompany my group; he had delegated a man named Dan to be our group leader. We followed him toward one of the boats.

"We're on assignment by the Legislature," Dan called out to those on the boat.

The crew let us on, and as we climbed onto the deck, I couldn't help but think that everything had gone too smoothly, too easily.

Dan and the others immediately strutted to the railings and took up posts, cradling their guns in their arms. Paul, Tim and I, who didn't have guns, acted like we were keeping watch. Not knowing when Dan would order us to overtake the boat, all I could do was watch and wait, and my nerves were starting to set in. Tim had suddenly become an irreplaceable asset, and my first thought was his protection.

Another boat appeared on the horizon. There were six now—two burning, four approaching—and my eyes burned with emotion. Didn't they see the burning boats and know to stay away? I had no way of knowing which boats my brother, or Jez, or Rueben might be on. Or whether it was too late to save them.

I watched in my peripheral vision as the other members of the Faction boarded the other boats that were still docked. Dan motioned me toward him as our boat left the harbor and started moving into the open sea. We were keeping pace with another city boat that seemed to be on a path toward the boats that had fired the missiles. Were they grouping together?

I stood by Dan and waited for his instructions.

"Wells is going to let us know when we'll take over this boat," he said, keeping his gaze forward as if he weren't speaking to me at all. "All the boats we're occupying will be taken over simultaneously, then we'll attack the city boats already in the ocean."

I exhaled and asked, "What's my duty?"

"We'll get you a weapon, and you'll stand guard over our captives," he said.

"All right," I said. "And what's the plan from there?"

"You'll be given information as necessary." Dan went silent then, and I moved back to my post.

I could do nothing until Wells sent over the signal. Another boat appeared on the horizon. The members of the Faction were easily outnumbered by both the city militia and the rebellion. And even when we took over the city boats,

Lake Town wouldn't know that we were on their side. They'd think we were just more militia.

Dan left his post and strode toward me. "Follow me," he said, then gave the same command to the other men. We walked to the front of the boat where the captain stood. He turned as we approached. The captain was an older man, which surprised me, and there was a wealth of knowledge in his eyes. I suddenly wished there were another way—that we could convince him to join us instead of capturing him.

"What's this?" the captain asked.

Dan lifted his gun and aimed it directly at the captain's face. "We're commandeering this vessel. Turn around."

The captain grabbed for something beneath the steering wheel, but Dan rushed him and knocked him on the side of his head with the butt of his gun. The captain collapsed, and within moments Dan had lashed the captain's hands behind his back with thick cuffs.

A cry went up all over the boat. Dan shoved the injured captain my direction, then turned, his gun raised, and shouted threats to the crew members.

Tim and Paul rushed among the crew members, cuffing them, then forcing them to sit against the railing on the wet deck.

"Take this gun," Dan said, handing me the weapon he'd prevented the captain from reaching.

I took the heavy object in my hand and gripped it tightly.

"Take the captain over there with the others," Dan said, and I obeyed.

The captain was strangely docile as I gripped his arm, maneuvering him toward his crew. Just as he sat at the end of the row, the boat lurched, sending me off balance and into the one of the crew members.

I grunted and scrambled to get off him. Dan had sped up, and we were speeding toward the other city boats.

I regained my balance, and, with one hand on the rail, I kept the gun pointed at the crew. I hoped that none of them could tell that I didn't know how to use it.

I watched as Paul and Tim positioned a missile and fired it off. The screech sounded like it was inside my head, and I clapped a palm over one of my ears, wishing I could use both hands. The missile landed on the city boat closest to us, and the explosion nearly blinded me with its brilliant flash of yellow. Black smoke rose, and men scrambled to put the flames out.

With a strange mixture of fascination and horror, I watched as some of the men on the inflamed boat jumped over the side. One man limped toward the railing and lifted a gun in our direction. Dan fired first, and the man crumpled to his knees, then pitched forward.

The sight of the bleeding man tumbling over the side of the boat and disappearing beneath the ocean water jolted me. I knew he was the enemy—at least he had been when alive—but it was disconcerting to see him alive and defending himself one moment, and then gone the next.

I swallowed back my emotion. My eyes stung, and my throat burned from the smoke billowing in our direction. The rain was no match for the leaping flames. Dan lowered his gun and returned to driving the boat. We made a wide berth around the burning vessel, only to come into view of another city boat.

A third boat targeted the second city boat, sending off two missiles. There wasn't even a chance for their crew to jump ship. Everyone and everything seemed to be instantly incinerated. My stomach roiled hard, mimicking the up-and-down swells of the ocean.

The missile firings continued until the Faction-controlled boats had decimated the city's original fleet. Dan called Paul and Tim over, but I was still guarding our prisoners, so I didn't hear our next orders until Paul crossed over to me.

"We're moving again," Paul told me just as the boat picked up speed. One thing was certain: Dan wasn't afraid to use fuel. The other Faction boats were already moving toward us, following.

Paul's face was covered in grime, and his eyes were bloodshot, but the smile on his face was bright. "We'll disembark on the other side of the city and let the rebellion move forward with their invasion. They certainly must be confused about the city boats attacking one another. But we need to disappear before they decide to attack us."

"What are we doing once on land?" I asked. "Can we separate from Wells?" I asked, lowering my voice to prevent the other Faction members on board from overhearing.

"We'll find a way to escape," Paul said, fully understanding my meaning.

I wanted to break into the control room with Tim, but I also wanted to find my brother and join Lake Town.

CHAPTER 29

Jez

I had wondered at some point if I might see the city again, but now that it was looming in the distance, I was wondering if I'd ever see Sol again. The burning boats upon the ocean only reinforced my dread. Was he alive? Had he been Executed? Altered? Banished? If he'd sent those warnings, then perhaps it was too late anyway. But I didn't have time to let my heart break.

Chalice and Rueben stood with me at the rail as we peered through the growing darkness and rain. Smoke billowed from several boats. "What's happened?" I whispered.

Rueben put his arm around me and pulled me close. Even his warmth couldn't comfort me now. Chalice had folded her arms, bracing herself against the wind. "They're city boats," she announced, triumph in her voice.

"They are?" Hope swelled inside of me. If the city boats were burning, did that mean our invasion had been successful?

"Wait," Rueben said, pointing to the south. "Those boats are from Lake Town."

I stared, taking in the whole scene. Two of the burned boats were from Lake Town, and I tried to comprehend what that meant. It didn't seem like there was a victor. Both sides had been destroyed. Both fleets burned. Just like I'd learned in A Level. War never had a winner.

Had our entire plan been derailed? If Jude had been killed or his case of chemicals destroyed, where would we be then?

"We'll go and see if we can help anyone," Rueben said, releasing me and hurrying over to Gabe.

The journey toward the burned Lake Town boats was made in silence, the rain drowning out our unanswered questions. The boat was charred beyond repair, and I knew no one could have survived such destruction.

Chalice and I gripped hands as our boat reached the blackened vessel. Rueben said he didn't think either of the burned boats was Jude's, but I felt we had to prepare for the worst. There were at least thirty people on each boat.

And then I saw something floating in the distance. "Look over there!" I said, and Rueben and Chalice squinted through the rain.

Some sort of raft was floating in the ocean, and it looked like people were on it. Moving. Alive.

"Gabe!" Rueben shouted. "We've got survivors!"

Gabe issued orders to lower the rowboats tied to the side of our boat, and Rueben and Michel jumped in them. I was right behind Rueben with Chalice at my side.

"Are you sure you want to come?" Rueben asked.

I didn't answer, just settled at the other end of the rowboat from him and picked up an oar. Chalice joined

Michel, and the four of us rowed the two boats hard toward the raft. Now I could hear voices—someone calling out to us.

One voice was familiar: deep and raspy. *Jude.*

He was alive, along with a few others who were on the raft. As we neared, I saw that there were even more survivors than I had thought. Several men were floating in the water, one hand on the back of the rafts. Jude stood tall on one of the rafts, his face and body stained with soot, and his clothing wet. And he held a metal case tucked beneath one arm. The chemicals. They were safe.

Despite the way I'd dismissed him in the past, I was grateful to see him alive and grateful to see that he still had the chemicals. I couldn't stop the tears from falling as I rowed with renewed strength. We reached the rafts, and Jude began helping the injured into our boats. We were able to fit six people in with Rueben and me, and Michel and Chalice loaded up with the remaining five, Jude included.

I looked across the space between the rowboats at him and smiled. He didn't exactly smile back, but there was relief in his eyes.

The journey back to our boat was quiet, and one woman cried softly. I didn't know her name, and now wasn't the time to ask.

Once we reached the boat and helped everyone get onto the deck, Becca and a few others gave them water and brought out jackets to cover them.

"Thank you," Jude said as I pulled myself up the rope ladder that ran along the side of the boat. He held out a hand and hoisted me the rest of the way to the deck.

"Are you all right?" I asked. I could see he'd been through a lot. But he seemed uninjured for the most part.

"I will be," Jude said, looking over the boat. "Did the storm blow you off course?"

"Yes," I said, peering at him. "How did you make it through so quickly?"

He looked back at me, one of his eyebrows lifted just so, the same way I'd seen Sol do it so many times before, and my stomach flipped at the likeness. "We lowered the sails in time, I guess."

He was being modest, but this was the first real and honest conversation we'd had, and I wasn't going jeopardize it.

"How many have you lost?" Jude asked. As always, he was perceptive.

"More than a dozen," I said. Then I told him about the battle with the islanders and how Chalice had saved us. His gaze strayed to where she was helping those we'd rescued. I was grateful that Chalice was with us, but had she walked from one death trap into another?

"What about your burning boat?" I asked Jude. "What happened?"

Jude hesitated, then said, "The city sent missiles, but then . . ." He looked past me to where Rueben and Gabe stood talking to some of the others that we'd rescued. "Rueben," he said, not loud, but Rueben turned his head.

Once Rueben joined us, Jude continued. "Something's not right in the city," he said, lowering his voice to avoid alarming the others. "The city vessels fired at one another, and then the ones that were firing turned completely away from the Lake Town boats and went to the other side of the island."

I stared at Jude. It didn't make sense.

Rueben looked equally confused.

"Are they resupplying with more weapons?" I asked.

"We have no way of knowing," Jude said. "But we've

lost militia, you've lost mechanics, and one of the medics' boats was burned."

Rueben nodded. "We're out of time."

"Correct," Jude said. "We've got to get into the city tonight and get the power shut down with whatever resources we can. Some of us might have to help fight; others will have to help the mechanics." His eyes moved to my face, and it was like there was an unspoken conversation between us. *We have to find Sol.*

"We'll reorganize and reassign," Rueben concluded. His eyes were on me, too. "Jezebel will stay with me. We'll go with the mechanics and help with the powering down, until the time is right to start up the generators."

Jude's jaw clenched, and I thought he was going to argue with Rueben. But he only said, "Be careful."

He turned away without another word and strode to the survivors from his boat. I couldn't hear what he was saying over the wind and rain, but I sensed the increased anticipation from everyone on our boat. We'd finally come to the pinnacle of our plans. For some reason, the city boats were nowhere in sight, and we were being granted access to land on shore. I didn't know whether that was good or bad, but staying in the ocean until the morning could mean a new kind of danger.

Gabe and Michel sent out signals to the other Lake Town boats, and by the time night had completely enveloped us, we were moving slowly toward the shore. The waves were almost silent as they lapped around the boat, and the rain grew gentle, and could have almost been calming, if I were tucked in a warm bed inside a building.

As we grew closer to the docks and the shore, there were only a few dilapidated boats harbored there, and they were obviously abandoned. Beyond the stretch of rocky earth, the cliffs rose, black with the color of night. The glow of lights seeped out of the towering buildings above the high stone wall that encircled the city like a fortress. Someday, those walls might be the only things keeping the ocean out.

As we drew closer, I expected an attack from the city militia, but the shoreline was quiet. Perhaps too quiet. Someone came to stand by me at the railing, and I sensed it was Jude without even turning to look. Although he didn't say anything, I felt a sort of camaraderie as we both stood on the deck, watching the city together.

Emotions and memories crashed through me as I visualized the streets and the buildings of the city and the B Level apartment where my caretakers, Naomi and David, had raised me. I heard the whispered counsel from Naomi about hiding my emotions, not letting anyone see me cry, laugh, or even smile. *Don't show affection, Jezebel. Don't let them see you cry. Don't . . . don't . . . don't . . .*

And then I tested into A Level and spent every waking moment in diligent study so that I could earn my way to the University, become the scientist that Naomi hadn't been able to, and find a way to start the ancient generators.

"This is for you, Naomi," I whispered in words too quiet for even Jude to hear. It was for Sol, too. For Chalice. For Rueben. For Lake Town. And for the citizens who never stood a chance upon their birth. My entire life until Sol sent me into the cavern had been lived in fear of letting the world know my true self, my true thoughts, and my honest emotions.

I was so caught up in my own swirling feelings that I didn't see the lights disappearing from the towering buildings at first. But as Jude leaned forward, grasping the rail and exhaling, I saw an entire building go dark.

"Oh no," Jude said.

Every sense of mine went on full alert, so Jude's next quiet words came loud and clear.

"Someone else is shutting down the power grid."

CHAPTER 30

Sol

I knew that Jez could very well be on one of the boats. Or maybe she'd remained at Lake Town. Or maybe she was beneath the waves of the ocean, not having stood a chance against the city's missiles. Wherever she was, I had a job to do. And with our attack on the city boats, I hoped that Lake Town was taking advantage of the break and would continue with their invasion plans, which I knew included shutting down the power grid.

But that only gave me less time to break into the control room.

"We'll wait here for orders," Dan said, crossing over to me where I still guarded the crew. We'd docked on the far side of the city from where the Lake Town boats had arrived, and the other overtaken boats had joined us, also docked and waiting.

I nodded and said nothing. I didn't want Dan to know that I had other plans—I just wasn't sure how to get off the boat and away from Wells. Time was certainly growing short.

Once Dan moved away, I looked over at Paul. He was securing the ropes about the rowboats tied to the vessel. I couldn't see Tim and assumed that he was below deck. We had to find a way to coordinate our escape.

Then Tim appeared from below deck. He glanced at me with a nod, then crossed to Dan. Their voices rose in argument, but I was too far to hear them clearly over the sounds of the ocean and rain. Paul joined them, staying silent during the argument, but listening.

Tim broke away from Dan and strode toward me, Paul right behind him. "We're going now," he said to me. "Wells had orders for us. Paul will guard the crew."

Paul nodded and turned his weapon toward the crew. "Go," he told us in a low tone. "I'll try to join you, but it's impossible for the three of us to leave without too much suspicion."

I hurried after Tim without a glance in Dan's direction, and we climbed off the boat, landing on the dock. The other Faction members in the other waiting boats saw us, and one of the other leaders shouted to Tim, asking him what was going on. Tim waved him off and increased his pace. I kept up, trying to stay calm, and hoping . . . hoping that Wells wouldn't appear.

Once we stepped off the dock, Tim moved even faster, until we were jogging toward the towering cliffs. When Tim judged that the darkness hid us well enough, we started running full speed.

"Where's that tunnel to the cavern?" Tim asked.

"We can't go back in there—the place will be incinerated." Just as I said it, the sound of gunfire erupted behind us. We dove to the ground in sync and rolled a few feet. Another spatter of gunfire, and then silence.

"Wells?" I asked.

"Possibly," Tim said. "Or even Dan." His eyes were dark as he looked over at me. "How do we get to the University from here?"

We didn't have time to come up with another plan, so I told him the only way I could come up with. "We'll have to scale the wall."

Tim looked up at the cliffs and the walls that rose even higher above them. "We'll trip the alarm."

"Yes," I said, "and probably more than one. But the only other way in would take us half the night to reach."

"Can you climb?" Tim asked.

"We'll find out." I wasn't as strong as my brother, Jude, that was for sure. I'd always been the more reasonable one, and he'd been the more daring. I could picture him climbing the wall without a second thought. For me, it would take every bit of strength I had left, and I'd be depending on adrenaline. I pointed at the rising ridge above us. "Let's follow the ridge for a couple hundred yards so that we get out of the line of fire from the boats, then we can find a way up."

Tim didn't protest, and in a moment we were both hunched over, running as fast as we could over the rocky earth and beneath the dark sky. My back and thighs ached, but no more gunfire sounded as we moved along the ridge. Every place that I scanned looked just as steep as any other, and I wished we had equipment to help us scale the wall.

"Here," Tim said, pointing upward.

I slowed and looked. It didn't appear any better, or worse, than any other cliff wall. "All right," I said.

We began to climb, slowly, stretching and fitting our fingers and toes into every available groove. We relied mostly on protruding rocks since the dirt was wet and slick. Every misstep sent rocks and mud dissolving into a small current. By the time we reached the base of the stone wall, we were sprinkled in mud.

After resting, we turned toward the wall. It was straight up, but Tim pointed out the grooves and protrusions in the stone that we could follow. I started up first, and after slipping twice, I finally made progress.

Once I neared the top of the wall, I chanced a look below me. Tim was struggling and was only about a third of the way up. I didn't want to hoist myself over the top yet since that would trip the security alarms, and with Tim so far below, I might get a bullet in the neck before he caught up to me.

But I couldn't hold my position much longer. My arms and legs were already trembling with exertion, and the adrenaline that had gotten me this far was quickly turning into exhaustion.

"Hurry," I hissed down at Tim.

He didn't respond, just stretched out his hand to find the next protrusion to hold onto. I focused on each of his movements and tried to ignore the fierce aching of my muscles. When my breathlessness turned into panting as I tried to stay upright, Tim called up in a strained voice, "Go over. Just go over!"

I couldn't wait any longer—not if I wanted to make it over the wall. It was either trip the alarm or slide down the wall back to the cliff tops.

I groaned with the effort as I slung my hand on top of the wall and hoisted myself up. I'd no doubt the alarm was now signaling security, and we'd be confronted any moment. I straddled the wall and looked down at Tim again. "Come on, you're almost here."

Tim just grunted and felt for the next foothold and handhold. It was then that I noticed he was squeezing his eyes shut.

"Only a few more feet, and I can grab your hand," I said, hoping it would encourage him. But even in the darkness, I could tell his face was very pale.

"Come on, Tim," I encouraged, raising my voice a little. "We've got to get over the wall. Security has already been alerted."

I watched as he struggled to make a final effort, and then he was within my grasp. I used the last of my strength to haul him toward me, and he made it to the top of the wall.

Somewhere a siren sounded, but I didn't think it was for us. Sirens were reserved for city emergencies, and it had to be related to something more serious than two men climbing over a wall.

I met Tim's gaze. "Are you all right? We need to get off this wall and to the University."

Some of his color had returned, but he was still unnaturally pale. I didn't think he'd been injured more than me, but then I saw the blood on his pant leg. From a scrape?

"I'm ready," Tim said in a shaky voice, and we faced the narrow alleyway alongside the wall.

I leapt first, half falling and half jumping. I tried to help Tim as he descended, but his right leg crumpled beneath him, and he cried out in pain.

"What happened to you?" I asked. Then horror shot through me. "Did you get hit by a bullet?"

"I think so," Tim said, grimacing. "We don't have time

to do anything about it now, though." He took a couple of steps before he stopped, groaning.

"Here," I said, looping my arm beneath his to support him.

We hobbled like that for a ways toward the nearest tram station. "I don't think I can . . ." Tim gasped. "Leave me here and escape while you can. I'm sorry."

I swung him up and over my shoulder, and, despite his protests, I carried him the rest of the distance to the tram station. I was grateful we didn't encounter other people yet, as someone probably would have reported our unusual activity.

While we waited for the tram, I pulled up Tim's pant leg. The side of his calf had been hit by a bullet, and the wound was ugly. I tore a strip of fabric from the bottom of my shirt and tied it above the wound, making the knot as tight as I could. Tim moaned a few times during the process, but he didn't cry out anymore. I didn't know if that was a good sign or not.

The sound of an approaching tram was a welcome relief. I helped Tim stand, and as we boarded, I heard someone shouting down the street. I didn't turn but just sat on the tram bench with Tim. The tram driver eyed us, then looked away. I knew we looked like militia with our weapons and dark clothing. I just hoped he wouldn't notice Tim's injury and blood-stained pants. As the tram pulled away, I saw a couple of security officers hurrying toward the tram.

Please don't stop, I silently pled with the driver. The tram picked up speed. Then time seemed to slow as we stopped at another two stops before arriving at the University. I helped Tim off the tram, and under his direction we made our way past the University to where the main government buildings sat. I had been in one of them with Wells, and now I was surprised to see lights on inside.

But I supposed I shouldn't have been surprised—not with all the Harmony implants we'd disabled. They were probably having some sort of an emergency summit meeting. Tim lifted a hand and pointed to the upper floor. Half of the windows were dark, the other half glowing yellow. "There's the control room."

"How do we get up there?" I asked.

Tim said, "I don't think I can climb the side of the building, so we'll have to manage the stairs."

"Can you get us inside?"

"Of course," Tim said. "That's the easy part. The hard part will be getting out once we've shut things down."

He led me toward the side of the building and a series of entrances that I hadn't known were there. Tim's breathing was labored, but he seemed to be moving more easily. Maybe the tied-off bandage was helping to stop the blood loss. He typed a long sequence of numbers into one of the keypads by a door, and in a moment, it clicked. Tim turned the handle, and the door swung open.

"I had to use the master code, and that will send an alert to the control room," Tim said as we stepped into the cool, dry interior. "What they won't know is that we're heading their direction."

Tim led me through a labyrinth of hallways, and whenever we heard voices, we stole into the shadows until we were sure no one was coming our way. Tim then unlocked another door with his master code, and we entered a narrow stairwell.

Tim started up the steps first, and although he moved quickly, he was heavily favoring his right leg.

"Are you going to be all right?" I asked at one point as I was beginning to doubt that the staircase had an end.

He glanced back at me, and in the dim lighting, his face was still pale. "I'll need a long nap after this, and maybe a medic to remove the bullet."

"Hopefully that will be sooner rather than later," I said, trying to keep my tone light when everything inside of me was twisting with dread. Without Tim, I couldn't get into the control room. As selfish as it sounded, I had to keep him functioning. The burning boats flashed through my mind, and I knew I'd do almost anything to help Lake Town succeed.

"We're here," Tim said, stopping at one of the landings.

The stairs continued, and I assumed they went to the roof.

"It could be a battle," Tim said, shouldering his gun and looking pointedly at me.

But we opened the door to an empty corridor. Light spilled out from beneath shut doors, and I could hear a murmur of voices behind some of them as we walked silently down the hall. We stopped before the control room door, and I could barely breathe as Tim entered the code.

I didn't know what to expect when the control room door slipped open, but I didn't expect Dr. Wells.

CHAPTER 31

Jez

"Do you know how to swim?" Jude asked me.

Just the thought of plunging into the cold ocean below sent a shudder through me. "I've swum before out of desperation, but I wouldn't exactly call it *knowing* how to swim."

Jude gave a short nod, then turned his attention back to the rising buildings of the city. Only a few had lights on now, while the rest had gone dark in the past few moments, sending a wave of speculation throughout the boat.

Rueben crossed over to us and said what we were all thinking. "Either Sol is behind this and is shutting down the power grid early, or there's another rebel group."

Jude released a short laugh, and I looked at him with surprise. "What's funny?"

"Nothing's funny," he said, looking at Rueben, "but I think you just figured out what's going on. There's a rebel group fighting the city—and we're fighting on the front lines for them."

"Not likely," Rueben said, but I could see that he was considering the idea.

"It would explain why the city boats fired on one another, then took off to the other side of the island," Jude said, then pointed toward shore. "It would also explain why everything's gone quiet now, and the power grid is being shut down as we speak."

"So what are you saying?" Rueben asked. "There's another rebel group that we'll now have to fight against as well?"

One side of Jude's mouth lifted. "Possibly. It's certainly keeping things interesting. But meanwhile, we'll stick to our original plan—at least what's left of it."

I looked around the boat at our now-ragged band of militia, medics, and mechanics. The other boats seemed in better shape, but not by much.

"We'll have to swim," Rueben said, looking at me. "Stay by me. I won't let you drown. We'll get as close to the shore as possible, but we won't be able to dock."

The buildings on the island went completely black then, taking away what little guidance to the shore they'd provided.

I shivered, and Rueben wrapped an arm about my shoulders. "We'll be getting a lot colder before we get any warmer," he said. Rueben was always so naturally affectionate that I hardly noticed, but I still felt Jude's steely gaze on me.

I didn't move and allowed Rueben's arm to stay there, because he was right. Soon, I'd be swimming in cold water, and then who knew when I'd be warm and dry again. The clouds had seemed to thicken overhead with the disappearance of the city lights, and I looked up as the rain dripped down. I wondered if I'd ever see the sun against the blue sky again. Lake Town people had already lost their lives in this invasion, and we hadn't even reached the shore yet.

"Uh oh," Rueben said, then swore.

Jude and I turned to see three boats speeding their way toward us, all lights blazing aboard. I latched onto Rueben's hand and gripped hard.

"Are they the city militia or are they the rebels?" Jude said.

Rueben tugged me back from the railing. "I don't think we should wait to find out." He handed me a thick jacket with padding. "Put this on. It will keep you afloat."

I looked down at the jacket. I'd never seen anything like it.

"Now, Jez," Rueben said, then rushed away, shouting orders to the other people to lower the rowboats.

My mouth fell open. This was really happening, and it was happening now. We were too far from shore to swim. Even if I were an expert swimmer, the cold water would keep me from surviving that long of a distance.

"Come on." Jude was tugging my arm now. "Put that jacket on like Rueben said."

"What about you?" I finally managed to say. I saw Chalice up ahead, guiding people toward the rowboats. A couple of people were wearing the padded jackets, but most weren't.

"I'm militia, remember?" Jude said in my ear as the sound of the speeding boats grew louder by the second.

I pulled on the jacket, but my hands were trembling too much to fasten the buckles. Jude stepped in and finished doing the buckles himself, then practically shoved me toward a rowboat. I stumbled forward, and someone's hand steadied me as I climbed down. The rowboat was lowered seconds afterward, and it was with relief that I saw Rueben was at the front of the boat.

"Grab an oar, everyone," he called out.

I scrambled to find an oar, the number of people and the darkness making it a bit difficult to accomplish anything. Then finally, I was rowing with the rest. They were rowing fast and silently, but I could see the fear in my comrades' eyes.

I scanned the water to see where the other rowboats were, and I thought I identified Chalice, Becca, and Jude in the same boat.

The city boats continued speeding toward us, not slowing, and I watched with horror as the first boat crashed head-on into the boat we'd just vacated. It hadn't even slowed down. The sound of splintering and groaning wood echoed above the sound of the waves.

"No!" I cried out.

"Row faster!" Rueben commanded.

I didn't think it was possible, but somehow we all obeyed.

The other two boats flew past the wreckage, heading toward other Lake Town boats, and it didn't take too much deduction to know what was about to happen. I wondered how many lives would be lost.

As I tried to keep up with the blistering pace of the others, I wondered why a city boat would go on a suicide mission. Had they run out of missiles?

And then Rueben was shouting at all of us. I looked over and saw another city boat speeding in the water, and this time directly toward us.

"Jump in!" Rueben cried out, and before I knew it, people all around me were jumping into the water.

The rowboat began to tip with the surge of waves heading our way, and someone tugged my arm. I plunged into the water and felt and heard nothing but icy cold black surrounding me. And then I started to move upward as fast as I could. My padded jacket slowed me down, and I wished I hadn't worn it.

When my head broke the surface of the water, I gasped for air, and then immediately inhaled seawater. I coughed viciously, and when I finally could breathe again, I looked about to orient myself.

"There you are." It was Rueben's voice, and his tone flooded me with hope.

He latched onto the shoulder of my jacket and dragged me alongside him. I kicked my feet, knowing I had to stay afloat, but soon realized that I needn't have bothered; the padded jacket was doing most of the work. We just had to catch up with the others now. Dark forms were swimming in front of us toward the shore. I heard plenty of coughing and splashing, and a few yells as the rebellion members called out to one another.

As we swam, my feet went numb first, then my calves, until it felt as if lightning were shooting along my legs. I stiffened as my left foot went into a severe cramp.

Rueben noticed and said, "Just keep moving. Even if you can't feel your legs, just keep moving them."

And I did, concentrating on staying close to him and trying to keep as much seawater out of my mouth as possible. But the water continued to surround me, cold and salty and numbing. Somewhere up ahead, I heard Jude's voice, and then it grew closer. He was telling people to call out their names.

"What's he doing?" I asked Rueben.

"Trying to keep people alert," Rueben said, his voice rough. And then he called out, "Rueben!"

And I went next, calling out, "Jezebel!" But it sounded more like a strangled shout.

I focused on the names that were being shouted above the dark water and was relieved to hear Chalice's name shouted, then Becca's.

The speeding boat that had caused us to bail out of our rowboats was heading our way again. I had grown so numb that I couldn't feel anything below my waist, and I was positive that the only reason I was still swimming was the padded jacket. I had no idea how Rueben and the others without jackets were able to keep their heads above water.

People all around us started moving faster, as impossible as it seemed. My eyes stung with the seawater, but I estimated we were still at least fifty yards from shore. So close, yet too far to make it. The boat was gaining with each second, its lights bearing down on us.

"Come on," Rueben shouted at me. "We're almost there. We can make it."

It took a moment to decipher what he was saying; it seemed my brain had gone numb as well.

"I can't make it," I said, not sure if my voice was audible over all the noise.

"You can," Rueben said, sounding far away.

And then I couldn't hear him at all. The roar of the boat was practically on top of us, and I realized my last breaths would be through a numb body submerged in cold water just yards from safety. What would Sol do when he heard about my death? Chalice? Rueben? Strangely enough, it was Jude I thought of last. He'd been so confident that we should invade the city despite the warnings on the tablet. But from the minute we left Lake Town it seemed that everything had gone wrong. Even Mother Nature had been against us.

I didn't realize that I had been pushed underwater until the seawater burned in my mouth and stung my eyes and clogged my ears. As darkness closed around me, I let my eyes shut, and I imagined the cold water turning warm as it rushed past me.

I couldn't explain the rushing sensation. It felt like I was moving upward instead of drowning and sinking lower—like something was pushing me forward. And then it hit me: the boat had passed right over my head.

CHAPTER 32

Sol

"So, you've arrived, just as I thought," Wells said, his arms folded over his chest as he stood in the center of the control room. Behind him sat two other men, both of them probably dead, based on the way they were slumped over in their chairs.

The room smelled fetid—of blood and human waste. Wells's eyes narrowed as he studied Tim and me, our guns raised and pointed at him. "What happened to you?"

"Shot," Tim said, stepping fully into the room. I followed, and the door triggered and slid shut behind me.

A flicker crossed Wells's eyes, and then his gaze was on me. "How did you get past my guards?"

I didn't know which guards he was talking about. "We climbed over the wall."

He laughed at my answer.

I didn't know what game Wells was playing. Did he not believe us, or did he just find us amusing?

"I've been waiting for you," Wells said, as he clasped his hands together casually. "I'm so glad you're finally here. It makes things so much easier."

"What's easier?" Tim asked in a weak voice.

A glance in his direction told me that he needed to sit down somewhere or he'd be passing out soon.

"Put down your weapons," Wells said, "and I'll explain."

"We're done listening to you," Tim said. He cocked the gun, keeping it steady despite the trembling in his voice. "Sit over there."

If Wells was surprised, he didn't show it, but he surprised me by sitting in one of the empty chairs that was positioned in front of the long counter running the length of the room. Monitors scaled the walls, and they were all set to display different sectors of the city.

Tim gave me a slight nod, and I took it to mean that I was to guard Wells. So I did. I moved toward him, keeping the gun that I'd never fired aimed right at his head. Wells just smirked.

Out of the corner of my eye, I watched as Tim sat in front of a console next to the dead men and started typing on the tablet controller. The monitor above his head flickered to a new screen and displayed the security portal he'd hacked into before.

"Ah, so that's how you did it," Wells said to no one in particular. I couldn't see any weapons on him, but I knew enough to not underestimate the professor-turned-Faction-member.

With Wells, I watched Tim select and delete mass amounts of ID numbers, group after group.

Wells chuckled. "You like chaos, I see."

I wondered why Wells wasn't trying to stop Tim. Surely

the Faction would prefer that the people be easily controlled.

Tim worked quickly. Something sounded outside the door, and Tim spun around in his chair and hobbled to the keypad, typing in another combination.

"That will only delay them a few moments," Wells said, folding his arms across his chest, a satisfied smile on his face.

"I only need a few moments," Tim said, going back to his work, selecting and deleting. I watched in awe as hundreds and thousands of lives were changed with a tap on a screen.

Someone shouted through the door, although I couldn't quite make out the words because of the thickness of the metal. And then the banging started.

Perspiration shone on Tim's neck as he continued to select and delete.

"Can I help?" I asked, but Tim ignored me.

"If you follow us, you die," Tim told Wells.

Wells lifted his hands in mock surrender. "I'm just enjoying the show. When you're finished turning lives upside down, I'd like to propose a job." His gaze moved to the door and the pounding on the other side. "Although it might be too late. If they break in, which they will, it will take me a while to break you free from whatever punishment they give you." He looked at the two dead men. "Especially when they find out you killed their controllers."

Tim looked over at me. "I need your help now."

I was by him in an instant as he grasped the tablet, his knuckles turning white as his face drained of color. "Enter the commands I give you, and then repeat them for each power grid."

"What are you doing?" Wells asked, rising to his feet.

I took the tablet as Tim raised his gun and aimed it at

Wells. Then Tim told me the combinations of numbers to enter as I clicked on the master icons of the power grids. One by one, the grids were confirmed "Off," but I could no longer hear Tim over the pounding that had grown louder on the door.

Wells lunged toward us, and Tim fired his gun. The two of them tumbled to the ground, knocking against me, and the tablet flew from my hands. I scrambled to recover it. Wells was lying on top of Tim, completely inert, his eyes wide and lifeless.

"Finish," Tim said, "then get out of here. Only the control door still locks in a power outage, but the others should be deactivated. I've lost too much blood to come with you. A small sacrifice for your plan."

With trembling fingers, I finished turning off the final power grid. Which, I found out in the next instant, included the University and the building we were currently in.

The darkness was complete, and if I hadn't had the glowing tablet in my hands, I wouldn't have been able to see anything.

The pounding and shouting from the corridor stopped long enough for Tim to whisper the door code to me. "Turn off the tablet and they won't be able to see you when you leave."

I rose to my feet and set the tablet on the counter, then I rolled Wells off Tim. With a grunt, I hoisted Tim over my shoulder. For the second time that night, I was grateful that he was a slight man.

"No," he protested, but his words were faint, and I retrieved the tablet and used the light from it to type the code into the keypad.

The door slid open, and I switched off my light source and moved to the side of the room.

Expecting someone to charge inside firing a gun, I was surprised to be met with silence.

My time was limited, and I left the control room. The corridor was completely dark, and voices and whispers, even groans, echoed around me. There were still people on this level, but they were cowered against walls and staying inside rooms. A couple of tablets glowed in one room, and someone called out to me, asking who I was. I continued past to the staircase.

Just as Tim had said, the door was deactivated, and I opened it easily. Down the stairs I went in the dark, knowing that I could lose my balance at any moment. I winced when parts of Tim's body bumped against the walls. He hadn't spoken since we'd left the control room, and I wasn't even sure if he was still alive.

When I reached the bottom, my arms were completely numb, and my legs burned from supporting Tim's weight. I set him on the bottom stair, then sank down beside him. There was no sound above us in the stairwell, so I figured we could rest for a few minutes.

"Tim?" I said. "Can you hear me?" When he didn't respond, I touched his arm and moved my hand up to find his face. His skin was feverishly hot.

But he was breathing, at least.

"All right, let's get you some help." I rose and stretched my aching muscles, then I picked up Tim again. This time he felt like dead weight.

I pushed through the unlocked door and stepped out into the night. Rain dripped down from a metal awning, and the buildings that normally had a few lights on at this time of night were completely black. It was like everyone and everything was sleeping.

But then I saw pinpricks of light on the sidewalk leading to the University campus. A group of people had gathered, holding umbrellas, with their wrist lights turned on. I could hear some sort of argument going on.

I hurried toward the group to see if anyone could help. When I reached them, I called out, "This man's been shot. Can anyone help him?"

Several people heard me and turned to look, their expressions a mixture of curiosity and fear. A couple of men rushed to help, and one of them said, "Let's get him to the University medical clinic."

Grateful, I followed as they hurried across the dark campus. Every muscle in my body ached, and although I was exhausted, I was much better off than Tim.

"Strange things are happening," one of the men said. "We've heard of other people being shot, too."

"What have you heard?" I asked.

"Just that there've been rebellions rising up all over the city," he said. "Enemy boats are trying to land on shore as well. Did you hear the missile launches?"

I had been in the middle of it, but I didn't admit this.

"Is this guy a rebel?" he asked.

I looked at Tim's pale face. "No," I said. "He works for the citizens. He's probably lost a lot of blood by now."

The medical clinic was as dark as the rest of the campus, but small spots of lights shone through the windows, which told me that people were inside. Hopefully there was a doctor who could help Tim.

We pushed through the doors, and a woman came forward. "The clinic is closed. We've lost power."

"The entire city has lost power," I said. "This man has been shot and needs immediate attention. Anything you can do will help."

Her expression was doubtful, and I wondered what was going through her mind—if she even comprehended the changes going on with her emotions.

"It's crazy, isn't it?" one of the men said. "Everyone is freaking out—we've all been altered or something." His voice dipped to a whisper as if he were speaking treason.

The woman hesitated, as if she were struggling to make a decision. "You can put him on a bed, and I'll tell a doctor. Two of them already left, after an . . . argument." Her voice trailed off as if she couldn't believe two doctors had argued.

We followed the woman into another room where a row of beds stood. A few of the beds were occupied, and we placed Tim in one of the empty ones. He didn't moan or make any sound, which worried me more. I placed my hand on his forehead again, finding it warm.

The woman did the same thing, and I could see the concern in her eyes. "How long ago did this happen?"

"A couple of hours ago," I told her, although I couldn't be entirely sure.

"I'll be back in a moment," she said, then left the room.

"Thanks for your help," I told the men who'd carried Tim. They both nodded and left as well, without asking more questions.

When the woman returned, she was carrying an IV bag. "I don't know where she went." Something told me that she wasn't telling me everything.

"Will she be coming back?"

"I don't know that, either," she said, moving around the side of the bed. "I can give this man antibiotics, but nothing else until a doctor comes."

I nodded my understanding. "That will have to be enough for now. Thank you for your help."

I saw a myriad of emotions in her eyes, but she kept her lips pressed together as if she were trying to hold back from asking questions or telling me anything more. Even though it seemed that the woman's Harmony implant had been deactivated, she'd spent her entire life acting and speaking one way, and that wasn't going to change overnight.

I looked down at Tim, wishing that the bullet had missed him. He'd helped the Lake Town invasion more than he could ever know, and now he might be paying for it with his life. There was nothing else I could do for him right now. I left the medical clinic then. If Lake Town was able to carry out their plan, a group of mechanics would be heading toward the underground generators, and Jez would be right alongside them.

If she was still alive.

CHAPTER 33

Jez

I took a breath, and then another. By the third, I realized that I was either alive, or my lungs were working in whatever paradisiacal state my dead body was now in.

"Jez," a woman's voice said. A familiar voice.

Chalice? My brain seemed to be working, although I couldn't bring myself to speak.

And then the pain came. It stabbed me with the ferocity of a dozen knives piercing my skin at once. My feet, my calves, my thighs, my hands, my arms. My lungs felt as if someone were holding a flame to them.

"Jez," another person said—a man this time. It might have been Rueben. How were they speaking to me if I was dead?

Then I felt a new pain as someone touched me, sliding their arms beneath my bruised body and moving me. I was rising, being lifted and carried.

I tried to open my eyes, but I couldn't. I tried to speak; my throat seemed to be swollen shut.

I slowly realized one thing. I was still alive. Somehow, I had survived the speeding boat rushing right over me. Somehow, I didn't drown, and someone must have pulled me to the shore. My stomach suddenly wrenched, and I threw up seawater.

The person carrying me barely hesitated—just continued moving at a fast pace. All around me, I sensed people moving and shifting, and low voices filtered in and out of my subconscious. I couldn't comprehend any of the words, but their tones were urgent, even desperate.

And then finally, I dragged my eyes open. We were near the cliffs, and I knew that Rueben was leading them to one of the tunnels that connected to a passageway leading into the city.

I looked up at the person who was carrying me. "Gabe?" I was relieved to see that he'd made it off the boat and out of the ocean.

He looked down at me. "Good to see you're awake."

"Let me walk," I said, my throat feeling like it was on fire. He slowed and set me down.

My legs throbbed, but I was standing, and that's what mattered. People moved past us, glancing over at me, but not saying anything. Their expressions were ones of exhaustion and fear. None of us had expected to be this beaten so soon. But I wanted to join them, on my own two feet.

Chalice came up to us and grasped my arm. "How are you?" she asked, and then Rueben was there, too. The three of them were staring at me with concern.

In truth, I was dizzy, and my stomach was clenched tight.

"I'll be all right," I said, looking at Rueben. "Thank you for saving my life."

His nod was brief. "We've got to hurry. If you're too weak, we can carry you."

"No, I can walk."

This time a smile touched his face, and he slipped his hand into mine. It was as if his strength flowed into me. I took a few steps with him, my muscles readjusting as I moved.

I looked about us as we walked. The darkness of the night had become our ally. Behind us was the ocean, and the burning wreckage made a bright display upon the water. The city boat that had been speeding toward us had disappeared somewhere. Or maybe it had simply gone dark.

Everything seemed too quiet, and that made me feel uneasy as well. Rueben led the way now, having moved up to the front of the group. I didn't have the time to count those who were with us, but I knew it was less than half of our original number. Perhaps there were other survivors still swimming to shore; I could only hope they'd make it.

Chalice passed into the tunnel ahead of me and turned on her wrist light. I turned mine on and spotted glowing wrist lights moving back and forth up ahead. We crouched for a ways until there was enough room to fully stand up. The passageway was narrow, with just enough space for an average-size man to pass through.

My lungs burned with the effort of walking, but I refused to complain or slow down. No one else could be doing much better than me, and I didn't want to be a burden. Yes, the rebellion had been training and developing their strength for the invasion, and I was months behind them in my physical abilities; but I'd also been given more concessions than the rest of them. My padded jacket and Gabe carrying me were like symbols of my weakness; I couldn't slow everyone down again.

The tunnel took a sharp upward turn and then opened up, forking to the right and left. Rueben went left, and as the ground gradually sloped upward, I heard the sound of trickling water. Then we were splashing through a shallow stream, and I was reminded of when Sol first sent me down into the cavern. That night seemed so long ago that sometimes I wondered if it was a different lifetime, where a different Jez existed. One who was naïve enough to think she'd be safe as long as she didn't show emotion.

Now I knew that nothing was safe.

"Jez?" Rueben called from the front of the group.

"I'm back here."

The people in front of me moved to the side as I made my way up toward Rueben. He was standing in front of a metal door. I lifted my wrist so that I could have more light to examine the door. There was no handle or lock on it, and the metal looked like it had been coated in a thick, transparent substance. When I looked at it from an angle, it seemed to ripple.

"What's on the door?" I asked.

"It's a polymer substance, and the Carrier key can dissolve it," Rueben said.

I must have stared at him with disbelief because he gave a short laugh. "Here, come stand near the door and see what happens," he said.

As I stood near the door, I felt my shoulder warm up, and my mouth fell open as the polymer shifted like the waves of the ocean until it seemed to have dissolved altogether.

It was only then that I saw the keypad on the door. It had been concealed by the polymer.

"How did that happen?" I asked, peering over at Rueben, who gave me a broad smile.

"If the Legislature knew what you could do, they would have never let you leave the city."

"Well, technically, they never did," I said, fighting back my own smile. "You pretty much smuggled me out."

His brows lifted. "That was Sol's idea."

At the mention of Sol's name, I felt the familiar twist of longing spread through me. But I pushed it away. I'd barely survived, and my job now was to help the rebellion.

"Now what?" I asked.

"Now we open a door that was sealed nearly forty years ago."

I stared at Rueben. "The generators are behind *this* door?" I said it in an awed whisper.

Rueben took my hand and squeezed it gently. "There's one more thing that I need to tell you before we go through this door."

I had no idea what he was talking about, but I did notice that Jude had woven his way through the crowd to come and stand by Rueben. With both of them looking at me, I started to worry. "What is it?"

Rueben looked to Jude. It was the first time I'd seen him show the other man deference.

"You know that starting the generators with your Carrier key will affect you physically," Jude said in a quiet voice.

"I know," I said, glancing at Rueben. "I know what happened to your grandmother."

"You might react differently," Jude continued. "There's been no way to test it, of course. But you might fall unconscious or become ill."

When I looked into the intensity of Jude's eyes, I realized that he thought I might back out. But I'd made my decision back in Lake Town, and I'd come this far. If I didn't follow through now, everyone's work over the past years would have been for nothing.

"Will you catch me if I fall?" I said, looking at Rueben and ignoring Jude's lack of faith in me.

"Always," Rueben said.

There was really no other choice for me. The city was falling apart. And the islands were even worse. I looked for Chalice. When I saw the proud smile on her face, I gave her a slight nod, then looked back to Rueben. "Let's open the door."

The edges of his mouth twitched as if he wanted to smile, but he only reached for my hand and wrapped it in his strong, warm grasp. I didn't care to see Jude's reaction.

Rueben guided my hand up to the keypad and pressed my palm against it. On the other side of the door there was only silence. The Lake Town people behind us seemed to be holding their collective breath. And then I felt it. Like all the energy inside me was drawn out in a flash. I nearly collapsed against Rueben. His arm anchored around me, holding me up.

The door started to move, a high screech accompanying it. If I'd had the strength, I would have covered my ears. As it was, I couldn't even lift my arms.

We were met with a rush of musty air—as if it had been waiting to get out of its cavelike confines for decades.

"Come on," Jude said, grabbing onto my other arm. As the two men at my sides propelled me forward, I knew there was no going back now.

The cavern was small and the ceiling low. The wrist

lights from all the Lake Town people glowed in unison, but still it was hard to walk across the uneven ground. I felt as if I'd been awakened suddenly from a deep sleep, and it was taking time to get my mind and body functioning together properly.

"Let's sit her down over here," Jude said, still on my left side.

I couldn't see exactly where he meant, but I was grateful to be off my feet. As the Lake Town people moved about the cave, inspecting their surroundings, I got a better look at everything. I realized it wasn't a cave—at least, it wasn't like the caverns I'd been in. It was a room that could have been above ground if I hadn't known we were inside the cliffs.

Rueben asked Chalice to sit by me, which she did, and he moved to the far wall. I leaned against Chalice, using her shoulder to rest my head against. "How are you feeling?" she asked.

"Like all my energy has been drained," I said.

She said nothing more. She knew as well as I did that this had to be done—whatever "this" was, and whatever it took from me.

Rueben must have found what he was searching for, because he was pressing against one of the walls, and with a whoosh it started moving.

A couple of people cried out and jumped back. Rueben moved back as well, and I watched as portions of the walls turned in on themselves to reveal tall metal containers. Rueben held up his wrist light, showing the sheen of the metal and rows of what looked to be keypads—or touch pads—similar to what I'd touched to get the initial door open.

I thought about the prospect of pressing my palm

against each keypad and having the same amount of energy drained from me. Would that be what it took? I didn't know. Rueben turned to me then, and I knew that I would be a part of the next step in the plan.

"What do I do next?" I asked. My voice seemed to echo in the room against everyone else's silence.

"Now we wait," he said, looking around at the others. "When we know the power grid is under our control, then we can start the generators."

I exhaled. I still had time to regain my strength. But I didn't know how much.

"The lights in the city were shutting down when we were swimming to shore," Chalice said. "They're probably all off now."

"Yeah, but we don't know who exactly shut them off," Jude said, stepping into the middle of the room and coming to a stop by Rueben.

I had no way of knowing which boats or groups had made it to shore before we had arrived on the scene of the burning boats. "So we were the first group ashore?"

"It looks like it," Jude said, looking about the gathered people. "Our plans have to change, and we must work with what we have now. A few of us will remain down here with Jezebel."

I stared at Jude, sensing I wouldn't like where he was going with this. How could I sit in a dark room while the others went above and fought for humanity? And then my eyes burned with another thought. What if they didn't return? What if the hours—or even the days—passed, and no one came back?

I shoved up to my feet and said, "I'm coming, too. I don't want to stay here while you guys are doing all the work." My head felt like it was spinning. Chalice grabbed my arm just as I started to tip over.

Rueben and Jude both rushed toward me, but I held up my hand. "I'm all right."

Neither of them looked convinced.

"I'll stay with her," Chalice said. "The rest of you can go above. If we don't see you by tomorrow, we'll come up and see what's going on."

Rueben opened his mouth to reply, but Jude cut in. "Better make that two days. And at that point, just worry about saving yourselves."

CHAPTER 34

Sol

The quiet was startling as I hurried out of the medic center. The streets were deserted, and although it was the middle of the night by now, things didn't feel the same. I expected at least a glow from a wrist light or something in the windows of the buildings surrounding me, but everything remained eerily dark and still.

I had to trust that Tim would get help, and that it was better than me trying to carry him around. Then I heard a strange, low chanting. I spun around and changed my direction, heading for the sound to investigate even as I filled with dread.

I rounded the next corner and stopped cold. Now I understood why the buildings had felt so dark and empty. The city militia had set up barricades to block off the streets running toward the University. Hundreds—no, thousands—of people were out in the rain, huddled together in a giant mass. The militia had their backs to me, but I could see that they had agitator rods aimed at the people on the other side of the barricade.

The people didn't seem to be trying to get through—perhaps they were afraid of the firepower. But what were they chanting?

I moved closer, staying near the buildings to keep out of sight. And then I saw the platform in the center of the crowd. The citizens were focused on the man who stood on the platform, holding an amplifier. He started speaking, and the chanting died down.

The man raised a hand, and the crowd cheered. I stared at him, trying to see if I recognized him. He was speaking about the Faction, and the people were absorbing every word. I studied the faces that were closest to me, and the display of emotions across their features startled me, even though I knew their implants had been deactivated.

The size of the crowd grew by the minute, and they all started chanting again. This time their words were loud and clear: "Faction, Faction, Faction."

I had to get away. I had to find out what had happened to the rebellion members. What had happened to Jez. But the barricades would prevent me from accessing the tunnels leading underground to the shore.

I made my way back toward the University. I hurried between a couple of buildings and climbed the wall. This side was much easier than the cliff side, and I hoped that the militia would be too busy with their barricades to monitor any other alarms. And then I realized that the alarms probably didn't work without the power.

The thought gave me the final bit of strength I needed to pull myself to the top of the wall. The sea undulated beyond the shore, with the burning and destroyed boats floating on top like discarded toys. Not only the Lake Town boats, but the city boats as well. I undoubtedly knew some of the deceased.

Movement among the rocks at the base of the cliff caught my attention. I squinted in the drizzling rain and saw a few dozen people making their way toward the cliffs.

One person was out in front, scouting the best way, and he directed the others as they found their footing. I knew, or, more likely, sensed that they were Lake Town people. My own people. These were the survivors, and little did they know what chaos they were walking into. I tried to make out the faces on the people, but they were too far, and the rain too dense. I watched for a few more minutes, and then gauging where they'd reach the wall, I climbed back off my own perch. I needed to find something to help them over.

When I reached the part of the wall where the rebellion would arrive after their ascent, I climbed to the top and looked over. They were much closer now, and I studied their faces one by one. Rueben, Gabe . . . Jude. *My brother.* His tall form was unmistakable. It had been over a year since I'd seen him, but there was no doubt in my mind that it was him.

I moved to sit on top of the wall, and it wasn't long before Rueben noticed me. He halted and held up his hand, stopping the others in their tracks.

"Rueben," I called out into the rain. I didn't want to shout or speak too loudly, but I saw the recognition in Rueben's face when he started walking again, straight toward my part of the wall. And then Jude's gaze was on me.

I didn't know what our reunion would be like, but I couldn't think about that now. I was searching the other faces for Jez. Where was she?

By the time Rueben reached the base of the wall, I was starting to panic.

"Where is she?" I called down to Rueben.

He lifted his face to see me, and said, "She's with Chalice in the generator room."

"Is she all right?" I asked, not needing to specify that I was asking about Jez. At Rueben's hesitation, anger flared inside of me. The destroyed boats drifting in the ocean were a testament to my worry. "Was she hurt?"

"She's well," Rueben said, and then started climbing. I stared at him, looking for any more hints in his expression. I'd just have to wait until he was closer to ask more questions.

Next, I looked at Jude. He was standing there, staring at me, as the others shuffled past him.

When Rueben reached the top of the wall, I grasped his arm and helped haul him over. He jumped down on the other side. I stayed on the top of the wall and helped the rest. Jude was the last person to climb up. Jude's usual cockiness was subdued, and I assumed that it was from whatever they'd endured on the boats. When he reached the top of the wall, I extended my hand to help him, but he ignored the gesture and hoisted himself over. I couldn't say that I was exactly surprised. Jude hadn't been happy about my election to come to the city while he stayed behind in Lake Town.

When I jumped off the inner side of the wall to join the others, Rueben said, "What's going on here? The city boats were firing at one another, and now the power grid is off."

"First, tell me about Jez," I said. I didn't care that we had an audience.

"When she used the Carrier key, it drained her energy," Rueben said. "Chalice is there with her until we can return."

"Chalice?" I didn't have time for questions about Chalice's sudden appearance. "Is Jez all right?" I pressed.

What the Carrier key would do to a person when activated had been the one factor we didn't know how to prepare for. I looked at my brother and saw the hardness in his eyes.

I stepped up to him. He seemed to have grown taller and broader, but his size didn't deter me. "What happened? Tell me everything."

"It was like you said," Jude said. "The Carrier key uses the body as a conduit. Your Jezebel will be fine, though."

Even though I hated that Jude had been around Jez, and I hadn't, I tried to take comfort in his words, hoping they were true. We still had a lot of work to do once we got the power grid back on.

I released a breath, knowing that I was helpless as far as Jez was concerned until I could see her for myself. I turned to the others and explained about the Faction, and how Paul, Tim, and I had deactivated the Harmony implants, and how we had turned off the grid and how the Faction was going to use the Lake Town invasion for their own momentum.

The faces staring back at me were stunned. All of our plans and preparation had been derailed.

Rueben lowered his head and stared at the wet ground. I didn't have all the answers, but I knew we had to do something.

"Do we form an alliance with the Faction?" one of the Lake Town people asked, stepping forward. I recognized her as Martha, one of the group leaders.

"That's what Dr. Wells wanted to do," I said. "Before he died." I explained how the Faction still wanted the people to be controlled by the Harmony implants.

"The Faction can just reactivate them?" Rueben asked.

"They could," I said, remembering the expressions and emotions I'd seen on the citizens' faces, and considering what it would be like to have those all gone again. Now, it was chaos, and I knew it would be a difficult transition for the citizens as they learned to navigate their new freedom. We just had to show them how. But the thought of Jez being ill from just one transfer . . . What would happen to her when she powered on all the generators? "The Faction won't be much better than the Legislature," I added. "But more essential right now is to get the atomic globes created and growing."

I looked to Jude, wondering if he'd been able to save the chemicals he should have brought over. We could recreate them in the University labs, but that would take precious time.

"The case of chemicals is in the generator room," Jude said, as if he knew what I was thinking. "Take us to the power grid control room. If the city is in as much disarray as you say it is, we need to reroute the power as soon as possible."

He was right, but then Rueben said, "How do we make sure the Faction doesn't reactivate the Harmony implants first?"

Without the expertise of Paul, I couldn't guarantee anything. I didn't even know where those two men were. All I knew was that we did have to hurry, and if Tim was coherent, he might be our only hope.

"Come with me," I said. As we moved through the alley, I told Rueben and Jude about Tim—what he'd done and how he'd been shot. Once we reached the street, I found we were much closer to the massive crowd behind the barriers. They'd moved into any remaining space, and I wondered how long it would be before the militia started firing on them.

Rueben slowed his step at the chanting coming from the crowd and the booming voice coming from the Faction leader.

"Stay close to the buildings," I commanded the Lake Town people. With a couple dozen of us, it would be harder to hide.

Just then one of the militia men spotted us and yelled for us to stop. I started running, without looking back, and just hoped the others would follow me. I heard their footsteps, but when the bullets started flying, I knew we couldn't possibly all make it. And we didn't have time to carry the injured.

Someone cried out behind me, and I stole a quick glance. Rueben had stopped to bend over an inert figure. "We can't stop!" I yelled out, and he snapped his head up.

I continued to run, not able to see if he had followed. At least Jude was still by my side; he didn't seem to have any desire to slow down. When we finally arrived at the University gates, we found them unmanned.

"This way," I called out, taking a sharp turn and cutting through the line of trees that separated the main campus from the medic building. I didn't want to lead us all into the building, or we'd become sitting targets. I led the group around a couple of other buildings until I felt like we'd lost the militia.

Rueben had caught up with us, and if I was counting correctly, there were two or three more missing. So many were losing their lives tonight.

"Gabe," I whispered, pointing to the building where Dr. Wells had died. We needed to get back inside the control room. "Take the others behind that building. Wait by the back entrance." The building was completely dark, but that didn't mean we wouldn't meet any resistance.

Rueben and Jude came with me to the medic building, and I felt much safer traveling with just the three of us.

Inside, the place was dark, and I almost stumbled over someone lying in the middle of the floor. I didn't know if the person was alive or dead. I looked around for the nurse, but she was nowhere to be found. We moved into the room that I'd left Tim in, and he was still there, lying down.

I switched on my wrist light, creating a faint glow in the room. Tim had an IV in his arm, and I was glad that he was at least getting some antibiotics. "Tim," I said, touching his shoulder. To my relief, his eyes opened, but his focus was off.

"This is my brother, Jude, and this is Rueben," I said, hoping that he was lucid enough to understand what I needed to ask him. "They're from Lake Town, and we need to redirect the power grid before the Faction can take it over."

His eyelids fluttered, then stayed open. His mouth moved, but I could barely hear him. "Paul," he said.

"We don't know where Paul is," I said. "We need your help." I looked at the IV leading into his arm. Was it really doing its job?

"Paul," he said again.

I shook my head, frustration building up inside of me. Trying to find Paul would take too long, if we could find him at all. Then Tim's hand grasped my arm, and I looked at him more closely. "*DyingGeneration* is the code word."

A shiver crept along my skin at the password.

Tim's eyes slid shut, and he seemed to be in a deep sleep.

"Let's go," Jude said.

I looked over at my brother, then at Rueben, who nodded his agreement. Moments later, we were running through the rain from the medic center to the Legislature building. We found rebellion members huddled near the back entrance.

"Come inside the building, but stay near the exit," I told them. Then I met Jude's and Rueben's gazes. "Come with me." Jude wouldn't be much good with the technical stuff, but he'd be a sufficient bodyguard if we needed one. I just hoped that Rueben was as smart as we all thought he was.

CHAPTER 35

Jez

The dry air slowly moistened the longer Chalice and I stayed in the generator room. We'd turned off our wrist lights and sat in the darkness, waiting. I might have dozed a few times, but mostly I was awake, thinking and wondering. When I next heard Chalice stir, I turned on my wrist light and said, "Let's go to the end of the tunnel at least."

"Need some fresh air?" Chalice said.

"Something like that," I answered. I was already on my feet and moving toward the door. My strength was back, but part of my body felt slightly numb. I grasped Chalice's arm as we walked to make sure I stayed steady on my feet.

We wove our way through the tunnel until we could hear the sounds outside—rain, wind, and above it all, the crash of the waves against the shoreline. We stepped out of the tunnel and stopped on jutting rocks that rose with the cliff behind us. I looked above us and saw the dark shapes of the buildings above the cliffs. The sky had lightened, and I guessed it was midday, which meant we'd stayed all night and morning in the generator room.

The wind was strong, cutting a path through my clothing and making me shiver. I was also starving, but I knew that an empty stomach was the least of my problems. Chalice had turned away from the cliffs and gazed out over the ocean. More city boats were on the water, and it looked like they were patrolling, waiting for any sign of another Lake Town boat. I knew there were a couple of other areas the remaining Lake Town boats might attempt to land, but I had a feeling that they wouldn't be able to get through.

I pulled my jacket tightly against me, trying to ward off some of the wind and rain, but a storm was rolling in quickly. I watched as the boats pitched side to side with the growing waves, and the pieces of the burnt boats moored on the rocks of the shore, as scattered as the pieces of my heart.

"What's that?" Chalice said, pointing toward the sky.

I looked up to see a small, dark shape moving too fast for a bird. "It's a missile," I said, grabbing her arm and pulling her back into the tunnel. We'd just gotten inside when the missile struck somewhere along the cliffs. Chalice and I both fell to our knees and covered our heads. The explosion vibrated the rocks around us, and bits of rock and dirt rained down. I curled into a tighter ball, waiting for a cave-in. But the rumbling stopped, and nothing larger than a few pebbles had cascaded around us.

"Are you all right?" I whispered.

"Yes," Chalice said in a hoarse voice. She started to cough, and I reached for her in the darkness, dust billowing around us. And then I heard a grating sound.

"The door," I gasped. "It's closing."

Without any discussion, we both leapt to our feet and started running down the tunnel. The farther we went, the more rocks were strewn about the ground, and soon the air was so choked with dust that we both had to stop to catch our breath. I tugged the collar of my shirt over my mouth. Chalice was staring at me with wide eyes. "What if the generators are destroyed in a cave-in?"

I was thinking the same thing, and just then the tunnel vibrated again as if there were another blast against the cliffs above us. As the earth and rocks shifted around us, we had no choice but to huddle together and wait for everything to settle. When the silence came, I dreaded finding out what damage had been done to the generator room. We turned on our wrist lights and picked our way through the crumbled rocks. When we reached the final bend before the generator room, the first thing I saw was that the generator door was still open.

Inside, bits of rocks had tumbled down, but otherwise the generators looked unmarred.

"I think they're all right," I said, wondering how functional any machine would be after forty years of disuse. But my Carrier key had unlocked the door, so at least that process was working.

Chalice nodded, walking along the row of generators, peering in the dim light at them.

Another low rumble started, then grew louder—much louder and deeper than the last one. Chalice and I instinctively moved toward each other and crouched against the floor. When a cracking sounded overhead, as if the entire ceiling were about to cave in, I started to hyperventilate. Chalice half dragged me next to one of the generators.

As we huddled against the smooth metal, I squeezed my

eyes shut, flinching at the sounds of each rock that tumbled to the ground. Then dust bloomed, and I pulled my shirt over my face, trying to breathe as little as possible. I wondered if we'd be buried alive in this room and never see the rain or the clouds again.

Chalice's arms went around me, and I held on to her. At least I wasn't alone. At least I would die with someone I cared about.

I waited and waited, and an eerie silence filled the room. Chalice's breathing, mixed with my own, was the only sound I could hear. The rumbling had stopped, the falling rocks had settled, and the dust was beginning to fade.

"Are we still alive?" I whispered.

Chalice released a small groan. "I think so." She shifted away from me, and her wrist light flickered on. The generators still looked intact, but there was definite damage.

What worried me the most was that the entrance to the room was completely blocked.

"How are we going to get out?" I asked, my voice trembling. I turned on my wrist light and pushed myself to my feet. My head felt light, as if I'd been spinning in circles instead of crouched in the dark.

"We'll have to dig ourselves out," Chalice said.

I was glad that one of us could think logically. Chalice followed me to the pile of rocks, and we worked together moving one at a time. I could only hope that no more missiles were fired against the cliffs before we could get out of the tunnels.

But we weren't so lucky. Another missile must have hit because the rumbling started again. My entire body started to shake, and Chalice and I started to dig frantically. We were covered in dirt, every nail broken. I could taste the grit in my mouth and feel it in my eyes. But we couldn't stop now. More dust billowed about us as the rocks shifted, but still we clawed our way until there was enough of an opening for each of us to fit through.

"You go first," Chalice insisted.

"No," I said in a way that ended all argument.

The faster she got through, the sooner I could join her. When Chalice disappeared through the opening, I wriggled my way into it, the sharp edges of the rocks tugging at my clothing and scraping my skin. Just as the tunnel was starting to open up and I could see Chalice crawling up ahead, another missile struck. This one was incredibly close, and my teeth snapped together at the vibrations beneath me. But it was the sound of more falling rock that shot panic through me.

"No," I cried out, reaching toward the last place I'd seen Chalice. "Chalice!" I called. My eyes burned and my throat was raw, but I shouted again, "Chalice!"

I thought I heard her calling back to me, but the noise of the rocks and dirt falling cut off any other sound. The earth rumbled above me, and the space between me and Chalice started to fill back in again.

I scrambled backward, away from the falling debris, and quickly made it back to the generator room. It was filled with dust, and I covered my mouth to breathe.

Chalice and I were separated, and I didn't think I could dig myself out again without her help. I looked around the dim space, blinking the dust from my eyes. What if I couldn't get out? What if the damage to the tunnel was too great and no one was able to reach me in time?

The generator room had held strong during the missile attacks despite the crumbling passageway leading to it. I knew I could last several days without food and water, but beyond that, I wasn't sure. There was a battle raging above ground. The electric power was off, and the Legislature was fighting against more than the Lake Town rebels.

I might be forgotten until it was too late. Chalice might not make it out; she wouldn't be able to tell anyone what happened to me.

The air started to settle, and I lowered my arm and breathed more freely. The metal case of chemicals was here in the cave. And only I could start the generators that would give the globes their initial power.

I knew what happened when I used my Carrier key. All of my energy would be depleted for hours—perhaps a day or two. And the longer I waited, the less energy I'd have to give. If I was to start a generator so that an atomic globe could begin its formation process, I needed to do it soon.

I closed my eyes and listened. The earth's trembling had stopped, and I could no longer hear the sound of falling rocks or sliding dirt. Was it a reprieve? That I didn't know. I opened my eyes again, looking at the row of generators along the stone wall.

I knew what I had to do.

CHAPTER 36

Sol

It was the smell that hit me first. Then the sight of Dr. Wells's still body and the other dead men in the chairs made my stomach feel like it was going to turn inside out.

"Is that him?" Jude said, coming into the control room behind me.

I could only nod. The taste of bile in my mouth made me want to double over and wretch.

"Let's get the bodies out of here." Rueben's voice.

Jude and Rueben carried Dr. Wells's lifeless form, then the other two bodies, out into the hall.

I exhaled and tried to steady my hands as I sat on a chair in front of a console. I stared at the empty, dark screens of the tablets and monitors until Jude and Rueben came back in. We had waited through the rest of the night and the morning before entering the building. Until we were sure that we weren't being hunted any longer. I couldn't remember the last time I'd slept or the last time I'd eaten anything.

Rueben seemed unfazed as he picked up a tablet and powered it on. The tablet didn't need the power grid to run, and its L-battery only had to be charged every few months. Of course, this is what Tim would have done. Used one of the tablets to access the power grid.

But my mind was numb, and my hands felt heavy, useless. Seeing the dead body of Dr. Wells, knowing that Tim's life was in danger, having no contact with Paul, and not knowing how Jez was doing had finally pushed me past my tolerance level.

Jude's hand clamped down on my shoulder, and I was glad that I could at least feel *something*.

"He's broken in," Jude said.

"What?" I whispered, forcing the word out. Was it possible? I watched Rueben as he typed a series of commands into the tablet. He was in the power grid, and he was typing faster than I could follow.

"We have about two hours, maybe three, to get back to the generators and restart them," Rueben said. "We can get the atomic globes running and then strategize from there."

I nodded. We could at least complete one of our goals.

"We need to hurry before someone else takes over the power grid." Rueben looked toward the doorway. "Is there a way to lock this door?"

"Yes, but I don't know how effective it will be against the Faction or whoever is winning the battle at the moment." I moved to stand, but a wave of nausea seemed to cut me in half.

"Easy, Sol," Jude said. His hand gripped my elbow as he moved me through the room, Rueben following.

Rueben shut the door behind us, and I averted my eyes when we passed by Dr. Wells's body. I was never so grateful to be out of a building and standing in the rain as I was at that moment. The sky was gray with the afternoon light, and the wind was fierce. A storm was coming. The timing couldn't be worse.

Jude explained everyone's duties, telling us that we'd all stay together and return to the generator room inside the cliffs. There were less than twenty of us now, and it was no use splitting up. We didn't have the man power to protect ourselves.

As Jude spoke, I scanned the faces of the rebellion members. Some I knew, some I didn't, but all of their expressions were the same. We'd failed in our original mission, but we were determined to survive. We would carry out part of our plan for now, and then decide what we could do from there.

"Let's go," Rueben said.

We started across campus, keeping to the sides of buildings whenever possible, keeping an eye out for the militia. We reached the alley that led to the sea walls, and just as I was about to climb over, the first missile hit.

The explosion was close enough that my ears rang and the ground shook beneath my feet.

"What was that?" someone cried out.

I grasped the wall to brace myself as the tremor continued. When the earth stopped rocking, Rueben and I climbed the wall and looked over to see smoke and fire along the cliffs. I looked out to sea at the city boats. One of them had shot a missile at the cliffs—but why? Then my pulse shot up as I realized the missile had landed close to the tunnels that led to the generator room. Were the boats targeting the tunnels? How did they know about them?

All heat seemed to drain from my body. *Jez.*

I turned to Rueben, and the look in his eyes told me he'd come to the same conclusion. We scrambled over the wall and dropped down on the other side. The others followed, but I was focused on making my way down the rocks and toward the hidden tunnel opening. Jude soon caught up with us, and as we ran, another screech filled the air. We dove to the ground just as the missile sailed over us and struck the cliff walls on the other side of the tunnel, this time closer to the opening.

"No!" I cried out. We had to get to the tunnels before the entrance was blasted shut. I was on my feet again, half running and half stumbling.

This time Rueben was in the lead, leaping over rocks and finding the most direct path. I followed close behind. I didn't look back to check on any of the others—my thoughts were purely focused on reaching Jez.

Before we reached the tunnels, a third missile struck, this time above the entrance. My heart dropped as I watched the cliff implode. I covered my head with my hands as rocks and dirt flew in our direction. When the dust shifted enough to breathe, I lifted my head. I'd been hit by small pieces of rock that had torn my clothing and scraped my skin, but I couldn't get the image out of my head of Jez on the ground, hurt by falling rocks.

Rueben, Jude, and I sprung to where the tunnel opening had been. One part of me knew that we'd just made ourselves a viable target for the boat that was firing the missiles, but I put that thought aside.

The rain mixed with my perspiration as I worked lifting rocks and tossing them away. Soon all of the Lake Town survivors were working on the rock slide, and we started making swift progress.

A fourth missile hit, and we all dove for cover. The blast was to our left, probably misfired, and the shock reverberated through my entire body. I couldn't hear anything, and my vision doubled as I moved to my feet again. I scanned the rebellion members—no one was injured, but we were all covered in dirt.

I wiped the rain and dirt from my eyes and started working again on the rock slide, my movements slower this time, but equally desperate.

I didn't know whether I was unearthing a grave.

When we'd cleared a path, I went in first, turning on my wrist light. Rueben and Jude were right behind me.

The tunnel was a mess, and I knew it would take a while to make any progress. But still, I was impatient, and my heart screamed in pain. "Jez!" I called out. "Jez! Can you hear me?"

Rueben and Jude stopped walking so we could all listen to the dust-filled darkness after each time I called for her. But we were met with nothing but absolute silence.

CHAPTER 37

Jez

I was moving, but how could I be moving when I couldn't see anything and couldn't feel my own body? Was someone carrying me? Had I survived the tunnel collapsing all around me? I heard only a faint sound—like a soft breeze, only deeper. A rushing sound, or maybe . . . I tried to open my eyes. I was almost certain I was hearing the ocean.

"She's waking up," someone said. A voice that I didn't recognize, yet it was familiar.

I'm not dead. At least I didn't think so. And I was warm. I'd been able to start the globe, and it was working. Hope zinged through me. We'd done it; we'd started the generators. The city would be saved. The people freed.

Someone touched my shoulder, and the pressure made me wince. Another touch, and my eyes opened. It took a moment for me to realize what I was seeing. Not a cavern ceiling, but a blue sky—bluer than I'd ever seen before. And Sol looking down at me, his head and shoulders framed by the brilliant blue. To the side of Sol was the brightest globe I'd ever seen.

The sun.

Slowly, I blinked. But the sun was still there. The blue sky, too.

"Good morning, Jez," Sol said in his low, mellow voice. The voice I hadn't heard for months; the voice I'd dreamed about. The voice I thought I'd never hear again when the rocks rained down on me inside the tunnel.

"Am I . . ." My throat was absolutely raw, but I forced the words out anyway. "Am I dreaming? Are you . . . ?"

His hand on my shoulder again shot a mixture of pain and pleasure down my arm—pain because I was sure my arm was broken from the rock slide in the tunnels, and pleasure because I was alive, and Sol was alive.

"I'm here," Sol said. "And you woke up on Solstice."

A slow smile spread on his face, and my heart seemed to finally beat to life. I gazed at the yellow sun in the blue sky. I squinted, and my eyes watered, but I didn't want to look away.

"Jez," Sol said, touching my face and moving to shield me from the sun's direct rays. "You're going to blind yourself."

I stared up at him, amazed that he was here and that I was again looking into his gray eyes. I wanted to reach up and brush his dark hair from his forehead. But my limbs wouldn't obey.

"What . . . Where are we?" I whispered.

"We're on a city boat," Sol said.

I tried to lift my head to look around, but a sharp pinch in my neck stopped me.

"Don't try to move yet." Sol touched my forehead, smoothing my hair back from the blowing wind. "A few of us were able to get on this boat and away from the city."

I exhaled, and Sol shifted so that he was sitting next to me. The sun was on my face again, and I closed my eyes halfway to revel in its glare.

"What happened? Where's Chalice?"

Sol was quiet, and I waited, not pressing him. I knew lives had been lost. I hoped Chalice was all right. That she was somewhere on this boat celebrating the Winter Solstice.

"We found Chalice unconscious in the tunnels," Sol said quietly. "She was alive, so we kept digging and found you in the generator room. You were injured, but you had also managed to start one of the generators and create an atomic globe. I don't know how you did it. You seem to have broken a couple of bones."

"I don't remember anything after starting the generator," I said. "I didn't know if I'd make it; I didn't know what might happen." I winced as I tried to shift. "My arm?"

He nodded. "And your collar bone."

"And Chalice?"

"Just bruises." He paused, and I wondered what he wasn't telling me. Was he trying to spare me some awful news?

I looked into his eyes again. They were more blue than gray, and I knew it was because of the brightness of the day. "Who was with you? Did you find your brother?"

"Jude and Rueben were with me," Sol said. "And the other Lake Town survivors. We all worked to dig out the tunnel entrance."

"And that's when you found me?"

Sol blinked rapidly. "It was a sight I'll never forget.

There you were, on the floor, unmoving, with a small atomic globe suspended above you, glowing and throbbing and already warming up the generator room." He swallowed. "But I didn't care about the globe. I cared about you."

I lifted my good hand and brushed the side of his face. He was real.

"We got you out of there as quickly as we could," Sol said. "The missile firing had stopped, but we couldn't afford to stay near the tunnels any longer. We couldn't stay in the city, either . . ." He looked away from me.

"What is it?" I asked. "What happened?"

"The place is in chaos, Jez," Sol said, scrubbing his hand through his dark hair. "The Faction is fighting off the city militia and gaining more and more supporters. They aren't much better than the Legislature."

Sol told me about Paul, and Tim, and Dr. Wells, and how they were training and planning to let the Lake Town invasion give them the momentum they needed to take over the city. He explained how Tim had figured out how to deactivate the Harmony implants and how the Faction would be reactivating them again.

He told me how Tim had been injured and Dr. Wells killed. He told me about the mass assembly in the streets and the shots that were fired at him.

I scanned his body, and he shook his head. "I wasn't hit," he said. "You got it a lot worse. When the swelling in your arm goes down, we'll bind it up."

I nodded, then said, "Did Paul and the others come with us?"

"Paul is on the boat, too," Sol said. "We didn't have time to go back and get Tim."

The regret on his face was plain. I tried to look past him

to see who else was on the boat. Several people were on the other side of the deck basking in the sun, but from my position, I couldn't identify any of them. Sol leaned close, grabbing my good hand, and said, "We left the city two days ago. We had to make a hard decision. You started one atomic globe, which we had to be satisfied with. Our other plans were completely destroyed, and with so many deaths, we didn't have a chance—not with the Faction trying to take over as well. Jude and Chalice stayed behind and will protect the globe you started. Even one globe has the power to make a difference. He wants to transport it to a building above ground."

I was stunned. Both that we'd actually left the city, and that Jude and Chalice decided to stay behind together. "Did anyone else stay behind?"

"Rueben and Becca and the others are all on the boat," Sol said.

Rueben was here, and Becca. I was glad for that. "What now? We go back to Lake Town?"

"Yes," Sol said. "We were hit hard. Entire boats of people were lost. We need to recover and rebuild. We need time to heal and become strong again."

My eyes stung with tears as I thought about the losses.

Sol continued, his voice sounding distant. "Jude thinks he can start an underground resistance in the city. One that can prepare and train until the time is right to defeat the Faction." He shook his head slightly. "But that's what the Faction spent years doing, so I think they'll be on the watch. But Jude is convinced. He thinks the globes will show everyone that there is hope, and that the new hope will change people's hearts."

I watched Sol speak, wary of his brother's plans. Even

with what little I knew of Jude, I knew he was headstrong, and that not even Sol could have derailed him.

"I'll have to return," I whispered. "I'm the only Carrier. We'll need more than one globe."

Sol didn't answer. He didn't have to. I could see the answer in his eyes.

"Help me sit up," I said.

Sol looped his arm behind my back and supported me into a sitting position so that I wouldn't have to use my left arm. Then he sat close to me, and I leaned against the rail, the water at my back and the deck sun-warmed and spreading out before us. Someone in the group on the other side of the deck laughed, and the sound was good to hear.

"Sol," I said in a soft voice, reaching for his hand.

His fingers slipped through mine, and his hold tightened as he studied me with those gray eyes of his.

"What if we can't stop the flooding?" I motioned to the ocean with my good hand. "What if Summer Solstice and Winter Solstice are the only things we have to look forward to?"

He closed his eyes, and when he next opened them, he looked intently at me. "At least I will have you, and you will have me," he said, his voice falling to a whisper. "I hated being apart."

I couldn't speak; I could only stare into the depths of his eyes. I had spent months worried about him, thinking about him, and wondering if I'd ever see him again. And now here we were, finally together.

He released my hand, then slipped his arm around my waist, pulling me close. The sun warmed my bruised skin, but nothing could replace the warmth that the look in his eyes brought to my heart.

Slowly, he leaned closer and brushed his lips against mine. We'd only kissed once, and that was right before he sent me into the cavern beneath the city, and right before I learned that nothing was as it seemed.

But at least one thing in my life had been true all along—Sol. I wrapped my good arm around his neck, and even though I knew that the others across the deck might be watching, I didn't care. I kissed Sol back. Maybe I was right about not being able to stop the earth's flooding or to save humanity. Perhaps saving ourselves was all that we could do for now. And maybe that was all right.

As Sol's kiss deepened, and I tightened my hold, I allowed my mind to float and the sun to soak into my skin. It would be another half year of rain before the sun would shine again. And I intended to celebrate every moment of it with Sol.

THE SOLSTICE SERIES

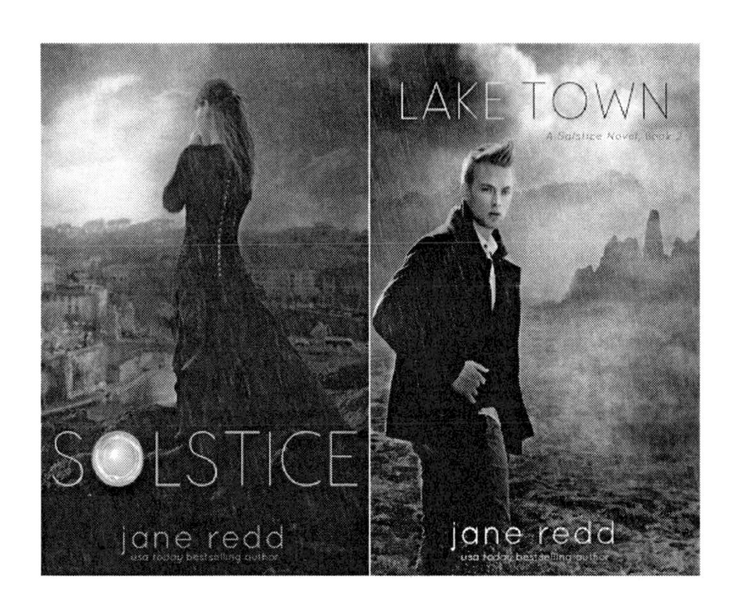

Coming Soon:
Book 3

ABOUT JANE REDD

Writing under Jane Redd, Heather B. Moore is the USA Today bestselling and award-winning author of more than a dozen historical novels set in ancient Arabia and Mesoamerica. She attended the Cairo American College in Egypt and the Anglican International School in Jerusalem and received her Bachelor of Science degree from Brigham Young University. She writes historical thrillers under the pen name H.B. Moore, and romance and women's fiction under the name Heather B. Moore. It can be confusing, so her kids just call her Mom.

Visit JANE REDD BOOKS on Facebook for series updates.

For book updates, sign up for Heather's email list: hbmoore.com/contact

Website: HBMoore.com

Facebook: Fans of H. B. Moore

Blog: MyWritersLair.blogspot.com

Instagram: @authorhbmoore

Twitter: @HeatherBMoore

CPSIA information can be obtained
at www.ICGtesting.com
Printed in the USA
LVOW12s1635190417
531396LV00004B/728/P